Edward Upward was born in 1903 at Romford, Essex, and educated at Repton and at Corpus Christi College, Cambridge, where he read English and History, and was awarded the Chancellor's Medal for English Verse. While at Cambridge he created with Christopher Isherwood a series of stories about the fictitious village of Mortmere. After graduating he became a private tutor and later a schoolmaster. From 1932 until his retirement in 1961 he taught at Alleyn's School, Dulwich, where he was a housemaster and head of the English department.

Edward Upward's first novel, *Journey to the Border*, was originally published by Leonard and Virginia Woolf at the Hogarth Press in 1938. In the 1930s he also contributed stories to *New Country*, *New Writing* and *Left Review* and was on the editorial board of the *Ploughshare*, journal of the Teachers' Anti-War Movement. For sixteen years he was a member of the Communist Party of Great Britain, but he left it in the late 1940s because he believed it was ceasing to be a Marxist party.

Between 1942 and 1961 Upward produced no new material, but in 1962 Heinemann published *In The Thirties*, the first part of his trilogy of novels *The Spiral Ascent*. The second part, *The Rotten Elements*, and the third, *No Home but the Struggle*, were published in 1969 and 1977 respectively. Edward Upward has also produced five volumes of short stories: *The Railway Accident and Other Stories* (1969), *The Night Walk and Other Stories* (1987), *An Unmentionable Man* (1994), *The Scenic Railway* (1997), and *The Coming Day and Other Stories* (2000). His other books include *The Mortmere Stories* (with Christopher Isherwood, 1994), a revised edition of *Journey to the Border* (1994), and the memoirs *Christopher Isherwood: Notes in Remembrance of a Friendship* (1996) and *Remembering the Earlier Auden* (1998).

Alan Walker was born in 1952 in Enfield, Middlesex, and educated at Enfield Grammar School and Queens' College, Cambridge. He has mainly worked in education, and for thirteen years was Director of Education of the Chartered Society of Physiotherapy. In 2000 he published *Edward Upward: A Bibliography 1920-2000*, and is currently engaged on a bibliography of the Enitharmon Press from 1987 to 2002, and on a biography of Edward Upward. He was awarded an honorary doctorate in Science by the University of the West of England in 2002.

OTHER ENITHARMON BOOKS
BY EDWARD UPWARD

Journey to the Border
introduced by Stephen Spender

An Unmentionable Man
introduced by Frank Kermode

(with Christopher Isherwood)
The Mortmere Stories
*introduced by Katherine Bucknell
and with images by Graham Crowley*

**Christopher Isherwood:
Notes in Remembrance of a Friendship**

The Scenic Railway

Remembering the Earlier Auden

The Coming Day and Other Stories

Also available

Edward Upward: A Bibliography 1920-2000
by Alan Walker

Edward Upward

A Renegade in Springtime

Selected Short Stories

Edited by Alan Walker

ENITHARMON PRESS

First published in 2003
by the Enitharmon Press
26B Caversham Road
London NW5 2DU

www.enitharmon.co.uk

Distributed in the UK by
Central Books
99 Wallis Road
London E9 5LN

Distributed in the USA and Canada
by Dufour Editions Inc.
PO Box 7, Chester Springs
PA 19425, USA

© Edward Upward 2003
Introduction and appendices © Alan Walker 2003

ISBN 1 900564 23 8 (hardback)
ISBN 1 900564 64 5 (limited edition of 50 numbered and signed copies,
cloth-bound by The Fine Bindery)

British Library Cataloguing-in-Publication Data.
A catalogue record for this book is available
from the British Library.

Typeset in Bembo by Servis Filmsetting Ltd, Manchester
and printed in England by
Antony Rowe Ltd

BOOKS BY EDWARD UPWARD

Journey to the Border (Hogarth Press, 1938)

* * *

THE SPIRAL ASCENT: A TRILOGY

In the Thirties (Heinemann, 1962; Penguin Books, 1969)

The Rotten Elements (Heinemann, 1969; Penguin Books, 1972)

No Home but the Struggle (Heinemann, 1977)

The Spiral Ascent was also published in one volume by Heinemann in 1977, and reissued in three paperback volumes by Quartet in 1978–79

* * *

The Railway Accident and Other Stories
(Heinemann, 1969; Penguin Modern Classics, 1972 and 1988)

The Night Walk and Other Stories (Heinemann, 1987)

* * *

Journey to the Border – a revised version (Enitharmon Press, 1994)
introduced by Stephen Spender

An Unmentionable Man (Enitharmon Press, 1994)
introduced by Frank Kermode

(with Christopher Isherwood)
The Mortmere Stories (Enitharmon Press, 1994)
introduced by Katherine Bucknell

Christopher Isherwood: Notes in Remembrance of a Friendship (Enitharmon Press, 1996)

The Scenic Railway (Enitharmon Press, 1997)

Remembering the Earlier Auden (Enitharmon Press, 1998)

The Coming Day and Other Stories (Enitharmon Press, 2000)

To the memory of my son Christopher

Contents

Introduction by Alan Walker	9
A Note on the Text	17
The Railway Accident	19
Sunday	53
The Island	59
The Procession	69
An Old-Established School	76
At the Ferry Inn	90
The White-Pinafored Black Cat	101
An Unmentionable Man	116
A Ship in the Sky	133
Emily and Oswin	150
Imaginative Men & Women	167
The Scenic Railway	176
Appendix 1: Publication details	195
Appendix 2: Edward Upward short story collections	198

Introduction

These twelve stories describe a literary career whose trajectory is unique. Edward Upward is now sole survivor of the celebrated 'Auden generation' of young poets and novelists whose outlook was forged by the political imperatives of the 1930s. Still writing and publishing as he approaches his centenary, Upward has never gained the wider recognition so freely accorded to the contemporaries he outlived. Until recently he seemed to have become, in his own rueful phrase, 'an unmentionable man'. Yet this is a figure whom Auden cited as a crucial influence on his early work, who was a lifelong friend and mentor of Christopher Isherwood, and who convinced Stephen Spender of the necessity of commitment to the communist cause. The scale of his importance seems matched by the depth of his neglect.

The roots of this predicament are both personal and political. Over a lifetime Upward has published only a fraction of what he has written. He endured a lengthy period in early middle age when he was unable to produce any work of substance at all. Only since his retirement from teaching in 1961 has he been able to devote the time and energy required for a sustained literary output. It is a curious fact that half of his published titles have appeared in the past nine years alone, under the Enitharmon imprint. It is also surprising to learn that seventy-six volumes of private diaries, together with a hoard of other writings – poems, essays and fiction, even abandoned novels and plays – have yet to see the light of day. Perhaps in consequence, Upward's renown as a writer is not as great as it could or should be.

Political factors must also be weighed. After the Second World War Upward never recanted his left-wing opinions. When he left the Communist Party in 1948 he did so not as an act of apostasy so typical of that era, but because he felt the Party was no longer genuinely revolutionary. He continued unrepentant as a lone practitioner of themes peculiar to his fiction, notably the tenor of life within the communist movement of the mid-twentieth century, and the barriers it created between artistic expression and political commitment. This was unpromising territory on which to rebuild a literary career in the midst of the cold war. Upward had difficulties in securing and retaining a publisher, and often drew the critical censure of the mainstream press. He was seen as an original talent that went willingly into the thrall of political dogma, his career more a cautionary tale than a record of achievement.

In truth Upward has repeatedly shown a capacity to revoke and renew his artistic direction while maintaining a consistency of belief. As a youth he filled thirty-eight notebooks with poetic juvenilia and won prizes for his verse at both Repton and Cambridge, but abandoned poetry for prose soon after submitting examples of his work to the uncompromising judgement of Auden. Upward is still perhaps best known for his dazzling early fantasy *The Railway Accident*, set in the mythical village of Mortmere which he first devised with Isherwood while undergraduates at Cambridge. *The Railway Accident* was written in 1928 but remained unpublished for twenty-one years. In manuscript form it enjoyed a *samizdat* status among Auden and other 1930s writers, and did much to create a literary aesthetic for that decade. By then, however, Upward had turned his back on fantasy and embraced the tenets of communism. Later still he was to destroy the bulk of his Mortmere manuscripts.

The Railway Accident is an altogether fantastic narrative in which plot takes second place to spectacle. The storyline – two men embark on a train journey which ends in violent collision, following which they are swiftly transposed to a treasure hunt in a country vicarage – is shot through with a displaced interior dialogue, non-sequiturs that seem to whisper directly in the ear:

'Fond of poetry?'
'I say, I'm frightfully sorry, I mean I'd no idea there was anyone else in the carriage.'

Introduction

'Hadn't you, ah ha. Well, I'll admit I slipped in rather on the quiet. Part of my trade you know. Otherwise you could never be sure what they weren't doing in the dormitories.'

The descriptive language likewise moulds a vivid cast of the unreal, a luminous dreamscape that reaches back to the summertime idyll of the *Alice* stories and forward to the psychedelia of the 1960s:

Up the bleached gravel drive, oppressed by ink-dark trees. Lilac bifurcated past the windscreen in perfumes of wan blue gauze. Odours of chimes of croquet hoops, tango of views of choirboys through the rustling privet. A lawn-mower wove its rainbow fountain among imagined rock and fern. Shreeve had fainted. The front door was held open by the brass head of a fox. Summer mildly billowed into a hall shadowy as a cave where Welken's geographical globes faded beneath clusters of hats. A rubber ball struck one of the windows.

Perhaps inevitably, Upward was unable to repeat this *tour de force*, though its example haunted him for years to come. The spirit of Mortmere walks visibly abroad in his first novel, *Journey to the Border*, published by Leonard and Virginia Woolf at the Hogarth Press in 1938, and in the short story *Sunday* which appeared five years earlier in the same publisher's formative anthology of 1930s writing, *New Country*. Both of these works deal with the act of initial commitment to the workers' movement, yet even here the world of fantasy cannot completely be excluded. *Sunday* begins with a statement by the protagonist, a neurotic and downtrodden office clerk, which appears to be exported directly from Mortmere:

I am going back to lunch. There is no ambush, no one will ask me to show an entrance ticket, I have not tampered with the motor-mower, no butcher-boy has chalked my name on the basin of the fountain.

This form of paranoid surrealism fits its subject well, but is notably absent at the end of the story. By this point, when the narrator has made the decision to engage in the political struggle, the language is simple: 'It will take time. But it is the only hope. He will at least have made a start.'

This disparity of diction is seen in another contemporary story, *The Island*, which first appeared in *Left Review* in 1935. The island in question is the Isle of Wight, which Upward had known since childhood and is here celebrated rather in the style of a Mortmere travelogue. The opening headlong paragraph sweeps the reader breathlessly into the narrative:

> What are you fond of? Is it the sun, is it the girls, is it mornings in rowing-boats, is it giving yourself wild primroses, or trickily nursing a frantic box-kite, or studying at first hand materials of history or of geology, or identifying distant liners, is it palaces on the screens of picture palaces, or the narrow strip of wheel racing beneath the silver-bright handle-bars of your cycle, or larking for hours with the kids, or walking for miles, or reading a serious book, dancing, wearing pink, just lying flat on the sands?

This all-embracing paradise, which seems to anticipate the vignettes of the future envisioned in Auden's *Spain 1937*, is challenged by a group of touring cyclists who are 'singing of hunger and war and social revolution.' When the holiday island is reviewed through their eyes the supposed seaside attractions are thrown into reverse:

> Or look with new eyes at the amusement arcade, the strings of coloured light-bulbs along the sea-front, the soft-witted advertisements outside the picture-houses – what are these but hypocritical decorations concealing danger and misery, fraudulent as vulgar icing on a celebration cake rotten inside with maggots, sugary poison to drug you into contentment?

The language in this paragraph is one of bitter rhetoric. The acute contrasts of tone in both *Sunday* and *The Island* prefigure all the problems of stylistic unity that Upward would subsequently experience. He possessed a natural flair for the unusual and the bizarre,

Introduction

which inspired him to beautifully loaded and balanced prose; but his political faith insisted that he wrote of plain facts in plain style. This dilemma eventually drained him of imaginative resource, and following the publication of two short prose pieces in the early 1940s he entered a literary silence that would last for twenty years. Once the everyday political struggle had been joined, it appeared there was nothing more to be said.

All of forty-five years and an entire literary cycle separate *The Island* from the next story in the collection, *The Procession*. The return to writing was long and painful for Upward, and to achieve it he was prepared to relinquish a great deal. In 1954 he began work on the autobiographical trilogy that would later be known as *The Spiral Ascent*. When the first volume, *In The Thirties*, appeared in 1962, many critics were hostile. It was felt Upward had harnessed his imagination to a literal style of narrative, with an overt flatness of tone and dialogue that bordered on the stilted. This process appeared confirmed when the second volume, *The Rotten Elements*, was published in 1969 with the subtitle 'A Novel of Fact'. Even here, all was not as it seemed. On careful reading the prose in these novels seems as intricate and deft as in any of Upward's works, while the dialogue is genuinely an attempt to capture the speech patterns used in left-wing political debate. Beneath the apparent realism of the books there hangs an intangible air of mystery that invests the suburban documentary setting with a sense of sleepwalking determination on the part of the hero, Alan Sebrill. Certainly *The Rotten Elements* can be read in diverse ways, not least as a psychological thriller.

Nevertheless Upward was stung by some of the criticism levelled at the trilogy. When he returned to the short story format in the late 1970s he wished to recapture the atmosphere of radiant strangeness that had come so easily to his Mortmere fiction. In *The Procession*, published in *The Night Walk and Other Stories* (1987), Upward describes the experience of a famous painter who watches from a balcony as what he assumes to be his own funeral cortège passes in the street below. At the end of the story Upward notes:

> This was not a dream. I have invented it, with help from an actual nightmare I had in bed at home several years ago. It is

A Renegade in Springtime

a fantasy, and not even a realistic one. Yet it may convince me that I can after all tell the truth about reality in a style that comes more readily to me than naturalism.

By these means Upward signalled at least a partial return to his early fantastic style. *The Night Walk* showed Upward able for the first time to assemble fantasy and realism within the same volume, or even the same story. Supposedly realistic tales include *An Old-Established School*, which recounts the travails of an elderly supply teacher who unexpectedly receives a supportive kiss from a beautiful female colleague. The reader may consider this fantasy enough, but the story is credible whether the kiss was real or imagined. Also straddling the two conventions lies *At the Ferry Inn*, a yearning account of a latter-day reunion between Upward and Auden at an Isle of Wight pierhead, which never in fact took place. Where the realism is triumphantly beyond doubt is in *The White-Pinafored Black Cat*, an unsparing yet tender study of loneliness and old age, quite without political content, in which the lead character is not, as Stephen Spender has pointed out, a fictional version of the author himself. This story is perhaps Upward's finest work in a naturalistic vein, and fittingly it was adapted for broadcast on BBC Radio 3 under the title of *The Sister Who Survived*.

Having at last been able to integrate the disparate impulses of his writing, Upward has undergone a remarkable late flowering, with his rediscovery by the Enitharmon Press and three further volumes of new short stories: *An Unmentionable Man* (1994), *The Scenic Railway* (1997), and *The Coming Day and Other Stories* (2000). In addition, the original *Mortmere Stories* written by Isherwood and Upward in the 1920s were at last issued by Enitharmon in 1994, along with a revised version of Upward's first novel, *Journey to the Border*. Memoirs of Auden and Isherwood have followed. As if these publications were not enough, Upward has lodged sufficient material in the British Library to furnish at least one further collection of new stories. The title of this volume, *A Renegade in Springtime*, is taken from one such story.

Many of the late stories are vibrantly surrealist, erotic, scatological. While they clearly proclaim their Mortmere ancestry, and

Introduction

have even earned Upward the title of a 'prose Magritte', they remain preoccupied with Upward's own socialist mission as a writer, and the popularity this has cost him. *An Unmentionable Man* is largely a linked series of short stories relating the dreams of an elderly writer, Stephen Highwood, who has been attacked in the street and admitted unconscious to hospital. The dreams are schematic and sequential, rather as those in medieval poetry. At the heart of their picaresque maze the narrative remains firmly under control, and even the most indulgent passages show a measured attention to detail, as in the portrait of a middle-aged woman in *A Ship in the Sky*:

> She could be in her forties. Her red hair had probably been dyed, and she wore a heavily jewelled necklace in several strands which gave only a few glimpses of the flesh that her low-cut evening gown would otherwise have revealed. She was perfumed, expensively perhaps, but the perfume failed to disguise a rich smell of alcohol.

The stories also move beyond Mortmere in their attempt to explore the depth of the irrational, rather than merely span its surface. In the same story the writer Stephen Highwood is heard to murmur in his sleep:

> 'What is it that's so scaring about the word "Andromeda"?
> I think it must be the hollow sound of that syllable "drom".'

This passing remark, highly characteristic of Upward, unsettles with its sudden shaft of fear, and serves as a timely prompt for the next dream-instalment, where the ship of the story's title is of course the *Andromeda*.

Not all of Upward's recent work has been surrealist in style, and he is still able to compose naturalistic stories that are all the more refreshing when set alongside the exuberance of fantasy. One story, *Emily and Oswin*, traces an instance of role reversal between a man and woman late in life; another, *Imaginative Men & Women*, is an atmospheric cameo of the Second World War, where a group of friends have tea in the garden while a nearby shipyard is bombed. The balance of tone within these stories, recounting everyday lives amid unusual circumstances, is as much a property of Upward's recent work as the rediscovered power of fantasy.

This equilibrium is displayed to masterful effect in *The Scenic Railway*, another story of old age that is the single most important work of Upward's latter career. Originally published in 1987, it was not collected for another ten years. The title obviously nods to *The Railway Accident*, and in some ways the two stories can be seen to act as prologue and epilogue to Upward's literary opus. In *The Scenic Railway* the lead character, Leslie Brellis (an anagram of Sebrill), escorts a group of the elderly disabled to an amusement park. Leslie, himself an old man, experiences a series of historical visions while riding on the park's scenic railway: the Christmas truce on the Western Front in 1914, the battle of Jarama in the Spanish Civil War. Finally he reaches a point where the visionary world he has entered supersedes his physical whereabouts, and he returns to his childhood home to be greeted by his long dead parents. In the final paragraph the act of sitting in a remembered chair becomes a kind of mortal regression:

> 'Home is a place where I am well thought of,' he said to himself as he sank into the comfort of his armchair, as he slid more deeply, more and more deeply, downwards into its safety.

This passage recalls Seamus Heaney's infant memory in the poem sequence *Lightenings* of sitting in a boat with his mother and aunts, 'three sisters talking, talking steady / In a boat the ground still falls and falls from under'. It is perhaps significant that the ready comparisons for Upward's work are with poets, Auden or Heaney, rather than writers of prose. Despite his early abandonment of poetry, Upward's gift is essentially poetic, and it is no accident that the hero of his trilogy *The Spiral Ascent*, Alan Sebrill, should be a poet. Like many poets before him Upward has discovered through experience that imaginative truth and literal truth are not exactly

Introduction

commensurate. It is a happy outcome of his long life that he should at last have found a means of expressing in his chosen language the political ideals he holds so dear.

ALAN WALKER

A Note on the Text

The editorial principle which has been adopted in the reprinting of these stories is to select the latest version authorised by Edward Upward himself. Thus *The Railway Accident* is taken from the version anthologised in *The Mortmere Stories* (Enitharmon Press, 1994), for which Upward made a number of minor amendments. *Sunday* and *The Island* are both reprinted from the edition of *The Railway Accident and Other Stories* published by Penguin Modern Classics in 1972 and reissued in 1988. *An Old-Established School, At the Ferry Inn, The Procession,* and *The White-Pinafored Black Cat* are all as published in *The Night Walk and Other Stories* in 1987, except for a number of minor amendments which Upward has made to the latter three of these texts for the present edition. All other stories are taken from the Enitharmon Press editions in which they were first collected. A publication history of each short story is given in Appendix 1.

The Railway Accident

'One more.'

'Thanks no, really.'

But Gunball had already signalled with a slow regardless movement of his forefinger to the girl wheeling a dumb-waiter on rubber tyres quietly through the tin wailing of milk-cans and the drawl of trolleys. I leant on the wood of the lowered carriage window, observing with the sharpened pleasure of an anticipated farewell the metropolitan morning striking down through risen straw specks, dust of horse dung, beneath the glass arch of the Terminus roof. A horse-drawn mail-van flickered red at the interstices of the platform barrier, there was frost in the air and I had, not intellectually but sensationally, a conviction of warmth which remembrance of the falsely tender coaching lithographs in Gunball's sitting-room would not have destroyed, since they would have been irrelevant to what seemed an impression quite unassociated with the past. Beyond the barrier a soldier in khaki carrying full marching kit was watching one of the horses. Another soldier had passed the ticket collector and had begun to walk up the platform. More were coming.

'What's the idea, I wonder?'

'Idea or no, the whole pack of them are getting on your train,' said Gunball. He carried two cups of coffee. I took both while he fetched out a flask from one of his angler's pockets and poured more than a little brandy into my cup.

'You'll need it. There's a nip in the air this morning. Spring-cleaning the gravestones. Well, I wish I were you. Give them all my love and tell them how sorry I am to miss the Treasure Hunt. My word, you'd not know we were in sight of the first of May.'

Nevertheless he wore no overcoat, seemed warm, and I recognized in his remark that advertisement, blatant or discreet, of the power of the weather which is necessary to most sportsmen who have left the country even for a few hours. Through the roof panes the sun froze whey-white on steam columns from the waiting engines. Other insignia of the bogus, curt and modern cathedral ceremony which in my daydream, induced partly by the cold, I had begun to arrange were the reverberating stammer of slipping driving-wheels on suburban trains and the fussing haste of porters loading the guard's van with wooden crates. Outside the station the air would be warm and I should remember clock-golf in the rectory garden, or there would be heavy snow recalling the voluntarily ascetic life I had often planned: there would be crocuses or vultures, it would not be the same as it was here. Immediately the train started everything would be changed.

'Just like the rector to have forgotten where he'd hidden the thing.'

'And then to have lost the plans.'

'Isn't it?' He guffawed without spite. 'All the same, beggared if I'd travel up there myself on a day like this *solely* in order to remind him. Besides, we could have done that by wire.' He smiled, ostentatiously shrewd. 'Who's the skirt?'

'Oh, the barmaid's Angora rabbit. Well, I'll remember to give him that message in your words.'

'Which?'

'"Try squinting under the damp beehive in the summerhouse."'

'All right: but don't harp on it for too long or he'll get fussed with the idea that one of the competitors might overhear you.'

'Anyway, what exactly is the treasure this year?'

'An ivory papercutter. Given by Harry Belmare. Good thing you took a first-class ticket. By the time they've loaded on the China Expeditionary Force, or whoever they are, there won't be room for a dry hug in the whole train.'

'I suppose Anthony Belmare's term won't have begun yet.'

'Probably not. That's another reason why I'm not over keen to be at the Hunt. The boy's all right, of course. It's the effect he seems to have on the others that I don't fancy. Shreeve and Wherry prancing about and imagining they're school kids again. Ten to one someone'll get a cricket stump pushed through his eyeball. Of course, I'm exaggerating but that's the kind of thing. You've got the carriage to yourself. You'll find chocolates in that newspaper and here's my reserve flask. Think that's gunpowder they're shoving into the van? There'll be meringues for tea if I know the rector's baker. My, I've a good mind to chuck up this shooting in the Black Forest and take a snooze on those cushions. Heads or tails, heads – tails, as it happens. Well, perhaps after all if it had been heads and I'd bought a ticket, something else would have gone against me; Griever might have got hydrophobia. Porter!'

'Yes, sir.'

'Just take a look at this window for a moment. No, not over there; it's this corner, I mean. Anything to attract your attention?'

'I don't think so, sir.'

'You couldn't suggest a certain rearrangement?'

'Well, sir, there's those golf clubs on the edge of the rack.'

'Oh, those are safe enough. Mr Hearn's not off on a sea voyage. But you might have noticed that the heating pipes are under the right-hand seat and that a suitcase placed against them is sure to protrude a few more inches than it would from under the seat on the left-hand side. You don't expect Mr Hearn to rub his ankles against that during the whole journey. Well, make a note of it. Myself, I've always found it a good plan before breakfast every morning to rehearse in my mind what I intend to do during the day; it lessens the chance of small oversights. Ah, one thing more: if you could procure an extra rug from somewhere I'll see you get a couple of pints for lunch. It's none too warm this morning by God.'

'What with the heater on and three rugs I shan't feel it much unless I pop off to sleep after ten miles.' I again glanced past him to watch a long corridor train with restaurant and sleeping cars which had drawn up on the opposite side of the platform. I should have taken a no more detailed mental photograph of it than most poets do of elaborate architecture if I had not been able to give it a place immediately in one of those non-technical elastic classifications, which alone satisfied my intelligence, of objects describable only by their effects on persons. My first thought was of a day spent in a racing motor-boat on a very calm sea. But the coaches, which seemed of a new triple bogie pattern crouched on concealed springs, were too heavily built, almost armoured, to sustain the image, and I remembered the picture in an illustrated journal of a man-carrying rocket designed by some scientific advertiser to be fired towards the moon from a gun. My instantaneous caricature of my own impression spoilt my chances of discovering what it really was; but there could be no doubt of the interest displayed by a middle-aged man wearing a plaid overcoat in the couplings and buffers between two of the coaches most nearly opposite my window. He was testing them with the end of a walking-stick. He turned, rapped heavily with his boot against the incurve of the coach-work, which I then knew to be what I had not supposed from distant inspection, cast steel. I remembered the face of George Wherry, architect to the Mortmere Rural Council, but was not sure that I had identified him.

'All those rats,' Gunball said, not explaining that he meant the soldiers, small cockneys with bow legs and peg teeth who now occupied the platform in groups from end to end of the train.

Wherry had finished his examination and had entered one of the restaurant cars. His face barely above the level of the lowest part of the embrasure peered from an oblong window. Like an electrically moved cardboard football in a sports outfitter's window it shifted almost surprisingly without revolving, devoid as cardboard of animation, towards the left-hand or rear-most corner of the window, then passed out of sight. The cast steel coachwork was painted grey, studded at intervals with visible rivet heads such as one sees on girder bridges or in the saloons of smaller paddle-steamers. Less space than I thought usual had been allowed for the windows. The panes, which seemed dark, were on the streamline principle, distinctly curved inwards towards a roof surmounted by scarcely projecting cone ventilators. However, I hardly supposed that the coaches were lit by gas and I wondered why ventilation could not have been obtained, as it usually is, through superimposed movable hatches above the windows. My impression of most details in the design of this train was that they were unnecessary or, if necessary, belonging to a world in which I should have felt as wholly disorientated as though, suffering from amnesia after an accident, I had found myself among hoardings bearing futurist German advertisements. I pictured myself leaning over a level crossing gate watching trains; I could not see this train pass until I altered the scene to weak moonlight with ravines and a sharp curve in the line allowing me to include all the coaches in a single and close view. Very long, tubular, dead, they turned with mournful speed at the bend, did not sway, plunged into the red earth and tree-roots of a landslip, emerged with the ease of a saw. Chambers of oblivion in which not one of the passengers returned to consciousness until a porter opening the carriage door shouted that the train had reached its destination.

'So I suppose this one will go there too,' I heard Gunball say.

'Where? Which one?'

'The train you're leaning out of at the moment. To Mortmere. But I was just saying I'd noticed that the other one certainly does. Look at that end coach; you don't see many of those on the main lines.'

It would have been too late to change. An eddy of hustling soldiers clashing water-bottles, trenching-tools, ration-tins, flooded between myself and Gunball who, like a bather surprised in the middle of a facetious gesture by a heavy wave, was scarcely able to shout: 'Anyway, yours will arrive somewhere.' A whistle blew with vicious sharpness, the train had started, the guard had rerolled his flag and vaulted on to the running-board of the luggage van. Then only, glancing through shifting gaps in the thinned but still racing groups of soldiers who had not yet been able to mount the train, was I convinced that the carriage which Gunball had designated was certainly of the out-of-date refitted type usually employed on the Mortmere slip-line. The narrow high body-design, compared with that of the preceding corridor coaches, had the top-heaviness and antique lines of an extended sedan chair, but it suggested also that this carriage could have negotiated very deep cuttings where the brambles had been neglected for years by the rural officials and where, as I indolently began to imagine, the signalman's eye must not be distracted by the vivid colours of fresh paint moving among the trees. If my train did not go to Mortmere I could get another the next day, or Welken might guess what had happened and send his car. The first gasometers, restful, solemn like stumps of semi-amputated breasts, curved past the window in frost-bright air. Wireless poles and drying pants in soot-black gardens with mustard and cress sprouting from window boxes would soon follow. Now for many months of complete summer I should idle in gardens warm with croquet and the tinkling of spoons, shadowed by yews. Naked bathing would be usual and the rector would fish for pike off log-rafts. Only the King may shoot swans. Do you eat mango salad, Mr Hearn? Yes, oh yes, certainly yes, though I have not ever, I now will.

'Fond of poetry?'

'I say, I'm frightfully sorry, I mean I'd no idea there was anyone else in the carriage.'

'Hadn't you, ah ha. Well, I'll admit I slipped in rather on the quiet. Part of my trade you know. Otherwise you could never be sure what they weren't doing in the dormitories.'

By chance I recognized him as Gustave Shreeve, but I knew that he did not know me and that it was only his exceptional self-conceit which made him forget that he wore no visible decoration to show that he was headmaster of Frisbald College. His large ears protruded almost at right angles to his temples – always a sign, to my mind, of an assertive, fussy temperament. He brought down a small suit-case from the rack, searched with vicious haste in the pockets of his country overcoat, mustard-brown and reminiscent of frosty afternoons on the touchline, for a pencil. He drew a fairly straight line freehand on a writing pad which he had produced from the case, stopped, glanced up to speak.

'Are you for Mortmere?'

'Yes.'

'Ah so am I.'

'Good, then I'm right after all.'

'Well, I see we've managed to secure a carriage in the safest part of the train.' I supposed he meant the rear. He laughed like a clergyman who has made a joke about a subject in which secretly he is seriously interested; then as if regretting his perhaps after all risky levity he added didactically: 'The safest part of any *long-distance* train.'

'You're not a keen railway traveller, perhaps?' I asked with deference.

'Very keen indeed. Of course I was joking just now. I'd as soon take my luck in the cab of the engine. Set me down anywhere on the track between here and Mortmere and I guarantee I'll tell you to within a sixteenth of a mile where I am. And not many regular travellers could do that. You know, speaking quite seriously, I believe there is nothing in this world of ours which if regarded from the right angle will not seem vitally interesting.'

'Yes, that's what I've always felt.'

'Yet you yourself,' he went on with approval, 'must already have knocked up against persons who can find nothing more intelligent to do during long railway journeys than sleep or read a novel.'

'I know.'

'Or play some footling card game on a mackintosh.'

'Not much chance of those chaps next door doing that.'

'Ah, why's that?'

'Well, look what a crowd of them there was at the station.'

'That's so,' he agreed with noticeable eagerness. 'Wonder who they are. Market gardeners, perhaps.'

'No, it's the troops I was thinking of.'

'What do you mean, troops?'

'You know, all that gang on the platform.'

'Ah, but they didn't get on this train,' he informed me. 'In fact, I should hardly expect to find troops travelling at all today, but if they did you can be pretty sure they would go by the other one, which is considerably the faster.'

'Then I'm afraid things have changed since you last came this way. Look at that door.' I pointed to the varnished partition separating the third from the first class section of the corridor. 'Well, I'll wager my return fare that that bulge in the upper panel isn't caused by the damp. Besides you must have seen them boarding the train when it started. The only thing I can't understand is why they're all keeping so quiet.'

'Probably you were misled, quite naturally, by seeing a few regulars giving their friends in this train, civilians of course, a good old military send-off.'

'Surely you can't have helped noticing at least one of them getting into the carriage next door to this – or next door to wherever you were when we left the station? It isn't as though their boots were soled with velvet.'

'Oh, I arrived pretty late, a last moment dash in fact, too late to have noticed my own daughter if she'd been there. But the fundamental point is this: You'll always find that troops, if they are present in any number, travel by express.'

'Well, if you arrived late I can't help feeling that that's just the time when you'd have had a very good chance of seeing them with your own eyes.'

'Excuse me, but this isn't the fast train.'

A terse crash of glass from the hidden corridor proved me right. Organized deafening laughter announced the success of some well-prepared booby-trap. At last they had begun. Hobnails rasped against varnish, rifles fell, a choir using toilet paper and combs played the first bars of the Forfarshire Stallion. The communication cord suddenly sagged, hung in a slackening useless loop.

'Lord. Well that's judgement with costs all right. So I suppose this must be the fast train after all.'

'Fast be damned,' he said with excessive vehemence. 'I'm sorry, but if you took the interest in railways that I happen to do you wouldn't make a statement like that quite so casually. I can tell you that alterations in the scheduled times aren't made over the breakfast table. If they are, well, God help us.'

'I know. Ten minutes late for an appointment and you lose a rattling good post in the colonies which would have made you for life.'

'GUARD.'

'Good God, what's happened?'

'GUARD.'

'Well, sir, I can't stand much nearer.'

'Of course this isn't the fast train, eh?'

'No, sir, you're right.'

'There you are.' Shreeve turned to me, less with triumph than with an absurd relief.

The Railway Accident

'Well, it seems the subject of our discussion has undergone an important alteration. The only statement of yours which I disputed was that there were no troops on this train.'

'Ah, I can see you are in the legal profession. It's a clever point. But I'm afraid the judge in this case is too old to lose sight of the issue. By the way, Guard, how is it that these soldiers have been planted on us at the last moment?'

'Change in the orders I suppose, sir.'

'But doesn't the Company raise any objections to this kind of thing?' I pointed towards the dangling communication cord.

'They get reparations, sir. Of course, we've come to expect trouble from these Territorials by now. The worst lot in the country. Colonel Moxon's English Rifles: though I believe Major Wherry has the command this Summer as they say the C.O. has gone abroad.'

'I saw Wherry in the other train,' I said absently.

The Guard's information exhumed no memories in Shreeve's mind. He seemed pleased, had an idea. The lax introverted smile of a nervous fisherman suddenly successful after hours of tension in a trippers' pierhead competition. He brought out an enamelled pencil sharpener barnacled with small wads of blotting paper, hair balls, husks of chicken food, from a waistcoat pocket, and used it rapidly on the pencil with which he had already made marks across his note pad.

'That sounds as though they're getting up a tug of war in the corridor,' I said. 'I wonder how much more the door will stand.'

'I don't know what it'll stand,' said Shreeve, 'but I know what I won't, and that's all this damned row they're making. Like a pack of girls.' He stood up.

'You'll only irritate them if you do anything,' I said. 'We don't want them all in here fooling about with bayonets.'

'Irritate them?' He was half-humorously amazed. 'Well that's one way of looking at sound discipline. Do you think the Colonel keeps a record of their individual fads and consults it every time he gives an order to form fours?'

'That's rather different.'

'It's a difference which made a tenth of the map red.'

The Guard had stepped out of the compartment and begun to retire towards his van. Anyway, that ought to show that the partition door is already locked, I thought. I turned to Shreeve: 'But seriously I think it would be better not to call attention to ourselves just now.'

'Well, if you'd rather not,' he said tolerantly, 'but I think it's a bad principle. Not because I'm a rabid spit-and-polish man. Only because I foresee that if we don't warn them of our presence now we shall certainly have to later on in the journey. I'm not going to suffer for any volunteer officer's incompetence.'

He replaced the sharpener in his pocket, began to draw carefully, his rigid knees resisting the jolts of the now racing train. I thought out what I should do when the English Rifles burst the partition door. Here's the man who thumped on the panel. Here; I've been cursed with him and his insults against the Army for over an hour. If as long. Probably longer, since we were passing the aerodrome and Camber Woods already. It wouldn't matter how ignominious: Shreeve would never be there to tell them. An airman in furs swung the propeller of a small monoplane. Someone was killing a rabbit with wire in the spinney. Seagulls on arable land far from the sea estuary circled for worms. A dung heap smoked in the damascene steel air. Woods passed like frozen paper. Further on, the girders of a bridge receded obliquely, very close to the window; the train's clatter changed to a lulling profounder rhythm.

'I suppose you've been wondering all this time what I'm up to.'

'I have, yes.'

'I'm making a rough map of our route, the various landmarks, you know, bridges, signal cabins, the main branch lines, etcetera. Any objects which can fairly be said to have a connection with the railway. It's a small thing I always like to do during a journey. If you were to ask why, I'm not sure whether I should be able to tell you concisely in a few words. I suppose it's because I've always felt impelled to take an interest in whatever happened to be going on round about me at a given moment. And, do you know, the man whom, as I realize more and more every year, I have truly to thank for that little habit is my old headmaster?' His wholehearted smile left no doubt that that gracious portrait had in a very few seconds been discarded in the portfolio for another more striking.

'I wish I had the knowledge to do something of that kind.'

'But it's not knowledge you need,' he urged keenly. 'Anyone could do it. Just take a look at this. Here's our main line – pretty roughly drawn, of course, but that's from memory – here's the central signal cabin at Belstreet Junction, here's where they control the points leading to the new slipline. Damn.'

The tug of war had probably gone to the team nearest to the partition door. A sharp crack from thin wood interrupted Shreeve's voice and I saw that the upper panel had split down the middle. It still screened from us the adjacent section of the corridor. I waited for laughter but heard only the exaggerated cheers of the winning team. Probably none of them had noticed.

'That's as much as I intend to stand.'

'Well I don't know. After all, they haven't been kicking up quite so much noise until now. I expect they'll get bored. They'll settle down on their own accord before we've done another few miles.'

'All right, here's an agreement we can come to between ourselves,' he said definitely. 'If there's any further trouble I go and tell them exactly what I think. That settled?'

'And ask them whether they're really there,' I evaded.

'Ah, now you're chaffing.'

'Well you'll admit that at first you didn't altogether believe me.'

'Yes, I admit. But then, not seeing them myself, and arriving as early as I did. . . .'

'Early?'

A slip of the tongue. He flushed. 'I told you I was late, I know. I'm afraid that was a bit of a fib. But when I've explained the circumstances I think you'll understand why.'

'Of course.'

'The truth is I was in the W.C. at the end of the corridor.'

'Ah.'

'Not actually using it, of course. Not while the train was standing in the station. There's nothing I detest more than that kind of failure to consider the comfort of others.'

'Yes.'

A Renegade in Springtime

'You're wondering what I was in there for at all, no doubt. Well, it's not a long story, but it's one which I don't care to repeat often. It might give the impression, quite unjustifiably as it happens, that I was patting my own back.'

'I see.'

'Well, some years ago I was taking a stroll one half-holiday . . . it was in June I think, as the river had sunk quite three or four feet below its normal level on the banks . . . near Gatley Weirs just outside Mortmere. All of a sudden I heard a splash. A large salmon leaping, I thought. Actually it was a man who had slipped off the footbridge and couldn't swim a stroke. I didn't see him till he had passed me by about ten yards. It was going to be a race; the question was, should I overtake him before he reached the weir? I hadn't time to take off anything more than my mackintosh. Well, I got there, just on the edge. It had been devilish hard going, I can tell you, with that icy current against me all the way. I brought him round with artificial respiration. Both of us had our clothes frozen almost stiff on our bodies. I got a passing farmer to loan me his trap and we drove to the nearest cottage. I thought this chap would never stop thanking me for having saved his life. Well, about a year later I met him again. He was still harping on his debt of gratitude, as he called it. I told him I had only done what any man in my place would have been bound to do. We met several times after that, and every time it was the same story; I had saved his life. What could I say? And when he started going over the whole thing in detail in front of my friends I at last felt I couldn't bear it any longer. Now the point I've been coming to is this: I saw him today at the booking office, fortunately he didn't see me, and I heard him ask for a ticket to Mortmere. Wouldn't you, if you'd been in my place, have made yourself pretty scarce?'

'I suppose I should. All the same I can quite see that he's got every justification for being very grateful.'

'Ah, rubbish,' said Shreeve, pleased. 'Anything to escape a scene on the platform.'

'So you don't think there's any chance of running up against him in the train?'

'Oh, he's sure to have gone by the other.'

'Now there's a point which has been puzzling me. The other does go to Mortmere?'

'Of course. It's the better train of the two, in fact. Starts twenty minutes later and arrives a quarter of an hour earlier.'

'I wish I'd known that before. It would have given me time to get a decent breakfast.'

'Well, perhaps you won't regret it.'

'Why's that?'

'Those new coaches they've been putting on lately are a bit stuffy.'

'That's what was my impression. Not from a close inspection, of course, and I really know nothing about the technical side of the thing.'

His smiling attention had wandered back to the map. He added a few lines, a semi-circle, began shading, did not look up to see whether I was watching. Another train going in the opposite direction to ours passed with a single sound. Watchers on a rapidly curving platform stared like dummies, were swept away by the burnt side of a steep cutting. Massed telegraph wires rose evenly and were flung downwards again at the pole. The river reappeared, passed slowly. The workman driving a tractor could never get on to this train. Nor could any of the married women or chauffeurs living in any of these houses. Metaphysically we were as remote as Saturn or the Plough. Our times differed. Between the dipping of the iron ladle and spilling of the tar on a road dotted with navvies, Shreeve had drawn a line more than a hundred yards long, though it looked only three inches on the paper. Another hour. Cucumber sandwiches. Afterwards the bed among birded wall-paper, feeling very full, sure of dreams. And in the morning at twelve I should go to the Skull and Trumpet for news and a game of darts.

'Yes, perhaps it's as well we're on this train,' Shreeve again smiled. 'I suppose you wouldn't remember the account in the newspapers some years ago of an accident which took place in Hainwort tunnel?'

'I don't think so.'

'Well, the train that was buried was the Mortmere express. And it started at the very same time as the one you regretted you'd missed will have started today.'

'Really. And what do you infer from that?'

'Nothing exactly.' He grinned with a mystifier's conscious relish. 'But I know that if you'd been travelling then and had gone by the slower train you'd have been saved.'

'There are two ifs to that proposition,' I readily argued.

'I don't see it.'

'All logical assumptions are quibbles.'

'Anyway in real life it was the faster train which went wrong. And one of the few survivors, a great friend of mine, gave me a peculiarly interesting account of something he'd noticed about twenty minutes before the disaster.'

'Did he?'

'Yes. It was like this. The train was passing certain grounds belonging to the Belmare estate (remind me to point them out to you) and there, not more than twelve yards back from the river, he plainly saw a fisherman dressed in green standing among the rhododendrons and winding his reel. Nothing queer about that. But when he looked again he saw only a horned sheep and two swans.'

'Pretty nasty.'

'It was, wasn't it? He looked again . . . his attention had been distracted for less than a second, perhaps by some slight movement in the carriage . . . and all he saw was a horned sheep and two swans.'

'So what did he do?'

'I never asked.'

'Now frankly, did you believe him?'

'I did. And I think you would have done if he'd told you the story himself. It was not the words that convinced me, they might have appeared in any book or play, but his face. That's a thing that never lies.'

'If it had convinced me I should not have cared to travel by this line again.'

'You would if you'd thought the position out. You see, the warning only applied to the faster train.'

'Then it'll be a sinister lookout for your admirer if we spot anything in the shrubs.'

He had a brief suspicion: 'For whom? Ah, you mean the cove who thought I saved his life. I wonder if he saw me.'

The Railway Accident

'Why?' I frankly asked.

'Because, well, if you'd care to know . . .' His voice stopped, far ahead of his fumbling experimenting thought. 'Because if we were to notice anything in the rhododendrons and the chap you mentioned happened to be one of the survivors, well, I know he's superstitious. . . . I mean he might even attribute his escape merely to having seen me on the platform.'

'And follow you about Mortmere telling everyone what a hero you were.'

'Ah.'

The interesting, superficially obscure explanation he had given me seemed to linger unpleasantly in his mind. A weasel looking out of a stone dyke, scared by footsteps. By bootsteps idly drumming on the sweaty tobacco-streaked floor. By Jews-harps and thudded tins. No, again he had not heard. Or perhaps he had, and what he'd said before was all bluff. Leaves were falling outside, from the woods. There were no woods and it was March. Of course, they were birds. Cigar-shaped like brown seagulls. Without wings. One of them struck the pane, softly, flattened out into a brown uneven paste. Ruffled cones of soiled toilet paper blew past. Shreeve was marking a corner of his map very heavily with the pencil. And of all those boys who through the changing years would constantly look up to him, not one dreamed that in the privacy of his room their headmaster was, profoundly and irretrievably, a coward. Ploughed fields were succeeded by grass, a lake, a private golf course. Gentleman's country. Here Disraeli wrote his novels. Breakfast is served from the sideboard. Turf mounds rotted in the damp shadow of the cypress avenue. The head gardener had invented but could not afford to advertise a herbal balm for eczema. It had cured the master and several of his friends. There were iron railings round the trees.

'We're not far from the place now,' Shreeve said.

'And is this part of the estate?'

'It is. Though we've some way to go yet before we reach the river. What's that?'

'Only those Territorials.' My tone excused him from remembering.

'You know what we agreed.'
'Yes, I do,' I risked.
'You'd think it wise to warn them now?'
'Probably.' I became confident.
'I mean you don't feel they might calm down on their own accord after a time?'
'Not now,' I definitely cornered him.
'Very well.'
I was quite wrong; he had hesitated merely out of consideration for my own opinion. Christ. I had sprung on to the seat, fumbled for the handle of a golf club, futilely released it. Shreeve was at the partition door, his hands curved to a megaphone. He shouted in padre's affected slang: 'Here, cheese that row you fellows.'

'Bligging spak a flunka blicking spug!' A few laughed. The lower panel split noisily. 'All together, ram the fliggering backer to bitching hell.' But already some other interest deflected them. 'Chuck over and hand back me Tin Lizzy. Look at this you gowks, Sandy's gone and cut his bum. That's his own funeral for shoving it through a closed window. Bleeding like a pig, is he? Here, take my neb-wipe.' Slowly they subsided, their voices merging in the clatter of the train. Probably we were safe.

'That's settled 'em.'
'Jolly fine the way you did it.'
'Oh, well, not really. I'm pretty used to having to deal with all kinds of ragging. Boys and soldiers, they're really just one big family. Of course I don't often address my boys in that particular tone.' He smiled finely. 'It was a bit of a joke. Anyway, how can it matter so long as they don't see me?'

It was true that they seemed to have quietened down. Too much so, I thought. But perhaps Shreeve was partly right about their being like boys. During the journey they might go through at least five successive crazes. They wouldn't persist in any of them for long. Perhaps they had now returned to the booby-trap. Well, at best all they could do would be to squirt water at us through the crack in the panel. But then I could move my seat to the other side.

'Hi.'
'What is it?'

The Railway Accident

'Look.'

'A river. Ah, you mean we're somewhere near?'

'We are. It's just beyond that first clump of pines. Ever seen a lawn kept quite like that? Think of the generations of gardeners who must have been born and died before they made it what it is now. Be ready to look along my arm when I point. A panther might come out of those trees in the height of the afternoon and you wouldn't hear even so slight a sound as an ant might make on lichen. Till it had sprung at your deck-chair. If ever in any age men have seen ghosts, I do earnestly believe that it is here, in gardens such as this, frosty, at full noon, that they have seen them. Not in the moonlit chancel or the abandoned graveyard.'

'Got the salts ready?' I partly sneered.

'Mind you,' he seriously, theatrically commented, 'I'm not guaranteeing you'll see anything. And if by any wild chance you do, it will be something so indefinable that afterwards you won't be sure that you haven't imagined it. The ghoul on the corkscrew stairs and the corpse in the frozen reservoir don't cut much ice in these critical days. No, it would be very different from that. Something, a stiff hedge or perhaps a tree which some fancy gardener has been busy on, would deceive the eye. Or let's say that some pattern in the landscape would strike a sympathetic chord in your brain. You know how in large cathedrals sometimes a certain note from the organ has sympathetically affected the roof, and suddenly a chandelier weighing many tons has plunged into the crowded nave. Perhaps it would be like that. A certain vibration of light. Do you notice anything to the right of those bushes?'

'No.'

'Very well. What's *that*?'

'I don't see.'

'Quick man, THERE.'

'Where? Mind out, you'll drop your handkerchief.'

'Oh, to hell with that.'

Straining from the opened window he violently, erratically pointed, his stiff arm shaken in the racing outer air, his fingers clutching a mere corner of what seemed less like a silk handkerchief than a small green flag.

'Didn't you see anything?' he absently hoped.

'No. Not where you were pointing.'

'What's up?' He suspected suddenly, with a forced explosive laugh: 'You're looking as pale as a horse. You didn't think I was serious, did you?'

'I really couldn't say.'

'Catch a glimpse of the fisher, eh?'

'I'm afraid not. But I saw someone I happened to recognize.'

'Well, considering the pace we were going I should think you were quite probably mistaken.'

'Why?' I flashed. 'Do you know who it was?'

'Of course not. I mean, how can I guess when I don't even know who you *thought* it was?'

'Harold Wrygrave. I saw him in a car. Standing up.'

'You're wrong,' he said with noticeable readiness, 'Wrygrave always takes the Upper Fourth in French at this hour on Wednesdays.'

'Well, he must have mislaid his timetable this morning. I know I'm right because I distinctly noticed that he'd recognized you as we passed. And I rather fancy that he was standing at the salute.'

'I'm afraid it would take more than that to convince me,' Shreeve said with faint irritation. 'Of course, if you're really quite *sure* that you recognized him, well, it is just possible. He's rather a hare-brained sort of cove. And there's just the chance that knowing I'm temporarily out of the way he might have risked taking a short holiday. Even the salute which you say you noticed mightn't have been altogether imaginary. You know the truth is, unaccountable though it may seem, that that fellow thinks absolutely no end of me.'

'Does he?'

'Yes. Mind you, I don't want to boast. It isn't because of any striking virtue he may have detected in me. If anything it's what might almost have been called a weakness on my part that he admires. On a certain occasion. I wonder if you can guess what I mean?'

'I believe I do. There were rumours at the time, you know.'

'Ah, then I shan't feel I'm giving the fellow away. What happened was that I surprised him in the act. I suppose he thought that no one would visit the dormitories during the afternoon. Perhaps I ought to have brought the matter into the courts. But then, though I'd be the very first to condemn that particular offence, when I considered that it would be generally known that one of my own masters . . . well, I think any man in my shoes would have hesitated.'

'Certainly.' I wondered what far more interesting subliminal train of thought had allowed him to expose so mechanically to me an incident which officially he would have been the first to deny.

'I look at it like this. Either you take action publicly and ruin the fellow for life, or else you deal with him on the spot in your own way, and instead of making a dangerous enemy you'll have a, if one can use that word, friend who'd do anything in the world . . .' He broke off with a sudden, almost fanatical inspiration: 'Perhaps you *imagined* you'd seen him.'

'I thought I'd told you pretty clearly that I was certain of it.'

'Ah, you don't understand. I mean perhaps what you saw was not Wrygrave at all but a shape, a simulacrum with his form and features.'

'A different kind of fisher in green,' I supposed.

'Yes. Yes. That's it. An omen, a warning in the quiet of the day, a visible prefiguration it may be of death as we comfortably roll through the frozen countryside.'

'Well, it's true I thought he looked ill.'

'Pale, was he?' Shreeve subtly foreknew the symptoms: 'Looked as though he'd had a shock? As though he'd seen an apparition himself? I quite understand. That's my friend's impression all over again. But let me tell you this; both that shock and that pallor were not his but yours, transferred from you to him, to it, to the *thing* which some premonition in your brain had conjured among the rhododendrons.'

'Conjured, ah ha.'

'Well, if you think I'm yarning there's nothing more to be said. For the present. Perhaps you're right, perhaps I am. Let's hope I'm wrong. But we shall know quite soon I think, as unless I've totally misread the timetables for the last six years the other train should overtake us in a very few minutes, and then it'll have less than twenty miles to go before it arrives in the vicinity of Hainwort tunnel.'

'Why "in the vicinity"?'

'You don't suppose it's actually going into the tunnel do you?'

'I'm sure I've no idea.'

'Haven't you? Well, that's the richest I've heard for many years. No idea whether it's going into Hainwort tunnel. Lord, man, if it went into that not only would it never come out but every passenger on board would be killed as surely as though the train had fallen five thousand feet into a ravine. Every man. Not one would escape. Not a single one. You see, it was the extraordinary collapse of that tunnel, on the first day of its use, which caused the original disaster. It has never been repaired. In fact, the slipline leading to it has only once been used.'

'Well I hope it won't be used today,' I sneered.

'Ah, God forbid. Let us try to believe that Wrygrave himself may really have played the truant this morning after all. It's best not even to imagine the horrible death which for the second time in the history of that train hundreds of persons would suffer owing to the incompetent engineering, or as some are inclined to think, the criminal guilt of one man.'

'But how can you assume, even supposing there's the least detail of truth in your so-called omen, that it will be that train and no other which will crash?'

He ignored my irritation: 'Oh, *we're* safe enough, if that's what you mean. And I think if you look at my map for a moment you'll see why.' He offered me the pad, adding: 'No one to interrupt our meditations this time.'

'Yes, it's extraordinary how quiet they've been since you warned them.'

'Oh, they know well enough whether you mean business or not. Now, where was I? Belstreet Junction? Follow my finger along this line. There it is. What I want you particularly to notice is that before we reach the Junction and for some three miles after we have left it the track consists of four parallel sets of rails. You may not know why that is. I'll tell you. These two lower lines, an up line and a down, are used exclusively for express traffic, but the other

The Railway Accident

two, the ones nearest the top of the page, are for goods trains and slower passenger traffic only. Now, we are at present travelling along one of the slow lines. And the reason why we are doing this is that in a very few minutes we are going to be overtaken by the Mortmere express, the train to which my friend's delusion, if you like to put it that way, referred. Look along the page a little farther to the right. What do you notice now? *That the four parallel sets of rails have become two.* You can understand that it would be impossible for any train to overtake another here. Therefore by the time we have reached the points uniting the slow with the fast line the other train will have had to pass us already. Follow my finger. Now we have reached the spot where the disused slipline branches off the main track. I want you to tell me: Which train do you think will arrive here first?'

'The other, I suppose.'

'Quite right. The other. And, God permitting, it will be the first to draw up in Hainwort Halt, the first to deliver its passengers to the care of the Mortmere busman. How simple, how ordinary that sounds as I say it. And yet this slipline, so easily rubbed out on paper, might be the indirect cause of death to all those people.'

'Why should it?'

'There you are,' he shrugged, 'why? Why did the tunnel collapse in two places almost simultaneously ten years ago? A minute error in trigonometry. Some urchin comes during the lunch hour and fools about with the surveyor's instruments, and afterwards nobody notices that one arm of the theodolite is bent a mere division of a centimetre out of the straight. You could pretend to accept that explanation, like the coroner. But if you'd stood as I have done for many hours among those terrible ruins it might have occurred to you to wonder whether after all it was an accident, an error, that the distance between the two collapsed sections of the tunnel almost exactly corresponded to the average length of an express train.' His spittle inspissated to a jellied cord clung between his softly gabbling lips, his hot face neared me, absurdly, disproportionately excited: 'No, my friend, there is only one explanation which will fit that fact. Deliberate foulplay.'

'And I suppose you've got a pretty close idea who did it.'

I had gone too far. For a moment his voice was suspicious: 'No, I can't say I have, myself.'

'Of course not. How absurd of me. As though anyone could possibly know; when even the coroner had to accept the other explanation.'

'Well, as a matter of fact there is someone who does know. Or says he does. A great friend of mine, the same chap, as it happens, who saw the fisher and was one of the very few survivors. I'll give you his words: "As surely as Wrygrave's vice is branded on his face, that maniacal crime is stamped on the face of the fiend who did it." He declined to say anything further at the time, but from various hints he had let drop I got the impression, perhaps wrongly, that he was referring to the designer of the tunnel, the man who is at present architect to the Mortmere Rural Council.'

'Wherry?'

'You know him, do you?'

'Quite well.'

'Oh, I can guess what you think.' Shreeve was on his feet and had begun to pace the compartment: 'That he's one of the most amiable and casual of men, the last fellow in the world to have carefully planned out even a comparatively innocent practical joke. I thought so too. But when my friend, though it's true he had not actually mentioned Wherry by name, began to tell me a few things about the man's record, how at school he had been known as a liar and a cheat and in later life had even been implicated in a scandal connected with the cricket-club funds, I almost wondered whether perhaps I hadn't been mistaken, whether after all this same man mightn't have had some presentiment of the Hainwort disaster.' It was plain from Shreeve's sweating face and the vicious jerking of his clenched hands that whatever crime of Wherry's he had in mind it was not one which had been committed some ten years before. He seemed to suspect my thought, for he soon added:

'The points leading to the disused slipline are hidden from the view of the nearest signalman by a bend in the mainline cutting. A child could tamper with them. Now suppose that the man who was at least partly responsible for the first accident is still living today and that his name might be Wherry. Suppose that there are several persons on the other train who are travelling to Mortmere in order to take part in a certain Treasure Hunt and that the treasure is known to be of considerable value. Mightn't he think it expedient to delay them?'

'It would be rather short-sighted considering he'd be on the doomed train himself.'

Shreeve was perceptibly checked: 'Yes, that's true.' He frowned, withdrew into his fanatic's incomprehensible daydream, suddenly resumed: 'That's true. You saw him, I know. But what if by some amazing coincidence something did happen to that train while he was on it. Nothing serious, of course. Just something that would make him believe for an instant that at last he had been called upon to give account for the part he may have played in the wrecking of that very same train, ten years ago. I am not a vindictive man, I shouldn't like to hear that he had lain for hours slowly bleeding to death in the suffocating darkness of the tunnel which he himself had designed. But somehow if he were to receive a severe shock or even to break an ankle I couldn't sincerely feel that the retribution had altogether been unjust.'

He mused, shaking with restraint, semiconsciously fumbled for his watch, regarded its face for some seconds evidently without reading the time. I noticed that we were passing through a large station.

'That train's overdue by two minutes,' he at last said, sharply.

A faint shattering of glass surprised us. The electric-light bulb above our heads had burst and fallen into the bowl-shaped glass shade which subtended it. A slurred thud sounded from the next compartment.

'Sympathetic vibration. Perhaps they're tossing one of their comrades in a blanket and he's hit the ceiling.'

'Well, I've had enough of it,' Shreeve said.

'But that's the first sound we've heard from them for over half an hour.'

'It's the last we'll hear for the rest of the journey.'

I had followed him into the corridor, ready to move towards the guard's van. He rapped briskly on the upper panel of the partition.

A Renegade in Springtime

'Unless I have complete silence for the next twenty minutes the whole lot of you will spend the week-end in the guardroom.'

There was no response. From a more distant section of the train the thudding sounded again. Like careful heavy footsteps. Shreeve was peering through a crack in the panel.

'There's no one there. They must all have gone up to the front part of the train.'

'I don't see how they could. It would be far too crowded already.'

'All right, then they've fallen through the windows if you like. It wouldn't be so very surprising; considering the lackadaisical bolshevik they've got for one of their officers.'

The problem did not occupy him for long. Outside three sets of rails raced backwards along the cindered surface of a high but gradually descending embankment. He tapped the glass of his watch, frowned. We had returned to the compartment.

'I shall positively have to get this old turnip of mine overhauled.'

'Really?'

'It's gained quite five minutes since I put it right by the station clock.'

'Awful curse when the things begin to go wrong. Once a watch-mender gets his fingers into them they're done for, in my opinion.'

'Ten minutes, more like. You see, we've got some way to go yet before we reach Belstreet Junction.'

'I thought we'd passed it already.'

'Did you?'

'Well, we've just passed through some large station.'

'You're quite wrong. Because if we had the express would have overtaken us by now.'

'Anyway you know the line better than I do. Look out of the window and judge for yourself.'

'Of course, I can quite understand what gave you the impression,' he maintained. 'We were passing through a wood. I noticed myself that the carriage had become darker for a moment.'

'I daresay. All the same I saw the platform with my own eyes.'

'Damned rubbish,' he almost shouted. His direct obstinate regard unapparently focused some object moving outside the window, became suddenly attentive: 'Good God.'

The Railway Accident

'Well, am I right?'

He was stiff with nervous terror: 'Good God. We're done for.'

'What on earth do you mean?'

'He may have time to pull up yet. A quarter of a mile. Listen. The brakes. Thank Christ. Don't you think you can hear them?'

'I think that if you indulge in much more of this bloody nonsense you'll make yourself mentally ill.'

'Oh my God, too late.'

'What for?'

'Christ forgive me.'

A self-balancing toy bird. He rocked woodenly, lightly on the seat. I turned to my window, less with ostentatious disgust than with irritation that his nervousness had genuinely infected me. Through the interior shadow of a passing signal cabin I thought I'd imagined I'd seen a man swinging an unlit danger lamp. The fields rose slowly to the level of the embankment. Cows moved against a large rock, across grass lozenged with flat stones. A cutting interposed, shallow-sided, deepening, slagged with frosted pebbles. The train suddenly swerved. We must have branched off from the main line. What an idiot, I almost thought we had. But of course it must have been some sideline that branched off from us. I did not look at Shreeve, unwilling to let him know how much I had been scared. In these parts they allowed weeds to grow between the sleepers. Reeds. They flickered against the pane. Oh my God. Where are we? Try not to be quite such a fool. You see, rector, I really couldn't for the moment remember that I'd ever heard that there were mountains. I can tell you I almost swore I'd attend Matins for six years. What makes the rocks look so white? Struth I'm sweating. Yes, and of course those blackbirds are really condors. How extraordinarily white. Rock above rock. When you get out of this you'll wonder how on earth you ever let that bloody imbecile half-convince you that something might happen. All the same, looking at it quite disinterestedly, you'll admit that the height of this cutting must be a record. For anywhere in Europe.

'This was my work. In a moment of jealousy temptation overcame me. Now I must pay the price.' Withdrawn into a trance of fear he had begun mechanically to confess. His pudding cloth face wilted. A pool of urine increased round his feet.

He would not see me at the window. I had rammed down the sash, leant out. Like a canyon the cutting deepened among organ-pipe rocks towards the still distant mouth of a tunnel. The English Rifles were walking on the carriage roofs. Some had already reached the engine. Exceeding sixty miles an hour it visibly left the rails, jogging the foremost coaches through spraying wood from ploughed sleepers, mowing the reeds. A blinding jolt had us into the inverted rack, dazzled with glass showering like luminous fish, ricocheting between punching upholstery. Jump. The brakes savaged the wheels. Calvary. Mater. The roses. Vesperal. Burial at sea. Slowing down. Shreeve stood at the uncertain door. He jumped like a rat. Had jumped, falling softly, not stunned, not even bleeding, my spine uninjured, my eyes safe. Buried in reeds.

Shreeve called, close by. On my knees I peered, saw the train entering the tunnel. Slowly. It had almost pulled up.

'Quick. Out of this.'

An iron echo approached us. Clambering the lower rocks I turned. The express had taken the points. Booster-fitted, excessively rolling, the racing Mogul engine rounded the curve, bounded into the rear of the carriage we had left. Coaches mounted like viciously copulating bulls, telescoped like ventilator hatches. Nostril gaps in a tunnel clogged with wreckage instantly flamed. A faint jet of blood sprayed from a vacant window. Frog-sprawling bodies fumed in blazing reeds. The architrave of the tunnel crested with daffodils fell compact as hinged scenery. Tall rag-feathered birds with corrugated red wattles limped from holes among the rocks.

'Another thirty seconds in that carriage and we should have been ... well. It makes you think. And I'm afraid poor Wherry will never see Mortmere again.' Shreeve gravely turned, designated the externally undamaged cast-steel coaches of the other train. Now hedged by flames. I noticed that the out-of-date sedan carriage which in the station I had seen at the rear of the train was no longer there.

'I am truly sorry,' Shreeve added. 'He was one of the best-hearted fellows I have known. You mustn't take too seriously the things I

The Railway Accident

may have said under the stress of excitement before the accident. He was a white man all through. And there's another thing I believe I said which might have misled you. Didn't I at one time make some remark rather to the effect, "This is all my own doing"?'

'You did.'

'Well, I can explain to you *now* what I meant. The fact is you must have been right after all in supposing you saw Wrygrave in a car. At first I was rather inclined to fancy you had been pulling the long bow. But from the moment when the train took the points the whole truth flashed on me. This was his revenge. He had waited to make sure that I was on the train, then raced us to the slipline. Because two years before I had justly thrashed him after making my discovery in the dormitories. That's what I meant when I said it was my doing. If I had neglected my duty this awful disaster would not have occurred.'

'Wrygrave's no more capable of a calculated revenge than a hen. It's malicious bunk. Though I admit I couldn't answer for what he might do under the influence of blackmail. You suggest that he bore you a grudge for thrashing him; but how could he foresee that contrary to all timetables the slower train would reach the points before the other did today? No,' I emotionally accused, 'if he intended to wreck any train at all it was not ours he had in mind.'

Shreeve made no defence. Above us a voice suddenly shouted: 'Here they are.'

'Lord, forgive me.'

'SHREEVE. HEARN.'

'You fool, it's Welken.'

'God. That you, rector?'

'Yours ever. Either of you hurt? Eh? Well, take it easy, old boy. No hurry. Got the car here waiting for you. We'll have you home in a jiffy, and then you can tell us all about it.'

The arum colocasia, lupines, lentils, the pomegranate, sycamore, date palms, yew, beech and privet, fenugreek, the meloukhia, the Acacia Farnesiana, carob tree, mimosa habbas, lemon verbena, nasturtium, rose and lily. Snakes hung from the elm branches; pigeons rose from black curtains of leaves, startled by the engine of the car. The river coiled through the woods, avoiding boles of pine and willow. Across the waters of the sun-white marshes alligator fishermen punted their raft. The seaman's monument on Belstreet Down like the gnomon of a sundial cast its shadow over the roofs of the village. A quarter to five. Blue-tiled houses which had grown like bushes out of the ground.

'Well?'

'"Try squinting under the damp beehive in the summerhouse."'

'Hoch, of course! Can't think how I forgot.'

Welken had manoeuvred Shreeve into a seat beside the chauffeur and was sitting with me in the rear. Descending rooks perched on the lowered hood. At the horse-trough outside the Skull and Trumpet, Alison Kemp balancing yoked milk pails returned the rector's amiable wave. Ducks slept on the toad-green water of the pond. Nothing has been moved. A fringe of chopped straw moustached the louvre slits in the church tower. Sergeant Claptree wore a joiner's green baize apron, was retenoning the struts of his henhouse. Facetiously he sprayed the chauffeur with disinfectant from a brass syringe. Ernie Travers opened the rectory gates.

'Are they waiting for me, my lad?'

'Yes, sir. Oh thank you, sir.'

Up the bleached gravel drive, oppressed by ink-dark trees. Lilac bifurcated past the windscreen in perfumes of wan blue gauze. Odours of chimes of croquet hoops, tango of views of choirboys through the rustling privet. A lawn-mower wove its rainbow fountain among imagined rock and fern. Shreeve had fainted. The front door was held open by the brass head of a fox. Summer mildly billowed into a hall shadowy as a cave where Welken's geographical globes faded beneath clusters of hats. A rubber ball struck one of the windows.

'So Wherry's safe after all,' I said.

Shreeve's drugged face was instantly alert. Round the screen of privet Tod Erswell and Boy Radnor swerved, Wherry overtaking them.

'Sloshed you both by inches. Now let's see if you can *run*.'

'Hullo, George.'

The Railway Accident

'Gustave by God.' But he easily deflected whatever amazement he may have felt into: 'Hullo Hearn. No idea we'd have the pleasure of seeing you after all these years.'

'The two rivals,' Welken shrewdly winked. 'Who's it to be this year? Gustave looks the more determined, but George managed to arrive earlier and I'll bet you he's been out with his footrule surveying the ground.'

'Pardon me. Just a moment.' Shreeve turned and hurried from us towards the garden.

'Watch him, George, ha ha. Stealing a march, eh? But perhaps you've got the Treasure in your pocket already, have you, George?'

'Didn't I see you on the fast train today?'

'Daresay you did. That's the one I came by. Slipped a coach at Belstreet Junction. It's far quicker than going on to Hainwort Halt.'

'Quicker than you may have thought. There was an accident.'

'Whew. Anyone injured?'

'Come on boys. Time we started the Hunt. I'm off.'

'Ta-ta rector. We'll be with you in two shakes. How many?'

'All your Territorials.'

'Poor beggars. They were looking forward to the holiday camp in Hainwort marshes.'

'Lucky you'd decided not to travel with them.' I couldn't repress a certain admiration in my tone.'

'You're right. A word in your ear: I had a premonition.'

'I'll wager you did.'

The trellised verandah supports. The lemon verbena like a tropic creeper. Wherry's Provençal hat and pirate's sash. How quiet and how hot the air is. You might drop a bomb into the sea and it would leave a more permanent sign than the shouts and chatter of the crowd on the lawn will leave. Welken mounted a wicker armchair:

'Before we begin I have a most interesting announcement to make. News has lately reached me of an engagement between Miss Belmare and Mr Reynard Moxon. They are to be married in July.'

Bellowing cheers. Centripetal faces turned. Miss Belmare with Dr Mears following curtly pushed her way to the front. He brought a tape-measure out of his waistcoat-pocket; ceremonially encircled her bust.

'Forty-five inches.'

'Hooray.'

Among the crowd Shreeve noticeably showed another immediate interest. In profile his chattering face aided by descriptive arm-gestures futilely strained to intercept Anthony Belmare's view of the ceremony. An interpreter. Grudging the boy's independent impression he was evidently explaining the scene. Anthony absently responded. An absorbed reader evading a wasp.

'Our only regret is that Mr Moxon has been unexpectedly detained at Karlsbad by the customs officials.'

Bombs of laughter.

'Otherwise I think you'll all concede there would have been little doubt, to use a pet expression of my old Dean's at St Salvador's, as to who would have been the successful *agonist* in today's contest.'

Serious cheers.

'I will now make the customary résumé of the rules. Ladies, gentlemen and boys, one of your number has been pre-informed of the whereabouts of the Treasure. When or if unobserved he will seek, unearth and clandestinely pocket it. (No, Sir Napier, "Unearth" is not an accidental hint.) The rest of you will have exactly half an hour in which to spot the concealer. The spotter wins the Treasure. If there is no spotter the concealer has it for keeps. I declare the prime of the hunt. You are advised to draw the kitchen garden.'

Wrecking shouts. They faded into the trees. The crowd separated into groups, solos. Miss Frorster in hygienic sandals and a hand-woven skirt. Sir Napier Bevan blue-lipped in the heat, gaitered and spurred, with checked breeches. Caesar Wrygrave sweating under the eyes, oyster-faced, deliberately observant. The boys from Frisbald College. Charles Wrythe. Andy and Mundy Shanks with a privately-made chart of the grounds. Gaspard Farfox with a terrier. The girls from Miss Frorster's Modern Academy. Mr Hards, scales of graveyard mud on his corduroy knees. Hynd and Starn, wearing faded college rugger caps. Wherry last but two, seriously conversing with the three choirboys. Ernie Travers, Boy Radnor, Tod Erswell in knickers. All descended the steps through the yew tunnel into the hedged kitchen garden. Only Anthony Belmare, still followed by Shreeve, remained on the lawn. Curtained by verbena on the shadowy verandah Welken said:

'I believe that boy's spotted you. But he can't get at you without being seen by Shreeve.'

'What,' I mused.

'Great Scott, I believe I forgot to tell you. You're the concealer. Hope you don't mind.'

'No. What do I do?'

'Simple as winking. Just walk into the summerhouse round the corner when no one's looking and lift the beehive. Pocket the treasure. Then mix with the crowd. There are no bees, I may say.'

'But someone is looking.'

'Never mind. The boy won't do anything while Shreeve is with him. Really it's hardly fair. I know what, I'll go and have a talk with Shreeve and give Anthony a chance to get away. Then if you're quick you can slip into the summerhouse without being noticed.'

'All right.'

Carefully parting the hanging verbena, Welken stepped out on to the lawn, approached Shreeve:

'Well, Gustave, got any ideas?'

'No.'

'I should try the kitchen garden. That's where the rest of them have gone. The concealer will probably be there.'

'Will he?'

'Ah, that's asking.'

Welken laid an emphatic forefinger on the lapel of Shreeve's coat. Anthony had already left them, begun to descend the steps through the yew tunnel. Shreeve's back was towards the verandah. The cowl on the blue cone-roof of the summerhouse veered as the damper air from the interior rose towards the sun. At the cool entrance brambles obstinate as wire had eaten into the doorless jambs. The beehive stood on a single-legged table spoked with warped cricket stumps. Whorled coils of black horsehair or blood sausage. It broke in my hands like cake, issuing dark treacle. Fortunately there were mulberry leaves. I cleaned the ivory paper-cutter, concealed it in my shirt.

A Renegade in Springtime

'Here he comes, boys.' Wherry's voice. At the back. A square in the trellis window was unblocked by leaves. Wherry with the three choirboys waiting in a clearing among the laurels. Bushes arranged like pincers having their axis at the summerhouse and a narrow gap between the far ends where Anthony Belmare carefully appeared.

Unnoticed, Wherry quickly hid.

'Challenge,' Ernie Travers shouted.

'Sucks, you're wrong,' Anthony said. 'Same to you.'

'Are we?' Boy Radnor ignored the returned challenge with a seriously spiteful sneer. 'How do we know you aren't lying?'

'How do I know you aren't?'

'Never said anything. What's more we've had enough of your cheek.'

'At him, dogs.'

'Go and eat worms.' Anthony briefly put out his tongue, began to run.

Ernie Travers smartly tripped him at the gap, had him by the ankle. Tod Erswell took the other leg. Boy Radnor's warted hands clipped beneath his armpits violently raised him. Anthony struggled with mock anger, the sleeves of his blazer slipping to his elbows, the thin watch-strap breaking on his wrist.

'You'll find some string in my pocket,' he offered.

'Pooh. We could fix you up with cotton.'

'You're going to be jolly well searched.'

Boy Radnor wrenched open Anthony's blazer, fumbled for the buttons of his silk tennis shirt.

'I don't know what you think you're doing.'

'Stop his gab, Ernie. The sash will do.'

'Dashed clever, aren't you. Three to one . . . You beastly rotters.'

Lost in pleasure, Wherry had frankly come out from the bushes.

'Look out, there's someone running.'

Wherry had no time to disappear. Branches snapped from the bushes at the gap, Shreeve plunged in like an escaped pony. Already before he had rounded the corner his arm had been raised to point; now it fixed on Wherry: 'You bestial fiend. I'll make you pay for it.'

'Buzz off.'

The Railway Accident

'They shall know about this.'
'Admit you've been properly fooled.'
'Rector. Here.'

A party of treasure-hunters whom Shreeve had easily outraced had now arrived at the gap. Charles Wrythe led them, sweating in drab herring-bone reach-me-downs, all out for the treasure, limping in tough boots through the hot grass. Miss Belmare followed, strong-buttocked, planting her heelless shoes heavily. Welken with a preconceived explanation of the scene scarcely observed it, was twisted with laughter:

'Blowed if they haven't almost torn the clothes off the boy's back. And the scream of it all is that you're both quite wrong.'

'The man who designed Hainwort tunnel . . .' Shreeve sinisterly began.

Whooha ha ha whoohaha ha.'

'Wouldn't go far out of his way for a treasure you could put in your pocket.'

'Whooha ha. Now Gustave, don't take it to heart. You're both in the same boat. And you've a clear twenty minutes to make it right or, whoohaha, wrong if we look at it from George's point of view. Try again.'

'Not until I've made an important statement.'

'If it comes to statements,' Wherry said, 'I believe I could make one about the headmaster of Frisbald College which would put daylight through several none too recent events.'

'What about a duel?' A voice asked.

'Whoo ha. Come now, shake hands like the pals we all know you really are. On with the Hunt. Time's precious.'

'What about it?' Miss Belmare persisted. 'With pea pistols. Reynard gave me a couple when we were engaged; he used to use them when he was a boy.'

Miss Frorster faintly sobbed.

'By great luck I have them with me,' Miss Belmare surprisingly drew two small revolvers from the V slit in her blouse, handed one to Shreeve.

'Gentleman to see you, sir,' Whinny Saunders the rectory maid standing at the gap addressed Welken.

A Renegade in Springtime

'Tell him I . . . Who is it?'
'Sergeant Ganghorn, sir. Motored up from the police station.'
'Very well. Awfully sorry, you people. Shan't be long.'
'May the worse man lose.'
He had gone. Miss Belmare handed Wherry the other revolver. Above the bushes I thought I saw the roof of a black motor van. Drawn up under the elms, on the drive.
'Is that a pea-shooter?' Charles Wrythe seriously asked.
Miss Belmare scoffed: 'It's a sweat syringe.'
'More like a six-shooter.' Sir Napier Bevan had come critically forward. 'If you value the judgement of an old sportsman you'll both put them away where they came from.'
Miss Belmare blushed.
Wherry: 'By God, I believe you're right. WAIT.'
SPAK. Shreeve had opportunely fired. Dropped the revolver with theatrical horror. Started forward. Mumbled: 'Awful mistake.' Dr Mears intercepted him:
'My job this time.'
Wherry writhed sneering like a rat on the ground with a bullet through his groin. Far off, from the sea, a first phrase of thunder warned. The crowd stood posed in self-conscious inactivity, aware of the tableau they formed. The laurels signalled in a fair damp breeze. Bees whirred. Beyond Belstreet Down the marine sky glittering like tin seemed the cymbals on which the vibrating note of a steamer's siren had been sharply struck. Dr Mears prised open a nickel instrument case. Everyone was chatting. At the gap, Welken had excitedly reappeared.
His face changed with difficulty: 'What's the verdict Doctor?'
'Not fatal I think, unless gangrene supervenes. Though I fear he will be permanently lamed.'
'That's a pity.'
'I can't imagine how Reynard made the mistake,' Miss Belmare said.
'A most amazing thing.'
Taut with news Welken finally released: 'Then what do you say to this: Harold Wrygrave has been arrested on a charge of train wrecking.'

Sunday

I am going back to lunch. There is no ambush, no one will ask me to show an entrance ticket, I have not tampered with the motor-mower, no butcher-boy has chalked my name on the basin of the fountain. This is a public path, no discrimination is made against persons not moving on a definite errand, against women without tennis shoes, men who aren't easily called Freddy by their colleagues. I have as much right to walk here as anyone. I am invited, everyone is invited, we are expected to stop and look at the mandarin ducks, to use the less direct path up the side of the valley, smell the lupins, poke groundsel through the wire meshes of the aviary. Why did the council put flood-lights in the trees round the fountain and build a thatched hut for the ducks on an island? Not merely in order to give the contract to their friends or because it's the fashion, but also because they want the town to have a good name with visitors. That's what civic consciousness really means, and it's a perfectly sound business proposition I suppose. They are really gratified that people come here, we are doing them a service, all kinds of people, dwarfs with diseases, young men with temporary jobs in the town, airmen and sailors, old women and public schoolboys returning from church, girls. There will be no inquisition at the park gates, no one is curious about your face, it is quite unnecessary to cross the grass in order to avoid seeming to follow the women who happen to be walking in front of you. Probably no one here knows anyone else. And suppose someone who did know you came up to you and suddenly asked what you were doing, you could say quite naturally 'I am going for a walk' or 'I am looking at the ducks'. You wouldn't have to pretend that you were exercising a terrier or going to buy a Sunday newspaper. That's the advantage of a place like this in a large town. There's no need to suspect that people are watching you from behind window curtains and wondering what you are doing. If anyone looks at you, you can see that he is looking at you, and you know he thinks you are merely walking through the park. And suppose everyone here were actually staring at me, suppose I were dancing or wearing sensible clothes, I should probably feel rather exhilarated. But as it happens I shall not be accused of anything, there is no kind of danger, not the least need to want to escape like a cat under the laurel bushes. I can't even flatter myself that I'm ill.

I am going back to my lodgings for lunch. Who will be there? Only the table, the flower with protruding stamens arching from its jug like a sabre-toothed tiger, the glass of custard, pleated apple-green satin behind the fretwork fleur-de-lis panel of the piano. The whole afternoon and evening will be free. Realize that, realize what I could do. All the possibilities of thinking and feeling, exploration and explanation and vision, walking in history as among iron and alabaster and domes, focusing the unity of the superseded with the superseding, recognizing the future, vindicating the poets, retiring between pillars as Socrates, desperate as Spartacus, emerging with Lenin, foreseeing the greatest of all eras. But unless I am very careful I shall sit on the sofa trying to decide not to go on reading the paper. I shall look out of the window. People will pass carrying neatly rolled umbrellas and after tea bells will toll. Everyone will appear quite at ease, fairly well-dressed, comfortably married, not at all furtive or sinister. Nothing will visibly suggest that they are all condemned, that what they stand for is already dead, putrescent, stinking, animated only by preying corpse-worms. I shall begin to doubt whether they are dead, whether it's not merely my own inefficiency which vomits when I hear them hint: 'In this funny old world of ours one must be a realist.' Hypocrisies which during the week seemed irrelevant abstractions will palpably promenade, bow, exchange smiles. I shall suspect that my work has been a drug, that all the week I have evaded this reality, that in future my leisure – the gaps between drug-takings – will become more and more impossible to bear. And the drug itself will never be anticipated with pleasure, it will always be feared. Perhaps that's why I've got nervous

Sunday

diarrhoea now. I feel as though I were in a waiting-room. Tomorrow I have to use a rotary duplicator for the first time.

Ah-ha, we are getting nearer to it now, we are becoming quite daring. The modest little secret has popped out at last. Now we are in our birthday suit. Oh, look, mother, there are spots all over his back. So that's why he was explaining that sunbathing permanently injures the brain cells. Is it credible? Yes, I am vulgarly anxious about my work. All other explanations are mainly decorative, shamming a greater horror, demon masks to divert attention. I am afraid that I shall not be able to understand the mechanism of the duplicator, that I shall not know how to fit the stencil on to the roller, I shall not get through what I have to do in time, shall perhaps damage the machine, be warned that my work must improve. Unless I am very careful I shall spend the whole of this afternoon uselessly trying to elaborate my fear into something monumental and flattering, and in the end quite frankly thinking of tomorrow.

Epictetus advised contempt for all things not dependent on choice. What's the worst thing, excluding murder and arson, in which I might be implicated tomorrow? I might be sacked without a testimonial. Epictetus would tell me that this is something outside my control, that I ought to be ready to accept it without complaint if it comes, that I should set my heart only on things which no external accident can endanger. He forestalled the 'His will is our peace' idea in less mystical language. Of course the idea is useless now, worse than useless, dangerous, sinister. Whether I am sacked or not depends at least partly on whether I make up my mind to understand the mechanism of the duplicator. I can't just forbid myself to be seriously interested in the success or failure of the copies, and then, if they fail, highmindedly submit to a thrashing from a slave-owner. No one would attempt to thrash or torture me, I should simply be asked to find another job. And if I found one the same process would begin over again, till in the end I should have no job at all. Things may have been different under the feudal barons. Then you were someone's property and you might be thrashed but you wouldn't be abandoned. That's what gave colour to the God the Father theory. But today real passivity is only possible to the leisured. Nevertheless there are thousands of people even now with jobs in this town who are made miserable by the idea that they ought to be at peace with their own souls. Though it's true they may not formulate it to themselves quite in that way – they may feel remorse for hating their wives, or they may wear an enamelled badge with the inscription 'Prepare to meet thy God', or they may make useless resolves to do their work at the office cheerfully. And what happens if they succeed in doing their work cheerfully? Suppose I became cheerful, suppose I refused to be alarmed by the duplicator. Then very soon I should be put on to something more difficult. And suppose even then I didn't revolt – I should soon be put on to something more difficult still. And in the end I shouldn't be a subordinate at all. I should have become one of those responsible liars and twisters who make a profit out of believing that drudgery and servility ought to be accepted cheerfully. But I am not likely to reach that position. I am much nearer to those other blunderers who, cynically regarding as a dishonour and a horror the work they have to do every day, try to preserve the old integrity intact within the blind enclosure of their minds. That is the maddest mistake of all.

It is mad to be content to hate every external danger, to be an ostrich, to accept any explanation which minimizes the importance of material gains or losses, to fail to try to find a real solution. It's no use pretending you are splendidly or redeemingly or even interestingly doomed. If you are doomed at all, and it is still possible for you not to be one of those who are doomed, you are doomed like a factory which excludes the latest machinery or like a migratory bird which fails to migrate. Don't flatter yourself that history will die or hibernate with you; history will be as vigorous as ever but it will have gone to live elsewhere. No, you are not a martyr, you are not a conqueror, you recognize that, you are aware that only history which is already living elsewhere can make martyrs and afterwards conquerors. Then where is it living, how can you get to it? Can it have disguised itself as a rotary duplicator, as traffic fussing in a smelly street, as electricity, as lying advertisements, as dingy and crowded tenements, as factory hooters, as any or all of those things which are so uneasily reflected on the surface of the old passivity? Stop just a moment. Aren't we becoming a little extravagant, almost

Sunday

metaphysical? Don't you think so? Because it's well known that comfortably-paid university experts have warned us again and again against mistaking abstract generalizations for concrete things. Don't you suspect that after all they may have been right, that history is nothing more than a convenient figment, an abstraction, and that only concrete things like motor coaches and duplicators and ultimately electrons – which though not perceptible to the senses would be if they could – are real? And why not go one step farther, why not say that electrons and duplicators and motorcoaches are nothing more than abstractions? Isn't that what you have been trying to convince yourself of all along? Day after day you have walked to work in the morning, trying not to feel sick, trying not to be degraded by petty fears, despising the genuine Jesus-gang who at least believed that evil was real, trying to dismiss the office buildings as an inconvenient dream, as a boring abstraction, as something neither pleasant nor unpleasant, without colour or shape or substance, finally as nothing at all – and every day you have failed completely. You have been jarred and stung beneath your pretences by the very reality which your pretences were designed to disguise. You have failed to deny history, as you always must fail until you are mad or dead.

History is here in the park, in the town. It is in the offices, the duplicators, the traffic, the nursemaids wheeling prams, the airmen, the aviary, the new viaduct over the valley. It was once in the castle on the cliff, in the sooty churches, in your mind; but it is abandoning them, leaving with them only the failing energy of desperation, going to live elsewhere. It is already living elsewhere. It is living in the oppression and hustle of your work, in the sordid isolation of your lodgings, in the vulgarity and shallowness of the town's attempts at art and entertainment, in the apprehensive dreariness of your Sunday leisure. History is living here, and you aren't able to die yet and you can't go mad.

But history will not always be living here. It will not always wear these sordid and trashy clothes. History abandoned the brutal fatherliness of the castle and it will abandon Sunday and the oppression of the office too. It will go to live elsewhere. It is going already to live with the enemies of suffering, of suffering beside which

A Renegade in Springtime

yours shows like silly hysteria, with people who are not content to suppress misery in their minds but are going to destroy the more obvious material causes of misery in the world. And the man who doesn't prefer suicide or madness to fighting – and how could anyone who has been at all near to suicide or madness prefer them? – will join with those people. He will look for history not in a Sunday afternoon's reading at his lodgings, not even in reading Lenin, nor in any of the excitements of thinking and feeling, but in the places where those people are. He will go back to his lodgings for lunch. He will read the newspaper, but not for more than a quarter of an hour. He will look out of the window and see the black hats and rolled umbrellas, but he will no longer be paralysed by disgust or apprehension. He will go out into the street and walk down to the harbour. He will go to the small club behind the Geisha Café. He will ask whether there is a meeting tonight. At first he may be regarded with suspicion, even taken for a police spy. And quite naturally. He will have to prove himself, to prove that he isn't a mere neurotic, an untrustworthy freak. It will take time. But it is the only hope. He will at least have made a start.

The Island

What are you fond of? Is it the sun, is it the girls, is it mornings in rowing-boats, is it giving yourself wild primroses, or trickily nursing a frantic box-kite, or studying at first hand materials of history or of geology, or identifying distant liners, is it palaces on the screens of picture palaces, or the narrow strip of wheel racing beneath the silver-bright handle-bars of your cycle, or larking for hours with the kids, or walking for miles, or reading a serious book, dancing, wearing pink, just lying flat on the sands? Social, brainy, daft, lazy, athletic, whatever your warmest pleasure is, so long as it isn't stealing or anything else illegal, there should be scope for it here.

Look across the real water; look, this island can't be a floodlit cloud, can't be a daydream through which you'll slip to find yourself back on the job and under the poisonous eye of a bullying foreman. One hundred and fifty square miles of it, and the sand is unarguably sand, the earth is earth, the limestone limestone, fluviomarine and estuarial, and roundly the real downs descend to the town, and the houses and bright hotels are crowding towards the pier, and the pier a pavilion-headed millipede is toddling through the springtime waves towards your paddle-steamer, this holiday steamer loaded with the first visitors of the year.

Nevertheless some of you are not wholly convinced, your faces show a certain listlessness – though you may not feel it – or even a certain rigour, you look almost as if you were confronted with things you are not fond of, as if you had seen something on the island which makes you apprehensive about rates and rents, or about feeding and clothing your children, or holding your jobs down. But there is really nothing here to force such anxieties upon you and you know that the cost of your holiday won't ruin you. Step hard on this deck, it isn't made of wishes, and you can't suppose that you'll be ordered below to work in the engine-room, or that the terrace of the yacht club like a redoubt behind its semi-circular sea-wall hides enemy cannon, or that the pier pavilion will bite your head off. You know you are going to have a good time, you knew it, you planned it weeks or months ago, and now you can feel it in the air, the sea smells of it, the wooded shore promises it, the canoe lake, the midget golf course affirm it, your eyes tell you it is true. This place must be a fact, this life fit for men and women must be real. How could you have doubted it? What weary imposture, what ghost-life, what Devil's Island in the heart have you allowed yourself to be cheated with until now? Did you mistake for realities those vile feelings, those arid panics in face of the future, those creeping apprehensions about losing your job, those sweating calculations before foodstalls in the market, all those nightmares which have been coming at you more and more venomously for so many weeks and months? Did you compromise with them, did you kowtow to them, eat dirt for them, did you betray for them this only life, this real life, this sea, this sun, this air brighter than diamonds or happiest tears? The moment is near now when you will be able to adopt a new tone, less diplomatic, less accommodating, towards all those ghost-miseries. The moment is here already, in a flash, as though it had been signalled by the sun-flashing windows of the pavilion. To hell now with that slave-life, that life not fit for beasts, down with it, drown it, throw it casually away as the sailor boy, the sea-boy emerging from the iron galley beside you, flings the used contents of a teapot into the thoughtless water. A good time, your birthright, has come.

Families, couples, hikers, cyclists passed along the two gangways and on to the concrete landing-stage of the pier. Other steamers just as crowded would arrive after this one, and in two or three days the steamers would go back crowded to the mainland. The social composition of the mass of visitors was difficult to determine, since it was obviously a mixture and contained both working-class and middle-class elements, but the office workers probably out-numbered the industrial workers, and there were possibly a few professional men with their small families, very few if any clergymen because Easter means business for the churches, and almost certainly no unemployed – owing to the cost of the journey – except perhaps one or at most two rich unemployed returning to their houses of retirement in the middle of the island. All tramped on to the deck of the pier, some to catch the train at the pier-head, others to walk or cycle or take the motor-tram to the pier-gates, and on the whole it could be fairly said that though none of them looked really gay all of them looked pleased.

One hundred and fifty square miles. Where will you go? Do your wishes whirl in a merry-go-round of indecision, uncertain which stopping-place to choose? There's no need for alarm, because whichever place you choose – whether here for automatic-machines and entertainments, or the downs for air and view, or the eastern bay for sand-cricket and the well-known chine, or that sun-trap behind the highest downs where east and north winds are unheard-of – whichever the place and whatever your tastes you are sure to find satisfaction. But this may sound like an exaggeration. Perhaps you are being kidded for the benefit of the railway company or the local councils. To dispel any such suspicions let it be added frankly that not all parts of the island would be equally attractive to all types of visitor. Obviously these severe-looking people gathering outside the pier-gates, these keen cyclists wearing the badge of a workers' sports club on their leather jackets, might complain if they found themselves riding over sharp stones along a cliff path – though surely they could dismount and wheel their cycles, and the view would go far to compensate them for their disappointment. Or again, you might be fond of crowds and find yourselves in some dead-alive village where nothing happens in the evenings and where there's nothing to look at except marshes and the flat-bottomed boats of the fowlers and cormorants perching on weed-hung posts – though what would stop you moving on at once to somewhere more congenial? But perhaps people exist who would discover nothing anywhere on the island to please them. The Commander's widow, for instance – that lady, that powdered marine fossil with her hair in whorls, who sits stuck in the bay window of her large modern cottage at the top of the hill, who never tires of believing that you have ruined the island for her with your voices and your clothes and your hiking and cycling, your cinemas, your lodging-houses, your crowds, your faces – though there's no reason why she should go on living here if she doesn't want to, since her property would make an excellent site for an hotel and she would have no difficulty in selling it, so possibly after all the island has its attractions for her as she leans against her crazy-pattern cushions in the window-seat, as she sits on guard over the past amidst her antique furniture and her superior knick-knacks, her bureau with the brass handles, her bowl of lavender, her china dogs and her real terrier, her framed samplers, water-colours, pestles and mortars, candle-lamps, toasting forks, teacups hanging from nails. It doesn't matter who you are or what you are fond of, it doesn't matter how energetic or crippled or intelligent or old-fashioned or frivolous you may be, this island should be able to provide something out of its variety to satisfy you. No strength should be denied exercise here, no weakness exposed or tortured.

What do you most want to do? Think – don't rush for a motor-coach or a train or go dashing off at once on your cycle. Lean back against the esplanade railing with the island before you, the wooded coast dwindling away on either hand, the town steeply retreating, the downs, farms, villages, streams, other towns, miles of brilliance and of fields, stretching invisible now behind ascending housetops. Are you bewildered, are you shaken by the daring or the queerness of your keenest wishes, are you tempted to smother them as fantastic and to decide on doing something you are only mildly fond of or not really fond of at all? There's no need for such caution, because however fantastic your wishes may seem, however vulnerable or high-flying or naïve, you should be able to fulfil them now. Uncover them, off with their wrappings of prudence and diffidence, expose them to the sun in all their fragility, their too-shy warmth, their over-excited tenderness – let them learn to live. No longing, no ambition should be ridiculous or impossible here. Do you want to be an engineer, for instance? You might think such a wish would be out of place on this island where there are no factories worth mentioning and no great works of construction in progress, and certainly you will not be given the opportunity here

The Island

of slaving at a conveyor belt or of sitting astride girders hundreds of feet above the ground. But why should you want to bind yourself to physical labour when it is possible for you to study the most up-to-date achievements of engineering at ease and without any material limitations or interference from machinery or foremen? Look back across the water and examine at leisure the aircraft-carrier anchored there. That elaborate weapon, which cost millions of pounds to construct, so trim and severe with its uninterrupted length of deck and funnels neatly on one side, with its barely visible guns, its concealed lifts and hangar, should teach you something. Though it may teach you more about destruction than about engineering.

But you may want to devote yourself to some more fundamental study. Go deeper, look with your mind now, see beneath this hill of houses, this pier, this broad concrete parking-place for motor-coaches at the end of the esplanade, beneath even this water, study the crust of the earth itself. And look with your eyes also: walk along the shore and see how the cliffs expose layer on layer of petrified ages, lucid almost as in a museum model, sediments of years on years when life struggled out of the warm oceans, life dying in millions, winning, growing carapace and fibre and preserving moisture in lungs, starving under frightful frost, luxuriating in the coal-measures, developing through aeons and aeons whose ruins teach you that the existence of the island itself is no more than a passing incident. And this knowledge will not condemn you to humility or to impotent reverence; on the contrary, the wider your understanding of nature becomes the less mystery will its laws have for you and the more confident you will be in your power to make it serve you. Though you won't get much chance of making it serve you here. And you won't be able to understand it very widely either, since two or three days' holiday will hardly give you time to gain anything but a smattering of geological knowledge. However you can walk under the cliffs and admire the strata without bothering whether they are called greensand, limestone, the grey Punfield shales, Blue Slipper or the Crackers, and if you are lucky you may pick up some beautiful jasper pebbles veined with dendritical figures.

A Renegade in Springtime

But you may feel geology would be rather a sterile study, you may prefer to occupy yourself with something equally serious but more human. Look beyond this complex of seaside living, these workers on holiday and what is provided for them and the inhabitants who live by providing it and the residents who are always on holiday, beyond this esplanade bandstand, these leather-jacketed cyclists, that large modern cottage at the top of the hill, this departing motor-coach issuing blue exhaust as its driver changes gear – consider the many historic phases that human society had to go through before it could arrive at its present state on the island. Many evidences in valley, in village, in town, on the downs, Celtic, Roman, Saxon, Norman, remain to tell you of past struggles, of gradual developments and cataclysmic changes, of new forms of society successively arising and decaying and being violently superseded by more vigorous and better adapted forms, just as the present form of society must decay and be superseded. And this knowledge will not fill you with pessimism and self-distrust but with confidence in the power of men to make even greater changes in the future than any they have made in the past, and with the determination that you will help in the making of those changes. Though it's true you are unlikely to participate actively here in a great historical movement. But isn't the island good enough for you already without its being convulsed by further struggles? And you aren't likely either to make a very profound study of history in two or three days. However you will be able to look at historical remains – earthworks, a burial ground, a Roman villa with a hypocaust and well-preserved tessellated pavement, churches, a whipping-post and stocks, the houses where Garibaldi stayed as a guest, the castle where Charles I was imprisoned, the site on which John Wilkes, fighter for freedom of speech, built his *Villakin* and erected to the memory of the poet Churchill a Doric column with a receptacle at its base for the storing of bottles of old port.

But you may consider this kind of history superficial and sentimental, you may conclude that since the shortness of your holiday makes any thorough acquisition of knowledge impossible you will do better to devote yourself to livelier and healthier forms of activity, to living rather than to the dry study of life. Think what an island of promise is before you, what sunlight, what fields for athletic leisure, for sport free from all taint of professionalism, for that fulfilment of the body which was long ago the ambition of the Greeks, what paths for love, what satisfied evenings for discussion, for the arts, for literature, for music, what a chance to begin a new life of culture and vigour. Come, begin now. But begin where? This flat esplanade offers no foothold for such climbing excitement. You cannot be a Greek here. And you aren't likely to find anywhere else on the island where you can begin a new life in two or three days. Perhaps there is nothing worth while anywhere here, perhaps the island has nothing in store for you beyond these freshly painted hotel fronts, this stationer's window crammed with humorous postcards, worthless china souvenirs, poker-work mottoes on bits of wood. Perhaps you will do nothing here, perhaps you will never succeed in throwing off the exhaustion and worry of the past, you are too weak, too injured to recover, perhaps you are done for.

What morbid bunk! This is the result of indulging in freakish fantasies and getting above yourself. Who but a fool would want to be a Greek? Come out of that sickly dreamland, that paradisial island of culture and everlasting joy, come and see the island as it really is and make the best of the ordinary human pleasures it has to offer you. Stop thinking and start moving, jump into a train or a motor-coach or on to your cycle, rush, drive, ride through the bright countryside, through woods, over bridges, down lanes, away to a real destination.

Arrive at the eastern bay. Come down to the beach. Feel your feet in the sun-warmed sand, every grain of it real. Walk on it, run on it, be free. Race, play cricket, fly a kite, dig ponds for the kids. Bathe, paddle in the real sea. Be lively. Be lazy, choose out a spot sheltered from the slight but chilly spring wind, lie in the sun beneath the esplanade steps or beneath the jutting sea-wall which surrounds the platform of the war memorial. Read a book or look at the other people. Make friends. Go to sleep if you feel like it; no traffic will disturb you here, and the forts on the cliff are taking a rest from gunnery practice for today. Be happy, be normal, make a joke of all pretentious fancies and morbid thoughts. Enjoy yourself

A Renegade in Springtime

like the other workers, the other clerks, other shop-employees. Like these men and girls playing rounders, those territorials in uniform strolling through the amusements arcade, this child scribbling with a coloured pencil on a piece of old newspaper. Like these leather-jacketed cyclists singing as they ride past the Cosy Café and down to the sea front.

But what's happened? Something seems to be wrong. It is as though everyone has for a split second stopped moving. Wooden groups with surprised faces are stolidly planted along the esplanade. Now everyone has become almost normal again. Very few people seem pleased, many are slightly embarrassed, most looked puzzled. Of three young men sitting together in the café one shouts out some hostile remark. The cyclists are singing of hunger and war and social revolution. They must be mad.

Could anything be more inappropriate on a holiday? And what have hunger and war and revolution to do with the island? There is every sign of prosperity here, people look contented, a new pier pavilion and swimming pool are being built, a section of the esplanade is completely blocked with temporary huts, sacks of cement, piles of steel rods, cranes, concrete mixers – there can't be much unemployment. And as for war – well, even the most unbalanced extremist would have to admit that the peaceful presence of a few territorials, forts, guns, is hardly the same thing as actual fighting. What right have these cyclists to try to spoil your enjoyment, to remind you of feelings which you wanted to destroy?

Vile feelings, feelings which you wanted to fling casually away, arid panics in face of the future, apprehensions about losing your job, sweating calculations before foodstalls, nightmares which you tried to drown for ever in the real sunny sea. Feelings which have been coming at you more and more venomously, which are coming at you even now. The sands will not cover them, the sun will not burn them out, you cannot exorcise them, they are not ghosts, are not mere nightmares, not mere psychological ailments to be cured by playing lively games or by sunbathing on the beach. You know that they come to you from the real mainland, from the real life to which you will return in two or three days, the life which has cancelled in advance all the opportunities for culture offered by this

The Island

pleasant island. And look more closely at this island: get up from the beach and walk to the back-streets of the town and see there some of the filthiest overcrowding that can be found anywhere in England. But you need not get up: look at this woman shuffling along in dirty canvas shoes, searching among the lines of rubbish left by the tide – seaweed, shavings from the construction work on the pier, dead crabs, straw, ice-cream cartons, blackened banana skins, a gouged-out hemisphere of grape-fruit filled with sand – hoping to find something that may be of value, perhaps as food. Or consider those forts on the cliff and see them not in their apparent stillness as grass-grown mounds beneath the mild sun, but in their real movement of preparation for a world-wide war. Or look with new eyes at the amusements arcade, the strings of coloured light-bulbs along the sea front, the soft-witted advertisements outside the picture houses – what are these but hypocritical decorations concealing danger and misery, fraudulent as vulgar icing on a celebration cake rotten inside with maggots, sugary poison to drug you into contentment?

The cyclists are not mad. You know they are right to sing here on this island about hunger and war. And yet there is something worthwhile here, something that is not poison, some freedom, some joy, some real leisure, something that you cannot easily abandon for a life of grim revolutionary struggle, some beauty that seems to invite your trust and your love. But while you trust in it enemies are attacking it, powers of destruction are undermining it, the powers of hunger and war, the powers that are driven to destroy because further construction means their ruin, because your life means their death, your awakening their disaster, the powers that would have you sit still and trust in dreams. Or would have you fight for dreams. No doubt the three young men sitting together in the café are aware of something rotten in the island and would explain it as due to the materialistic attitude of people like the worker cyclists, to your attitude, your desire for a decent life now and in this world, no doubt they feel there is too much liberty here, too much selfishness and indifference to the things of the spirit, they would gladly tighten their belts in the service of some great spiritual cause and would gallantly obey orders.

A Renegade in Springtime

Your view of the island will be different from theirs. You will see rottenness not in the leisure and the opportunities for enjoyment, however meagre these may be, which the island offers you, but in the forces that are working for the destruction of all freedom and culture. You will remember that such inadequate liberties as you possess at present have been won by bitter struggle, and you will recognize that now more than ever it is necessary for you to fight to defend them, to fight to extend them, to fight till you have made them adequate and made them secure, till you have destroyed their destroyers. And if ever in the setbacks and the tortures of the final struggle you think of the island, let the thought bring to you not the weakness of regret, not nostalgia for a ghost-place dazzling with false promise in the spring weather, not remembrance of the island as you saw it from the steamer today, but the strength of the certainty of a real place, the island as it can be, a place fit for men and women, as it must be, as it will be.

The Procession

On a balustered balcony five storeys or more above the unexpectedly crowdless street I stood waiting for a procession which I foreknew would be significantly unlike the Lord Mayor's Show my mother had lifted me up to look at from a similar balcony in my early childhood seventy years before. What I was about to see now might be a military parade or a funeral or a political demonstration rather than a carnival of any kind. It seemed a long time coming. When I stopped staring up the street for a while I noticed that I was by myself on the balcony and that a stone ledge extending from one side of this along the face of the building as far as another balcony at the same height fifteen yards away might not be broad enough to give a hesitating suicide a foothold for more than a few seconds, and could be slippery too with all the grey-white droppings deposited there by night-roosting starlings. A gilded spike pointing up towards me from the top of the lantern of an iron street-lamp far below must have held my interest for longer than I was aware, because when I looked away along the street again the first walkers in the procession were already very near.

Walkers, not marchers. Without music from drums or fifes or brass. No one was singing or shouting. And there were no small bright balloons with faces or slogans colour-printed on them floating from strings above the faces of the walkers, no flowery tableaux formed by tiaraed young girls in rising tiers on lorries with decorated wheels like revolving rosettes, no huge wicker-work or papier-mâché images of Gog and Magog or of John Bull. But if I was seeing a funeral it was not a state ceremony in which a riderless horse with reversed Wellington boots fixed to the stirrups would be followed by a flag-draped coffin on a gun-carriage.

Although the walkers were so noiseless along the street that I could almost have supposed the women as well as the men must be wearing rubber soles and heels, they were casually dressed and did not try to keep in step with one another, or they might even – as anti-militarists – be purposely keeping out of step. It could be a political demonstration. I thought I recognised a fair-haired girl there who when I met her once at a left-wing meeting had told me I was her favourite painter, and I had believed her. I was sure that the two exceptionally tall young men in the procession, not walking together nor seeming to be known to each other, were two students, a Latvian and a New Zealander, who had on separate occasions come to ask me questions about the relationship between politics and art, my art in particular, and I had called them 'giants' afterwards when I had described them to my friends. But if I was watching a demonstration why were there no banners? There was only an unframed painting on canvas which one of the walkers was holding up by its lowest corners. Its prevailing colour was woodland green, and it was frighteningly familiar, yet I could not wholly understand what made me afraid until I saw coming on close behind the painting, and pushed like a barrow by three or four of the walkers, a low-wheeled vehicle carrying an exposed coffin. Though the lid was not, as in a Greek Orthodox Church funeral, removed from the coffin, I knew whose corpse was inside.

The voice of my dear love who was standing suddenly quite near me said consolingly to me, 'We never expected we would be lucky enough to go together. One of us had to be first. I wish it had been me, just as you would have wished it had been you if it had been me.' Before I could turn towards her I heard myself crying out in protest to all the street, 'I don't want to die yet. There's no reason why I should be dead now. I haven't been ill or in an accident.' When I did turn to her she was not there, must have gone back into the large room which led out through wide-open French windows on to the balcony. But my cry had been heard by the broad-bodied elderly man in a conspicuously well-tailored suit who was coming along the balcony from the room unhurriedly towards me. I was in no doubt that he was Everard Axtell, who had been my friend when we were younger. The brightly flower-patterned shirt he wore now might seem too young for his hair which had become entirely white, but his features had aged so little that he would have been instantly recognisable by me even if I hadn't seen recent photographs of him so often in the newspapers. He took a second or two to recognise me, then said, 'That funeral is not yours.'

There was a kindliness rather than any real kindness in his voice. He could have been a professional healer speaking to someone unwell. 'If the funeral were yours you would not be standing on the balcony here. You would be down there in the coffin.' As though he thought I was insufficiently impressed by his reasoning, he went on with less kindliness, 'You will never have a public funeral, not even a third-rate cockney one such as you have been watching.' I became aware of him as having the kind of face and figure which would have made him appear 'distinguished' even to people who had never heard of him. He could have been taken for a famous former rugby player – a three-quarter back more probably than a forward, since he was not tall – or a diplomat, instead of the well-known art critic and collector he actually was. But it came to me that what he had been saying could be true, and evidently he guessed he was beginning to convince me; his voice changed, was more kindly again. 'You might have been able to expect to have a public funeral some day, though only a small and unofficial one, if you'd gone on painting in the style you'd already begun to develop in your early twenties.' I still said nothing. He asked with genuine but controlled exasperation, 'Why did you abandon the kind of realistic fantasy you were capable of when you painted *The Wormhouse Gate?*'

I wondered whether what exasperated him might mainly be that he thought of me as having thrown away a capability he wished he himself had possessed.

'I doubt whether I know why,' I said.

'We all of us admired that picture. Admittedly we saw an element of parody in it which bordered on farce here and there. The violent viridian of the moss on the huge rocks among the oak trees obviously referred to some of Courbet's forest scenes – I remember how highly you thought of him as a painter then – but whereas his forests give an impression which is anything but peaceful and one feels that

A Renegade in Springtime

a sportsman's gun might be fired from behind a tree at any moment, your oak spinney is almost ludicrously sinister (he spoke that word in a complimentary tone) as if somewhere in it just out of sight a poacher was about to step unawares into an iron-toothed mantrap; and I find it quite miraculous that at the same time we are somehow reminded – perhaps it's a case of extremes inevitably suggesting their opposites – of the dreamily hazy springtime leaves in a Corot birch wood. Was there a sapling in the left foreground of your picture with a few very small rhomboidally-shaped leaves growing on it?'

'Yes there was.'

'Well, that may partly account for the Corot effect. But of course the central thing in the whole design is the Poussin-like sepulchre glimpsed between oak-trunks in the middle-distance. One can imagine one sees the words *Et in Arcadia Ego* incised in the stone lintel over the sepulchral doorway, yet when one looks closely the lettering turns out to be nothing more than accidental vertical markings on the stone, and the lintel itself is only a horizontal slab of rock which some geological happening has left balanced over a door-like boulder. And the Arcadian shepherds one thought were there on either side of the doorway are just not there at all; nor is the medieval Mayday morning party of horse-riders whose bright clothes – malachite green for the women and gold on blue for the men – seemed distantly visible in the sunlit interstices between tree trunks at the farthest edge of the spinney; nor is the early twentieth century one-cylinder motor-car which had appeared to be coming along the palely buff-coloured lane you placed near the right-hand lower corner of the picture, though some rather shapeless dark vehicle is in fact represented at that point. And there are other objects and people and also animals – from various historical and prehistorical epochs – you managed to suggest and bring together in this painting without actually representing them. You were called a surrealist by some critics at the time, but I think this was a complete misnomer. You were essentially a representationalist, and nothing physically impossible or even improbable was depicted in any of your paintings – such as women with knob-handled chests-of-drawers in place of bosoms, or giraffes with their

The Procession

manes on fire. But you were a representationalist of a new kind. You were unique.'

I couldn't help showing the gratification he made me feel, but my feeling was quickly changed by what he said next:

'Why didn't you develop that style farther instead of going on to produce the flat and unallusive naturalistic stuff you've confined yourself to for the last twenty-five years – utterly without undertones or overtones or warmth or atmosphere or wit, bare of all feelings except the most commonplace and dubious political ones?'

'I couldn't have gone on in my earlier style however much I'd wanted to. I couldn't have ignored how shallow and false it was as a response to the real horrors of the contemporary external world. Some art critics may think that art needn't tell the truth about any reality outside itself, but I think that if it doesn't it becomes fraudulent not just morally but also as art.' Not caring whether he might assume that the anger I knew I was failing to disguise might be due simply to his having wounded my personal vanity, I continued: 'I wanted my paintings to deal with things of fundamental concern to ordinary people today and I wanted to paint in a way which would be generally intelligible. I didn't want to be the kind of painter who disguises his lack of content by being superficially as elaborate as possible.'

Axtell appeared not to have been listening to me. 'If you'd gone on in your earlier style,' he said, 'you could have been at least a partial success, like –' he paused and then named two names which, though he spoke them clearly enough and though I felt they ought to be familiar to me, I couldn't recognise. But I was certain that neither of the names was his own. He hadn't paused out of modesty. I could see that he thought of himself not as a partial but as a complete success. At the same moment I noticed a decoration pinned to the cloth of his suit just above the breast pocket – a ribbon with a garish and cheap-looking medal attached to it. Presumably it had been awarded to him by the State and presented by the Monarch. I thought, 'You did not cost them much', and I had a quick temptation to speak these words aloud, but I was helped to restrain myself by remembering how unseemly and sordid it is when old friends quarrel with one another in old age, and the words were driven utterly out of my mind by my sudden realisation that the painting of mine he had just been describing – *The Wormhouse Gate* – was the same one that had been carried by a walker in the funeral procession.

I jumped forward towards the balustrade, ignoring Axtell, and I leant over the white stone coping to stare after the procession which by now had moved on so far down the street that I couldn't be sure whether I saw where the coffin was any longer. I cried out in agony, 'It *is* my corpse they are carrying there.'

'No, it is not yours.' The voice that said this from behind me wasn't Axtell's. I turned and saw a very old man, short and thin and strikingly insignificant-looking compared with Axtell (who was no longer on the balcony), and I knew him at once as J. R. Sedgely, whom I revered more than any other painter of the twentieth century.

'It is not yours,' he said again. 'It is the corpse of the better artist you had it in you to be, but never were.' I was conscious of the characteristic slight lopsidedness of the features of his understanding face as he went on, 'Don't think I'm one of those who praise the richness of your younger style in order to seem all the more unprejudiced when they completely damn your maturer plainness. I don't doubt at all that your later paintings are better than your earlier, though those had something of imaginative value which if you had been able to retain and develop and meld it into your later work could have put you not in the first but in the second rank at least of the European painters of the last two centuries.'

I looked at him with gratitude, believing he meant what he said though I did not believe it to be true; but I said nothing.

'It is the same for all of us – not just the artists, but everyone alive in this century, even the luckiest of the lucky, and three quarters of the human population of the earth are not among the lucky. We are none of us able to be what we have it in us to be. It is the same for me.'

'No, no,' I passionately said. 'You are one of the truly great.'

'I don't think so. I have no illusions about my work.'

Mildly smiling he moved away from me and went in through the opened French windows at the back of the balcony. I followed him quickly, but not quickly enough. A wide and jagged crack appeared on the stone floor in front of the windows, and it rapidly deepened and lengthened along the whole balcony, which began to tilt downwards. I knew that within seconds I must fall into the street and be killed.

This was not a dream. I have invented it, with help from an actual nightmare I had in bed at home several years ago. It is a fantasy, and not even a realistic one. Yet it may convince me I can after all tell the truth about reality in a style that comes more readily to me than naturalism.

An Old-Established School

Quite soon on the first morning of term at an old-established school a temporarily appointed elderly schoolmaster, Henry Mitchell, realised that a number of the pupils were referring to him among themselves as Austerlyn Greenholt. The name was spoken in matter-of-fact tones, not disrespectfully at all, by someone in each of several groups of adolescent boys and girls who were lounging against multiple-shafted Victorian gothic pillars as he walked along the cloisters to look for the classroom where he was due to begin his teaching at this school. He did not resent the name – it was like an amalgam of two or three eminent names he couldn't immediately remember, and he was even a little pleased he was going to be known by it here (after all, he had been called worse things at some other schools) – nevertheless the promptness with which it had been invented could indicate a spiritedness among the pupils that he might do well to be wary of in good time. Unfortunately he would be less punctual in finding those of them who were waiting for him unsupervised in the classroom now than he need have been if the Headmaster's directions to him about how to get there had been less perfunctory.

He passed a pillar behind which a boy and girl were embracing each other, or rather the girl was embracing the boy, who stood still with a smirk on his face. Austerlyn's pretending not to notice them was made easier by the approach towards him at the same moment of another boy, tall and serious-faced, who said to him politely, 'The form you will be taking are in there, sir,' pointing to an arched doorway twenty yards in front of them along the cloisters. This boy – he was presumably the form-captain – walked slightly ahead of Austerlyn until they reached the doorway, where he stood aside to let the master go in first. It was not a classroom that Austerlyn came into but the Great Hall of the school. It seemed larger than any school assembly hall he had been in before, with what looked like a church organ at the farther end of it and at the nearer end a high gallery from the middle of the bow-shaped front of which a white clockface mercilessly stared, and overhead there was a shadowy hammer-beamed roof. The form that had been waiting for him appeared to him at first sight to be a fairly small one – the appearance being no doubt due both to the comparatively little space its members took up in the Hall and to their orderliness as they sat there – but he soon estimated without having to count them that they might be as many as thirty-five, the boys and girls sitting in separate groups mainly, though there were a few pairs. He beckoned to the form-captain, who was on his way to sit down with the rest of the form.

'I understand this is to be a Chemistry lesson,' Austerlyn said, and the absurdity of it struck him even more now he was in this Hall than it had done when the Head had told him it was to be so. Austerlyn had raised the objection that he was not qualified to teach Chemistry but the Head had insisted, saying that this was only a 'one-off occasion' (what an expression for the Head of such a school as this to use, – or was the school, which had recently become co-educational, not really of the old-fashioned kind that Austerlyn had expected?) and the Head had finally added, giving Austerlyn a positively admiring smile, 'with your long experience you should have no difficulty in improvising.'

The tall form-captain looked respectfully puzzled, and said, 'Mr Birkett, our form-master, told us we were to bring our Geography exercise books and atlases, sir.'

'Well,' Austerlyn said, raising his voice so that other members of the form would be able to hear, 'the Headmaster told *me* it was to be Chemistry. And that's what it will be.'

He was suddenly glad of this. He had already improvised quite a bit of the lesson in his mind while he had been finding his way to the form he was now with. He would talk about the lives of famous chemists, or at least about those aspects of their lives which most interested him and which he knew a little about. Starting with

Robert Boyle, mentioning the famous law about the relation of the volume and pressure of gases (but no more than mentioning it, since he had long ago forgotten its details) then concentrating on Boyle's battle against the obstinately surviving reactionary alchemical concepts of his day, such as the four elements. This would enable Austerlyn to generalise for a while on the entrenched prejudices which new ideas had come up against in every age. Next, Joseph Priestley, who discovered oxygen and had his house set on fire by the Church and Crown mob because of his sympathy with the French Revolution. What a pity Austerlyn would not be able to mention Gay-Lussac, about whom he knew nothing except his fascinating name.

He moved away from the form-captain and advanced towards the form. He came to a stop facing the middle of their front row. He raised his head and took into his view the whole thirty-five of them, individuals with interesting and even startling differences between them, but he felt he must be seen to see them as a group or else he might fail to get their full attention as individuals. He found he had stopped directly in front of an adolescent girl the skin of whose face had an astonishing baby-like delicacy of colour and texture. Just in case he might give the impression of having placed himself there not by accident but because she was attractive to him (as she was), he shifted his position quickly – though avoiding precipitancy – nearer to the rather heavy-faced boy who sat next to her. He spoke to the form as a whole, clearly and no more loudly than was necessary to reach their back row.

'I am going to talk to you this morning about the lives of famous chemists. There was a time not long ago when such a topic might have been considered out of place in a Chemistry lesson. It certainly would have been considered out of place as long ago as when I attended my first Chemistry lesson.' He noticed no smiles anywhere along the four rows in which the form sat. 'Strangely enough I was quite excited at the idea of learning science – before I actually started learning it.' There was not a single snigger or titter from any of them. And very rightly. He knew that by suggesting there had been something odd about his having been keen to learn science at school he was trying to ingratiate himself with them in a quite disgraceful way; and, worse still, if the cap of his criticism happened to fit the chemistry-teaching at this school and his new colleagues got to hear of what he'd said, he might be held guilty of unprofessional conduct. But he couldn't prevent himself from adding, 'Chemistry soon came to seem nothing more to me than Bunsen burners and pipettes and litmus paper and substances in bottles which had nothing to do with life outside the lab.' The form looked monolithically stolid. He turned away from them and took a pace or two in the direction of that end of the Hall where the gallery was, with its merciless white-faced clock. Movement, he knew from experience, was often a useful ploy (what a word, but he had found lately that slang could sometimes help his thinking) to hold attention at moments when he wasn't sure what he wanted to say next. He saw, below and in front of the gallery, a large blackboard and easel. Almost surprised that someone had had the forethought to provide this, he went forward to it. He was oddly confident that no one in the form was playing up behind his back. There was even a new stick of yellow chalk ready for him – it had been placed on the thick felt of a new board-duster, which was tri-coloured like a dingy neapolitan ice, and the wooden holder of the duster had been carefully balanced on one of the pegs that held up the board. The names of two more chemists came quickly into his mind. Lavoisier and Cavendish. He would tell the form that it was Lavoisier who totally and finally overthrew the phlogiston theory which Boyle's experiments had already called in question, and they would be interested to hear that Cavendish discovered hydrogen which led to early experiments with balloons, and he could tell them a thing or two about Cavendish's eccentric private life as well. He turned to face the form again, and their unshifting gaze convinced him that their eyes must have been on him all the time he had been walking away from them towards the blackboard.

He wrote the name Robert Boyle in large script at the top of the board. He began to speak about Boyle, more loudly than he had spoken about his own first experience of Chemistry lessons, but not more loudly than he saw was sufficient now to be clearly heard by the listeners in the back row. Yet before long he found he had to raise his voice a little, and then again a little. He didn't immediately know why he felt that this increase of volume was necessary. The form were not beginning to show any obvious signs that he was becoming inaudible to them. At last he noticed there was another sound competing with the sound of his voice; and its volume must be increasing at a faster rate than he was achieving, otherwise he might have noticed it even less soon. The noise did not come from the form, was not any kind of visually undetectable subversive humming. It did not come from anywhere inside the Hall, but from the cloisters outside. It was produced by the footsteps and voices of another form who now arrived at the open doorway and entered the Hall, becoming quiet as they did so. At their rear was a woman teacher; and while they walked on quietly to seat themselves near the other end of the Hall, well beyond the form that Austerlyn was in charge of, she detached herself from them and came towards him. She was dark-haired, about thirty years old and so startlingly beautiful that he averted his eyes, though only for a moment, from her face just before she spoke to him:

'I'm so sorry about this, but I'm afraid it's quite typical of the way things go on the first morning of term here. Particularly at the beginning of a new school-year.'

'Oh that's quite all right,' he said, not averting his eyes.

She was obviously well aware of her beauty, but altogether indifferent to it at present or to its effect on him. She saw him as a colleague, which he knew was how he ought to see her.

'Operation Chaos we call this,' she said.

'Well, I'll admit I was slightly surprised to be asked to give a lesson in Chemistry, which I'm ignorant of, and to discover I had to give it in this Hall.'

'I hope my voice from the other end of the Hall won't distract you.' She certainly didn't mean to use that word in the way it could have been taken by him.

'And I hope my lesson won't disturb yours.'

'No problem,' she said.

With a colleaguely smile she went away from him towards her group of pupils – she seemed to have even more than he had – who had sat down in rows with their backs to his lot and at a distance of some ten yards from them. He began to speak again about Boyle, but before long he became conscious of someone moving – or hesitating – just outside the open doorway. How many more interruptions would there be? His concentration on what he was saying about Boyle was not helped by the fact that the hesitater now stopped moving altogether and simply stood there in the doorway. Austerlyn abruptly decided it would be better to change this lesson from Chemistry to Geography, for which the form had atlases they could study while he was coping with the next interruption. He walked up to them to tell them what he had decided and why. They showed no surprise. He could not discover from any of their faces whether what he had been saying about Boyle had interested them much, but he sensed that the impression he had made on them, so far, had not been a bad one. He asked them to find the map of South East Asia in their atlases. He already knew he had something which interested him so much more deeply than Chemistry to say about this part of the world that he couldn't fail to arouse an answering interest in it among them.

He would still need the blackboard. He liked to draw large rough sketch maps; and the speed of his drawing would excuse the inaccuracies his watchers ought to detect in the map he intended to draw now. As he walked away from the form again he saw that whoever had been standing in the doorway was no longer there. He went up to the blackboard and taking hold of the neapolitan felt duster he wiped off the name of Robert Boyle. Without speaking he rapidly sketched a map showing the boundaries of Vietnam, Laos and Kampuchea, and he wrote the names of these countries within their boundaries. He began to talk of the terrible destruction that had been done there by the richest and most powerful nation in the world. He noticed that someone was standing in the doorway again. It was a boy, rather shorter than most of the boys belonging to the form he was speaking to but probably not younger than they were, though his cheeks were remarkably rounded and rubicund. Austerlyn all at once recognised him as the boy he had seen being embraced by a girl behind a pillar in the cloisters.

Although the girl's face hadn't been turned away from Austerlyn, not much of it had been visible to him except a softly swelling palely pink cheek and the corner of a large dark eye and of opened lips more deeply red even than the boy's face, which she was avidly kissing the unviewable farther side of, while her hands reached under the boy's open jacket and were stroking the sides of his brown woollen pullover with a slow circular movement. His smirk had had conceit in it, but also just a little embarrassment, as if he hadn't been totally sure he wasn't being made a monkey of. His face still showed a smirk as he stood in the doorway now, yet this time he was quite unembarrassed. Austerlyn stopped speaking to the form and directed an expectant glance at the boy, who made no response to it although he certainly saw it; but after a delay which was long enough to make the point that he was in no way influenced by Austerlyn's glance he strolled into the Hall.

He came directly towards Austerlyn at first, then went behind him, passing however in front of the blackboard which Austerlyn had stepped away from at the moment of ceasing to speak to the form. The boy's head, with its cheeks showing more shinily red than ever against the board, performed a sudden jerky stiff-necked quarter-turn, like the manipulated head of a ventriloquist's dummy, and faced the form with a fixed grin of such pertness that Austerlyn could hardly keep his anger cold as he said to the boy:

'You're rather late for this lesson, aren't you?'

Instead of saying anything to Austerlyn, and without even looking at him, the boy gave the form a crude and slow wink from one of his abnormally long-lashed eyes. This time Austerlyn spoke to him with a hard sharpness.

'What is your name?'

It seemed that the boy was going to ignore the question, but that suddenly he had a better idea.

'Laos,' he said.

'Repeat that,' Austerlyn said, controlling fury in case he might have misheard or in case Laos might by an almost incredible coincidence be the actual name of the boy and not an invention suggested to him by Austerlyn's having spoken it, and written it on the board, as the name of a country in South East Asia.

The boy walked on without answering and went to sit down at the right-hand end of the front row of the form Austerlyn was in charge of – the end which was farthest from the door and had no doubt been purposely chosen by the boy so that the progress of his late arrival in the Hall could be fully observed by the maximum number of his fellow pupils.

'I asked you to repeat your name,' Austerlyn said, in a tone he tried to make quieter than before, not wanting to heighten the drama of a scene he now sensed that the boy might have planned in advance.

The boy surprised him by answering this time at once that his name was Laos. However he pronounced it almost as one syllable – not Lah-oss now but Louss. Or Louse. He swivelled his wide-eyed gaze through ninety degrees along the front row of the form as if appealing for confirmation from them that he was telling the truth.

'It seems a remarkably appropriate name,' Austerlyn was horrified to hear himself say. Even if the name was a fake – which Austerlyn was nearly as certain it must be as he was of the impossibility of miracles – he had reacted to it in the worst way he could have: he had fallen into the double trap of allowing himself to be provoked by it and of being guilty himself of the cheapest and nastiest kind of traditional schoolmasterly provocation in return. And suppose that – by one chance in a billion – the name was not a fake: he would be guilty not merely of schoolmasterly sarcasm but of something that could almost be called inhumanity.

The boy did not respond for several seconds. Then he got quickly up from his seat and said loudly, though without shouting:

'Say that again, you wet geriatric slug, and I'll bash your face in.'

He came forward towards Austerlyn, who stood completely moveless trying to feel an absolute confidence that even at the present stage of world history his position as schoolmaster, if not his elderliness, still had sufficient charisma to inhibit any pupil from attempting an actual physical assault on him. The office makes the man and a dog's obeyed in office, he might have thought if he had had time to think, though he might also have remembered how in revolutionary periods be-medalled generals who have expected that their mere arrival upon the scene of a mutiny would be enough to quell it have been hauled from their horses and trampled to death by their men. But the boy, instead of trying to hit Austerlyn's face, walked straight past him, rather fast, and towards the doorway of the Hall.

Within a second or two Austerlyn, in rising rage, moved very rapidly after him, shouting from behind him, 'You will come with me at once to the Headmaster.'

The boy walked on and out into the cloisters, ignoring the shout. Austerlyn stopped in the doorway, realising that to go to the Headmaster's study would mean abandoning the form here in the Hall; and what would the Head think if he were to admit – as he could hardly avoid admitting – that he had been almost obscenely sarcastic about the boy's name, even if it was an impudently invented name?

Austerlyn turned and was beginning to walk slowly towards the form, trying to re-assume an outward calmness, when he noticed that he was still holding the board-duster and the stick of chalk, the duster in his left hand and the chalk in his right. He would have liked to take these back to the board at once, but he was deterred by the thought that he might not succeed in getting the duster to balance on the peg where he had found it and that the form would see him ridiculously juggling with it for a second or two in a useless attempt to catch it as it dropped to the floor. He went forward and put it and the chalk down quickly on an unoccupied chair not far from the door. The form were all of them watching him. He looked at them and was unable to discover from their faces anything of what they felt about him and Laoss. He saw no blatant signs of gloating. They could not be expected to take the side of a master – and a stranger too – against one of themselves, yet Laoss might be a type who would not be particularly popular among them. They might not be against Austerlyn, even though they couldn't be for him. He got the impression that if he had been capable now of going on with this lesson about South East Asia they would have been willing enough to listen to him. But instead he told them, as unshakily as he could:

'I want each of you to make a map of the three countries I have sketched on the blackboard. Consult your atlases, and you can use tracing paper, if you have some with you, to draw the outlines. Put in the main towns and the main physical features – rivers and mountains.'

An Old-Established School

It might be rather too elementary a task for a form of adolescents, he suspected, but fortunately they didn't appear to think so. They all had tracing paper with them and they got down to work promptly, though they had nothing to rest their atlases on except their knees. He walked slowly along their front row and back again, as if he was an invigilator at an examination, and his movement lulled the hurt that sulked in his nerves. Then the thought came to him that the woman teacher, whose presence in the Hall he had completely forgotten during the past few minutes, was likely to have been aware of at least something of what had happened between him and Laoss. He looked up over the heads of the form towards the far end of the Hall; and she was on the platform there, facing the large group she was in charge of, but not talking to them at the moment. Her control over them was evidently such that she would have had leisure to watch anything going on at his end of the Hall, if she had wanted to, though now she was watching them not him. The silent organ with its many pewter-coloured pipes of varying widths and heights looming behind her at the back of the platform made her seem like a singer on the stage of a concert hall, a famous soprano about to begin to sing an aria, while the awed music from the orchestra had become so pianissimo that he could not hear it at all. But the appearance she had of being totally unconscious of him at his end of the Hall convinced him she must have seen and heard every shameful detail of the Laoss incident.

He turned his back on her and on the form. He was incapable even of pretending to continue to take an interest in their map-drawing. The large white-faced clock, unavoidably visible in the middle of the bow-shaped front of the gallery above and beyond the blackboard towards which he paced now, startled him momentarily by showing that thirty-five of the forty-five minutes allotted for this lesson had already passed; but there were still ten more to go. Bitterness made him indifferent to what the form might do in that remaining time. He cared only about what he would do when the ten minutes ended: he would see the Headmaster, give instant notice, get away from the school for ever this afternoon, regardless of breach of contract and loss of salary. What was he doing here anyway? Why was he continuing to teach at his age? Why was he allowed to? He should have stopped years ago. He didn't need the money. Yet he went on and on, and at every school where he got a job he had to endure some vile humiliation sooner or later. It had happened here on the first morning and it could soon happen again if he didn't escape without delay. It might be happening at this moment.

There was a noise behind him and he turned and saw that the form were beginning to stand up from their seats. They did not look as though they were conscious of acting rebelliously, nevertheless it was obvious they were about to make their way out of the Hall. They moved unhurriedly towards the doorway. One of them even came back from there, threading his way through the others who were going out; he might have left his atlas behind and be returning to fetch it. Perhaps ten minutes had passed more quickly than Austerlyn had realised, and the form were leaving the Hall quite legitimately to go to their next lesson. Or at least they would be leaving legitimately if he had given them the signal to dismiss. Perhaps he had given it, unintentionally, by some accidental movement he might have made with his arm in the agitation of his feelings after he had turned his back on them and on the woman teacher. It was too late to stop them now: most of them were already out in the cloisters – although one of them hadn't yet begun to move from the Hall, was standing near the front row of seats at the end farthest from the doorway. This was a boy, possibly the one who had returned while the rest of the form were walking out. He seemed to be waiting for Austerlyn. He was Laoss.

His stance wasn't aggressive. He was not staring directly at Austerlyn but at the floor between them. It was possible he had decided that he couldn't escape the consequences of his offence against Austerlyn and that he might as well surrender to him now. His face offered no show of contriteness, but the pertness and insolence had quite gone from it. Austerlyn suddenly suspected, without knowing why, that the name Laoss was more likely than not to be the boy's real name after all. And perhaps the others called him Louse and this had caused him to have a chip on his shoulder and to behave in the objectionable way he did. Austerlyn moved a few short steps towards him, stopped while there were still several yards between them, then spoke:

'I am very sorry for what I said to you. I am very sorry. I ought never to have said it.'

The boy gave no kind of response.

'I suppose I thought you were much younger than you are.' This sounded as though Austerlyn was trying to justify himself, and also it could be taken as an insult, and anyway no matter how young the boy's face might look or how short his body might be – though his shoulders were broad – there could be no excuse for the disgusting sarcasm Austerlyn had said he was sorry for. He continued quickly:

'I'm not asking you to forgive me. That would be just as impertinent as if I were to say I forgive you.'

The boy came towards Austerlyn, in an unaggressive way, but said nothing, and still without looking at him walked past him in the direction of the doorway. At least he would know now that he wasn't going to be punished, Austerlyn thought with a little relief, watching him go out into the cloisters and noticing at the same time that the form which the woman teacher had been in charge of were also on their way out through the doorway. Then he noticed she was standing beside him.

She said with colleaguely sympathy:

'He's a problem all right, that lad. I know him well. He was in my form all last year. But I must say he surprised even me this morning.'

Austerlyn would have liked to ask her whether the boy's name really was Laoss, but if he did she might get on to talking about the boy in detail, and this would be repugnant to Austerlyn at present.

'I was as much to blame as the boy was,' he said.

'I think it was just one of those things that can always happen in our profession,' she said consolingly, though not contradicting him. 'They must have been happening for centuries, long before this school was rebuilt in Queen Victoria's reign and even before 1588 when it is said to have been founded.' She smiled. 'But formerly the taught and not the teachers were the ones who got hurt most.'

He had a brief impression that the Great Hall, now when her pupils as well as his had all made their way out of it, had become larger than ever, and its hammer-beams higher and shadowier.

'I was never cut out to be a teacher,' he said.

'You may say so, but I couldn't help listening to your lesson when I ought to have been minding my own business with my own class, and I watched your lot while you began to speak to them about South East Asia, as well as earlier on before you stopped speaking to them about Robert Boyle, and perhaps you didn't get through to all of them, but to some of them you did, and certainly to me.'

He said in a more relaxed tone than he had been capable of before:

'The trouble about taking temporary jobs in schools is that the pupils are apt to regard an elderly newcomer rather as they would a student-teacher, and he has to prove to them as soon as possible that he isn't fair game.'

'I'm sure that's not how they regard you here in this school.' She smiled again. 'If they did they might not have found such a distinguished-sounding name for you as the one I've overheard some of them using.'

She evidently kept her ears as well as her eyes open, he thought, though he wasn't in the least riled by her referring so uninhibitedly to the fact that the pupils had given him a name which wasn't his own. And she went on:

'Have you been called Austerlyn Greenholt at any other school before this?'

'No. Why?'

'Well, such things can travel. In no time and from one end of the country to the other.'

Abruptly yet vaguely he remembered a school where just before leaving he had heard the name Austerlyn Greenholt spoken but had not connected it with himself. Instead of telling her this he said with some vigour:

'As soon as my three weeks at this school are up I shall retire from teaching for good.' Then he realised that his talking with her had at least saved him from carrying out his irresponsible intention of giving notice to the Head at once and leaving the school this afternoon.

'I don't imagine you will really retire, even when you're no longer a schoolmaster,' she said. 'You may believe you're not cut out for teaching, yet my guess is you will want to go on with it – not for teaching's sake but because of something you feel you need to teach, though I expect you will teach it mostly to adults and not in any educational institution.'

He looked at her and was aware again, as he had failed to be while his disgraceful confrontation with the boy still dominated his feelings, of the extraordinary beauty of her face.

'You are too sensitive, Henry,' she said.

She moved nearer to him, and leaning forward she kissed him warmly on the cheek. Too soon she stepped back from him and said, 'Now I must get along to my next class.' She walked away briskly towards the doorway of the Hall, allowing him no time even to ask how she had got to know his real forename. But as she went out of the doorway she gave him a quick colleaguely smile before she disappeared along the cloisters. He was left in no doubt that the kiss had been a 'one-off' happening and that she was unlikely ever to kiss him again.

He made no move to follow her but remained standing where he was in the Great Hall, which now seemed to have become so large and so empty that he did not clearly see the far end of it, nor the hammer beams overhead, nor even the near end where the gallery was, though perhaps he did not try to see any of these things, as he was thinking still of her and of what she had guessed he would do after he had retired from schoolmastering. He recognised that no matter how grim the effort to go on might be for him he could not escape his need to say to others the kind of things he had said to his class this morning, and that his need would animate his day-time thoughts and his dreams at night for as long as he was alive.

At the Ferry Inn

Arnold Olney after forty years of estrangement from his once close friend Walter Selwyn had a letter by the first post one morning in Walter's characteristically almost illegible handwriting to say he would be arriving on the ferry-boat at 11.45 am and was hoping very much to have some hours with Arnold before returning to London for his flight back to New York the next day. Arnold was only momentarily disconcerted at the risk Walter had taken in giving him such short notice – so short that if the letter had come by the second post Arnold would not have seen it till the evening, because he had planned to be out all day, and what might be the one opportunity he would ever have of meeting Walter again would have been lost. When he got into his car to drive to the ferry he felt an extreme gladness, and he realised at last how profoundly during the past few years he had wished to be reconciled with Walter, though he ought long before now to have guessed this if merely from the frequency of his dreams at night about Walter as the young poet he used to know so well and to admire more than any other.

    The ferry-boat was coming out from the mouth of the estuary on the other side of the water as Arnold walked to the quay after leaving his car in the nearby car park. The boat moved against a background of high-masted small moored yachts and of trees dark enough to be firs or cypresses though their rounded cumulus-cloudlike shapes told him they were neither firs nor cypresses but possibly oaks or not yet diseased elms. Above them the sky was heavy with grey horizontal clouds. The boat turned gradually from the shadowed mainland until its bow was pointing directly towards him, so that he could no longer see its side or know whether its movement was slow or fast, and after a while he felt that his staring at its bow was making it seem to have stopped moving. He looked away from it, to the right and to the left, at the intermittently sunlit grey water, sparkling in patches here and there yet elsewhere as unrippled as though it had been smoothed over with a flat iron, and he saw a cormorant coming from a distance on his left in rapid straight flight parallel to the near shoreline and so low that its wing tips almost contacted their dark reflections on the water's surface. He watched it pass and go blackly on out of sight. He was taken by surprise when he noticed that the ferry-boat was already nearly half-way across from the mainland towards the quay where he was waiting. He could see the passengers on the deck, even their faces, though none of these distinctly yet. A quick fear rose in him. Walter might have changed so much as to be unrecognisable by him, might appear not just old but senile and decrepit. The thought of this was hardly bearable to him. When the ferryboat came nearer he could see no one on it who looked at all as he could have expected Walter to look, and he had a different fear: that Walter since writing to him might have had second thoughts and decided against making the journey to meet him. Even after the ferry-boat was alongside the quay and the passengers were beginning to walk down the gangway, Arnold could not see Walter among them. Then a young man still on the deck waved to him. Arnold was totally unable to believe for a second or two that this could be Walter. But as the young man descended on to the quay he did not seem so young. Rather than really young he was astoundingly well-preserved. He certainly was Walter — tall, broad-hipped, sloping-shouldered, his hatless hair thick and yellow, his cheeks plump and smooth-skinned as ever. He was wearing an alkanet-blue light summer jacket and was not carrying a raincoat or a bag of any kind or a book. His face as he came up to Arnold showed the kind of pleasure it would have shown more than forty years ago if they had met again after not having seen each other for a week or two.

'How glad I am you're here,' he said. 'I was afraid you might not get my letter in time.'

'How glad I am I did get it,' Arnold said.

'I ought to have written sooner, but I didn't start reading your new book till the day before yesterday. I think it's wonderful.'

A Renegade in Springtime

In an instant the anti-progressive attitudes and ideas which had been adopted by Walter during the past forty years, and had inhibited Arnold from trying to renew his friendship with Walter, became entirely unimportant to Arnold, and he said,

'There's no one I would rather hear praise my book than you.'

'It made me realise how much I needed to meet you again,' Walter said. 'I only wish I didn't have to go back to London so soon today.'

Though already knowing from Walter's letter that Walter wouldn't be staying for long, Arnold felt a brief chill of disappointment which he attempted to hide by saying in a lively way,

'Well, I hope there'll be time for us to have lunch together at the Ferry Inn just up the road here, and to have a drink beforehand.'

'Oh yes. Plenty of time.'

They began to walk along the cobbled road towards the inn. Arnold said,

'How extraordinary it is that you are actually here. It reminds me of that sonnet of Auden's which begins, "Just as his dream foretold, he met them all." I dreamt two nights ago that I met you here at the ferry.'

'And who were the others – "them all" – you met besides me?' Walter asked, with a keenness which suggested he hadn't yet lost the liking he'd had as a young man for analysing his friends' dreams.

'There weren't any others. Immediately after meeting you I woke.' Arnold, remembering there had been things in his dream that he didn't want to be led into describing to Walter – such as the shock he had got on seeing how saggingly old the flesh of Walter's face had become – hoped to deflect Walter's curiosity by adding,

'How well Auden's sonnet gets the inconsequent feeling of a dream, though not so marvellously as you get it in your poem about the Timor Sea, which is really a poem about Fear.'

'I was always glad you liked that,' Walter said, with such warmth that Arnold wondered whether in spite of Walter's having become world-known (or known at least to those minorities in the world who took notice of modern poets) he had felt a lack among his readers of the kind of whole-hearted enthusiasm shown for his poetry by Arnold in the nineteen thirties. But Arnold wasn't able to say anything further now in praise of the Timor Sea poem, because Walter asked quite eagerly,

'And what happened in your dream *before* you met me?'

They had already reached the front of the Ferry Inn, a genuinely old timber-framed building with a not very wide entrance doorway, and as they were about to go in through this Arnold said,

'A man wearing a green velour homburg hat handed me a suitcase in the street and said, "I'm afraid I've got to hurry so please put this down for me on the steps of the Imperial Bank over there", then left me holding the case which I at once went to get rid of outside the bank before walking very quickly away to meet you at the ferry.'

The passage-way they entered was lined with black oak panels and was narrow, dark and long. As they emerged into the bar-room at the end of it, which by contrast seemed light and was moderately noisy with talk, Walter said,

'So you deposited a bomb in front of the bank.'

The talk immediately stopped, at least from the group of navy-blue-blazered yachtsmen – or so Arnold took them to be – who were standing near the bar that Walter and Arnold were approaching. Walter had spoken in a clear unlowered voice, just as he usually would have done years ago when saying things to his friends which could outrage or alarm other people overhearing him, and he seemed just as indifferent now as he would have been then to the effect he had had on his overhearers. He gave no sign of noticing the looks on the faces of the yachtsmen as he stood waiting at the bar to be served – after insisting that he and not Arnold should be the one to buy the drinks, a schooner of dry sherry for Arnold and a large gin and vermouth for himself.

'A schooner of sherry,' he said to Arnold with interest; 'is that British yachting slang, do you think?'

'I don't know,' Arnold said, without giving even a half-glance towards the four large-bodied blazered men he was standing so close to. He wondered whether the hostility he sensed in them could be defused if he were to say now to Walter, 'I only dreamed I deposited the bomb', but something, he didn't know what, warned him that this might heighten rather than lessen their suspicions. He felt relief when he and Walter began walking away from the bar with the drinks which the impassive barmaid soon brought, though he was as sure as if he could still see the men that all four were staring hard at the backs of the two of them.

He led the way to a small table in an alcove at the far end of the bar-room where no one else was sitting. It was rather dark here both because of the oak panelling and because there were none of the windows with leaded diamond-shaped panes that made the rest of the room a little lighter than the long passage through which he and Walter had entered.

'It's like being born again in reverse,' Walter said after they had sat down. 'First the vaginal passage-way and now the primal snuggery.'

This time the yachtsmen did not appear to hear him, though he spoke no more quietly than before. All four of the men were facing the bar now. The broadness of each of their backs was made to seem still broader as they stood side by side together.

'A strange kind of womb,' Arnold said.

The alcove where he and Walter were sitting was walled on three sides by oak panelling with framed small colour prints of yachting and fox-hunting scenes attached to it, and all along the top of it was a ledge on which brilliantly polished brass horse-harness ornaments were arranged in a continuous row.

But Walter, who had never been as interested as Arnold was in external details, gave only a brief glance round the harness brasses and colour prints, then came back to what evidently interested him much more, Arnold's dream.

'That bomb you let yourself be tricked into leaving outside the bank,' he said with a hint of severity, though smiling, 'obviously represents a residual guilt in you after your years of left-wing political activity.'

Arnold, while unwilling to accept this interpretation, did not want to interrupt Walter, who went on,

'You were loyal for longer than the rest of us to "the clever hopes", as Auden afterwards called them, that we all fell for in the nineteen thirties, but your book has brilliantly rejected them at last, and without any exhibitionistic breast-beating or spitting on your youth.'

Arnold's unease at Walter's assumption that he had wholly changed his political views since the 'thirties was soothed by a recognition of the strength and genuineness of Walter's admiration for his book.

'I ought certainly to have become deconverted much sooner from my total faith in Stalin,' Arnold said. 'My doubts began quite early on, but I overcame each of them in turn, though less and less easily, until after he died and Khrushchev's revelations about him brought them to their climax. Then quantity changed into quality.' Arnold smiled as he used this dialectical expression, but he saw Walter wince slightly at it. Walter said,

'Your description of the moment of deconversion, when your central character realises how wrong he has been to trust the word of politicians rather than of honest imaginative writers like Gide, is one of the most moving things I have ever read. It reminded me of that last verse we used to be so excited by in Baudelaire's poem about the great painters where he says that art is the best testimony human beings can give of their dignity.' Suddenly Walter, in very English French – or Anglo-American French – and without raising or lowering his voice, spoke the lines,

'"Car c'est vraiment, Seigneur, le meilleur témoignage
Que nous puissions donner de notre dignité."'

There was an irony in his tone, implying perhaps that he no longer thought art quite as important as he and Arnold had once believed it to be, but the lines would almost have brought nostalgic tears into Arnold's eyes if his attention hadn't been abruptly diverted to a group of three youngish head-scarved and Fair Isle jumpered women sitting at a table near the bar. They were looking at Walter less with disapproval than with embarrassed concern, as though they suspected him of being a patient allowed out for the day from a mental hospital. They might be connected with the four yachtsmen at the bar, who were taking little notice of them however and also were giving the impression – which was likely to be a pretence – of not having heard Walter speaking French verse. But Arnold's uncomfortable awareness of the women and the yachtsmen did not make him forget his unease about Walter's apparent assumption that he had completely rejected his former left-wing views. At last, although he was very reluctant to risk lessening Walter's admiration for his book, he said,

'My disillusionment with Stalin didn't mean I became disillusioned with Marx or with Lenin.'

'I guessed that from your book. You obviously have quite a way to go yet before realising that there must have been something in Lenin, and in Marx too, which was bound to lead to an autocracy like Stalin's.' Walter's assertively authoritative tone caused no uneasiness in Arnold, who remembered how habitually Walter had spoken like this forty years ago when arguing about anything he considered important: and Arnold was glad that Walter seemed not to have formed his high opinion of the book in unawareness of its Leninism. Arnold said,

'Lenin can hardly be blamed for being revised and distorted by Stalin, any more than for being completely repudiated by Euro-Communists now.'

'If you think as you apparently do in your book that almost every existing communist party has gone "revisionist"' – Walter's emphasis on this word seemed to imply a criticism of it – 'how can you claim that the teachings of Marx and Lenin have any practical importance any longer in the world at all?'

'An anti-imperialist revolution has already begun in the Third World,' Arnold said, 'and whatever mistakes the workers in the imperialist countries may yet make they will ally themselves with it at last.'

'So you're hoping for a revolution still,' Walter loudly said, 'though no doubt you wouldn't disagree with Marx and Engels that class struggle has sometimes led to the common ruin of the contending classes, and presumably you've realised there could be final ruin this time.'

'There could be, but this will depend on whether or not the revolutionary movement can get sufficient support to break the power of capitalism before capitalism can destroy us all,' Arnold said not so loudly. He could not refrain from adding, 'The revolution needs support from poets too.'

At the Ferry Inn

'Auden was entirely right when he pointed out that poets didn't save a single Jew from the gas chambers,' Walter said, 'and he was right too in saying that a poet shouldn't be expected to come out with public statements about politics any more than a dustman should.'

'Auden wasn't being politically neutral when he made those two public statements,' Arnold said. 'He was helping the imperialists who want poetry to be silent about their crimes.'

Walter suddenly stood up, saying,

'I'm afraid I'll have to go to the lats.' He used their old word for it. 'I think I've got a touch of summer diarrhoea.' He added, as if to make clear that there was no connection between it and his conversation with Arnold, 'I suspected it after breakfast this morning.'

He glanced around the bar-room for a moment or two. Then like a homing pigeon that had found its bearings he went straight towards the end of the bar where the red-faced handlebar-moustached yachtsman stood glaring at him. Walter appeared to be about to speak to the yachtsman but actually he was looking well above the man's head at a pointed wooden sign with *Toilets* printed in gilt letters along it. He walked on, seemingly not noticing the man who glaringly watched him disappear through a doorway to the left of the bar, and who continued to watch the doorway for almost a minute after Walter's disappearance; but when the yachtsman gave up watching he turned to face the bar again, not to stare at Arnold. Evidently he was less resentful and suspicious of Arnold than of Walter.

Arnold sitting alone in the shadowy alcove soon began to regret more and more that he had been talking with Walter about things that divided them instead of trying to tell him how deeply he still admired his poetry. 'If I had not been his friend and known him as a living poet,' Arnold thought, 'I would never have known how marvellous human life at its best can be.' This was what Arnold needed to tell Walter, and would tell him as soon as he came back to the alcove. But Walter was taking a long time to come back. Arnold, looking towards the doorway through which Walter had disappeared, was all at once conscious that the yachtsman with the handlebar moustache was no longer standing at the bar. The man might have followed Walter out of the bar-room and might be physically attacking him now. An apprehensiveness grew in Arnold as minutes passed and neither of them reappeared. He got up and walked across to the bar and then through the open doorway towards the toilets.

He found himself in an even narrower and darker passage-way than the one by which he and Walter had come into the bar-room from the street. There were two doors along the left-hand side of the passage, and on the first of these Arnold was able to read the word *Wenches* inscribed in black lettering with a facetiously antique double V instead of a W. He opened the second door, hardly glancing at the similarly pseudo-antique inscription on it, which looked something like *Gallants,* and he came into a white-tiled Gents lavatory where a large man was standing alone at the urinals with his back to the door. It was the yachtsman. Walter must be in one of the three closets on the opposite side of the room. He might have become ill, perhaps ill enough to be incapable of getting out of the closet he was in. Arnold thought of going to listen at one or other of the closet doors, but he realised that if he were to do this it would almost certainly be noticed by the yachtsman who might assume it was some sort of obscene perversion and might compensate for his failure to beat up Walter by beating up Arnold instead – and the same could happen if Arnold did nothing yet except stand here waiting for him to go away. So Arnold went and stood at the urinals, though as far as possible from the yachtsman, the whole upper half of whose body now appeared to be gradually swelling up, as if he was drawing an immensely deep breath or had become tumescent with rage. At last the man buttoned up his flies and walked away to go out into the passage, morosely ignoring Arnold, who as soon as he had gone moved quickly over to the closets. Surprised that the engaged sign was not showing on any of their doors, Arnold opened the nearest of these. Walter was not inside, nor in the next closet, nor the third. Then just beyond the closets Arnold found a larger doorway already open, and he walked out of this into a yard which had wild plants growing between its flagstones and was enclosed on three sides by the windowed and

At the Ferry Inn

balconied walls of the inn building, and in the middle of the fourth side there was an archway that led into the street. This was the route that Walter must have taken, Arnold thought, as he himself walked across the yard and through the archway. But why hadn't Walter come back into the inn by the front entrance from the street?

Might he have missed the entrance by turning to the right instead of to the left when he had come out through the archway? Arnold stood looking up and down the street, which was quite crowded now, probably with people who had disembarked from the next ferry-boat after the one Walter had arrived by, and he was unable to see anyone who could be Walter. He decided to walk down the street to the right, against the main movement of the crowd. Without meeting Walter he reached the quay, from which the ferryboat was just beginning to move away. A black-jerseyed man had lifted the noose of a thick rope from a bollard at the edge of the quay, and at the stern of the boat another man was operating a capstan to bring the rope on board. Arnold was about to turn round with the idea of going back past the inn to search for Walter along the street to the left of the entrance, but his attention was caught by something he thought he saw, and then was certain he saw, on the ferryboat. It was Walter's alkanet-blue light summer jacket.

Walter was there on the deck among the other passengers. He was looking towards Arnold, without seeing him. The shock Arnold felt gave way after a moment to the bitterest remorse. His guess was that by criticising Auden he had given deadly offence to Walter who must have suspected rightly enough that the criticism was aimed at himself too. But when the boat began to move at full speed away from the quay Walter suddenly did see Arnold and smiled and waved to him as if nothing in the least untoward had happened. Arnold smiled and waved back, sure now that whatever unguessable reason Walter had had for so abruptly leaving him it didn't mean that the ending of their long estrangement had been illusory. They remained looking and smiling at each other as the boat moved farther away, until a cloudshadow passed over the deck, momentarily causing Walter's face to seem even more saggingly and

A Renegade in Springtime

horrifyingly old than in Arnold's dream two nights before, but Walter became younger again when the shadow had gone, though soon his features were indistinct in the renewed sunlight as the boat took him still farther from Arnold and nearer to the dark-treed overclouded mainland.

The White-Pinafored Black Cat

It might have been better if Esther Johnson and her brother Maurice had retired to a proper village with a church and a pub and four or five little shops, rather than to this hamlet without any of those advantages. What had attracted Maurice was the railway station here, a small one out of use as a station after the single line passing through it had been closed down early on in the post-Second World War period of railway dismantlements; and Maurice – a railway enthusiast since childhood – had discovered during a summer holiday with Esther in this district that the station house was up for sale to the public. The price asked for it was almost unbelievably low, and he decided at once to buy it. Esther acquiesced; though while she quite liked the prospect of retiring to an address that would intrigue her few surviving old friends, she could have wished it had been one that would have sounded a little more fashionable perhaps, such as 'The Old Watermill' or even 'The Old Coach House'.

But the station house was comfortable to live in, more so than a converted watermill or coach house would probably have been. It was well-built and pleasant to look at and on its south side it had a garden already plentifully provided with flowering plants, and also there was a lawn that sloped slightly downwards to a clear-flowing stream. Maurice would have liked to retain in the house the old ticket office together with the short passage-way which led out from this to the station platform on the north side; however, Esther was firmly against that idea, although when telling him so she tempered her firmness with a pun. 'I must absolutely draw the line at our pretending to be station-master and station-mistress here,' she said. She knew that few things would have pleased him better now than to be in charge of a rural railway station where real trains actually stopped and he could sell and collect tickets; and certainly she would have been glad sometimes if she could have made the short direct train journey to the nearest shopping centre instead of having to take the considerably longer road route there by bus or on her bicycle, much though she still enjoyed cycling. Fortunately, after they had found an efficient local builder who was able to convert the ticket office and its adjoining passage-way into one room where Maurice could set up a model railway track, he acknowledged that the conversion was an improvement.

Retirement was never a problem for him. Every morning he woke to an awareness of something interesting he would be able to do, either in his model railway room or outside at the end of the platform in the old signal box which became his workshop where he could make useful or ornamental things for the house or for his railway, and later on he took up pen-and-ink sketching, mainly of scenes that would have been viewable formerly by train travellers along the now rail-less track. It was just as well he could be so self-sufficient, Esther thought, as he was not a man who easily found new friends. He was inclined to be jokily outspoken in a way which seemed to her to be obviously not at all ill-natured, but it gave lasting offence sometimes to people who had not known him long. One of these was Dr Vallance their nearest doctor here, to whom Maurice had unluckily remarked when consulting him about an attack of indigestion, 'Of course you doctors nowadays are really Civil Servants', and after that Dr Vallance had refused to have him as a patient any more. Maurice, unworried, said to Esther, 'He never did my indigestion the slightest good. From now on I shall avoid all doctors for as long as I possibly can.' But Esther felt she needed to see one because of her arthritis – if that's what it was – which was beginning to affect her shoulders as well as the finger joints of her left hand, and being too embarrassed to return to Dr Vallance (though presumably he wouldn't have refused to continue accepting her as a patient) she had to go to Dr Pentelow whose surgery was a mile farther away than Dr Vallance's.

Maurice's jocular frankness didn't get him liked by any of the inhabitants of the hamlet. Not that any of them showed hostility to him, and to Esther they were always civil, though she sensed that — no doubt because of Maurice — their civility was unlikely ever to develop into friendliness. She did not mind greatly. She found friendliness — and one particular friend, Margery Horton — among the small congregation at the church of a nearby village, a beautiful seventeenth-century church not attended by any of the few other Anglicans living in the hamlet, who regarded Mr Liddicott, the rector, as standoffish, and preferred to go to a church in the nearest town or to listen to the Sunday service on the radio. It was Margery who gave Esther and Maurice the kitten they named Abigail which had such attractive markings — all black except for one large pure white oblong patch stretching downwards from just below the chin, like a pinafore. They were glad to have Abigail as a companion for Selima, their older cat which they had brought with them from their former home in London when they had retired. Selima was already ten years old now, and Esther had recognised that without a cat at all she, if not Maurice, might begin to feel increasingly isolated here in this hamlet as she too grew older. And she became more and more fond of Abigail, who seemed to show an attachment to her personally in a way that even Selima, affectionate but caring less for persons than for places, never did. Nearly always as she returned from the town on those mornings when she went shopping there she would find Abigail sitting upright just inside the garden gate, waiting for her, and she would say 'You faithful little creature'; at which Abigail would turn and precede her along the path to the station house. But one morning when she returned from taking Selima — who had been refusing food recently — to see the vet, she did not find Abigail waiting for her. Esther was tired as she walked into the kitchen carrying the wicker basket in which she had taken Selima on the bus to the town and back. She wished Maurice had been able to come with her to carry Selima, as he gladly would have done if he hadn't been feeling unwell after breakfast. Abigail was not in the kitchen when Esther opened the lid of the basket to release Selima there. Esther found Abigail dozing in the south room on the hearth rug at the sprawled and upturned feet of Maurice who was sitting dead in his armchair. The pain he had had after breakfast had been due to heart disease, not indigestion.

A Renegade in Springtime

The shock for Esther was very great, although its full effect was held back by the pressure of all the things she had to do now, immediately and during the following week, and without any help from the one person she would most naturally have turned to in a time of disaster, Maurice himself. She did get support, however, from her friend Margery, especially when arrangements had to be made with the undertaker and the rector for the funeral. In spite of arthritis which was more severe than Esther's yet was, Margery came over to the hamlet each day before the funeral and stayed at the station house for several days and nights after it to help with the shopping and cooking and to keep Esther company in the evening. But eventually Esther was alone there, except for the two cats, and her grief came fully into its own.

Perhaps only the cats, and the necessity of feeding them, made her take the trouble to go on preparing meals for herself also, though her thoughts and feelings were about Maurice and hardly at all about the cooking or eating or anything else she had to continue doing now. To have been able to talk about him with someone who had known him really well might have given her comfort, but none of their surviving old friends had been in good enough health to come down for the funeral, and their father and mother were dead and so were all their other relatives except for their cousins who lived in Australia. Yet she could get some comfort from talking about him in her thoughts, and the presence of Selima and Abigail in the room helped her to feel as if she wasn't talking entirely to herself. On the first evening that she was alone with them she did once speak directly to them about him, though not aloud. 'He used to stand at the back door and call you in by name every evening before it got dark,' she said to them in her thoughts. How anxious he would become if they did not return quickly, she remembered. His voice would rise till the whole hamlet must have heard it and perhaps laughed not very kindly about him and about those unusual names Selima and Abigail. He was afraid that the two cats might take to hunting together down by the river in the long grass where adders lurked. Or that they would 'go feral' and never come home to the house again. 'Feral' had been a favourite word of his ever since he had first read it in a boys' magazine during his schooldays.

He had never really outgrown his boyhood. He had not wanted to outgrow it, or to adapt himself fully to adult life. She had long realised, though never so keenly as she did now on her first evening alone in the room with Selima and Abigail, that this was a fault in him. He might still be alive and have several more years of life before him if his boyishly tactless jokiness hadn't offended Dr Vallance. Yet she had not at any time in the past wished to reproach him for his boyishness, and least of all did she wish to now that he was gone. How much more forgivable a fault his was, she thought, than the forgetfulness that some adults showed about their early years.

For many evenings in her aloneness with Selima and Abigail she told them, not aloud, the story of his and her childhood at the vicarage. She was two and a half years younger than Maurice, yet except during her earliest infancy he had shared his toys with her, so that soon she became as interested in his trains as he already was in her dolls. He was imaginative, not only about the dolls and the trains, and he shared his imaginings with her. There was one of his imaginings which meant so much to her now that she repeated the story of it on several evenings in her thoughts. It had come to him the day when he and she had discovered in the box-room at the top of the house an oblong tin which had once contained shortbread. The tin was brilliantly rustless inside, with only small spots of rust showing here and there through the tartan-patterned paper that covered the outside. He carried it downstairs, concealing it under his jersey and trying to conceal with his arm the bulge it made, and she knew it was to be a secret from everyone else in the house – their governess, their mother and father, even the cook and the housemaid. They took it on to the veranda, and from a corner behind the wicker armchair there he fetched out a strange-shaped white stone they had hidden after bringing it back from the seaside that summer. He put the stone into the tin and closed the lid over it. 'This must never be opened again,' he said. 'Now let's take it to the park.' They set out at once for the public park, which was less than a quarter of a mile away, and when they got there they walked to the far end of it where the disused sand-pit was. He pushed the tin into one of the larger of the many holes excavated in the face of the pit by nesting sand-martins. She helped to enlarge the hole, after they had made sure there was no nest inside it, and then to fill it up with sand around the tin. She didn't know why they were doing this, nor did she ask him. They stepped back when the tin was completely and deeply hidden by firmly pressed sand. They stood silent till Maurice said, 'This is the most important thing in the world. It is more important even than Mummy and Daddy.' She felt an excitement, yet she was a little frightened – not only because she suspected that their vicar father would have thought there was something heathen about what they were doing, and that their mother – although she was less strict in her beliefs and was fond of theatricals – would have been rather shocked. Esther was frightened also at the idea that anything in the world, except God, could be more important to her than her mother and father. And Maurice was saying that an old shortbread tin was more important. But she sensed that it wasn't just the tin itself he was thinking of. And then, not quite clearly at first yet clearly enough to cause her excitement to overcome her fear, she knew he was really saying that he and she, through their act of burying the tin in the sandpit, had become more important to each other than either their mother or their father was to them. After that, if not because of it, they became consciously closer to each other in affection and in understanding as they grew older, until the time came for Maurice to go away to his public school, while she, being a girl, went to the local High School. (Her mother would have liked her to go to Cheltenham Ladies' College if it had been less expensive and if her father hadn't believed that young girls should live at home.) But Maurice wrote to her often from his boarding school. She kept most of his letters. She still had them, though it was years since she'd last read any of them. She had brought them with her when she and Maurice had moved from London to the station house. They were in a cardboard box at the back of her wardrobe upstairs.

   She fetched them down to the sitting-room and began to read them in the evenings now, slowly and not aloud, each of them more than once. It had been usual for Abigail to jump on to her lap and lie there to be stroked while Esther talked about Maurice in her thoughts, but stroking Abigail while at the same time handling the letters wasn't easy for Esther, who was thankful that Abigail was such a good cat and didn't ever try to paw or claw at the letters out of curiosity, or out of jealousy because they were monopolising Esther's attention. Selima did not jump on to Esther's lap. Poor Selima was no longer able to do that. She had slowly been getting weaker, and the vet hadn't held out much hope that she could ever fully recover. So it was an additional sadness more than an unexpected shock for Esther to find her lying dead on the hearth rug one morning. Esther would have liked to make a grave for Selima at the bottom of the garden, but though still capable of pulling up weeds by hand and of planting small plants with a trowel, she could not dig with a spade any more. She had to get the vet to come and take Selima away.

After this she was even more thankful for the comforting that Maurice's letters from school gave her as she continued reading them in the evenings with Abigail on her lap. There was one of them in which he was enthusiastic about Thomas Gray's poem 'On a Favourite Cat, Drowned in a Tub of Gold Fishes'. It was a kind of poem he liked better than Gray's more serious 'Elegy written in a Country Churchyard' and he wanted her to like it too – which she did, – and nearly fifty years later their own Selima had been so named by them because as a kitten she had had a fondness for looking into bowls and vases of all sorts, though fortunately never meeting the same fate as Gray's Selima. At the age of fifteen Maurice began writing light verse himself, some of which he enclosed in his letters, and by the time he reached the Sixth Form several of his poems had already appeared in the school magazine. He was expected by everyone to do well academically. Their father hoped he would go to Oxford and from there into the Administrative Civil Service. But victory in the Great War was longer coming than their father had prayed it would be, and Maurice was called up into the army at the end of 1917. Esther could find no letters of his written to her after this. She couldn't even remember for certain that he had written any to her then, though it seemed likely to her now that he would have done. The whole of that year, from his call-up until the Armistice, had become vague to her, possibly because she had given so little thought to it

– she hadn't wanted to think of it – during later years. One evening while she was trying to make herself remember Maurice as he had been when he had come home from the war she fell asleep in her chair, and when she woke – or just before she was fully awake – she felt an intense physical pain, the most dreadful pain she had yet had in all her life, a pain that could mean she was on the point of death.

She could not locate just where in her body it was centred. At first it seemed to be in her chest and then in her throat and then it spread to her shoulders and her arms. It was a general, paralysing pain. But its intensity lessened as it spread, and when she became quite wide awake she couldn't feel it anywhere. Yet for many minutes she remained convinced it had been a physical reality, not just a horrible dream. She got up out of her chair, only then becoming remorsefully aware that Abigail, who was forced to jump to the floor, had been lying on her lap unstroked and unthought of by her all this while. But soon, remembering why she had got up, she temporarily forgot Abigail again. She had intended to go and telephone Dr Pentelow. She wished now more than ever before that the dislike Maurice had developed for the telephone during his years of office work in London hadn't made him refuse to have one installed in the house here. 'There's a call-box just across the road anyway', he had said, not considering the possibility that he or she might become physically incapable of getting across to it one day or even merely that the weather might sometimes be bad. She thought she could hear rain falling now. Yes, it was, heavily. And what would Dr Pentelow's response be when she did go across to the call-box and phone him? Would she be able to persuade him that she was ill enough to make it absolutely necessary for him after his day's work to get into his car and drive over at once to see her? No, she wouldn't be able to, because she was becoming less and less sure that the pain hadn't been a mere nightmare after all. She decided to postpone ringing up Dr Pentelow till the morning. She went back to her chair, at the foot of which Abigail sat waiting, giving no sign of grievance at having been tipped abruptly by Esther to the floor. To make amends for that unkindness Esther bent down and stroked Abigail fondly now, but did not get into the chair again. A feeling of shakiness caused her to think that the best thing to do would be to go upstairs and, early though it was, to put herself to bed for the night.

She went to see Dr Pentelow after her breakfast next morning. She felt no unusual pain now, only the usual arthritic one across her shoulders and also the one that had started fairly recently in her legs and was particularly noticeable this morning as she walked the five hundred yards or so between the bus stop and Dr Pentelow's house. She would certainly tell him about this as well as about her experience the previous evening. He took her blood-pressure, then applied his stethoscope to various places on her chest and her back, but he made no comment until she asked whether what she'd experienced could have been a kind of hallucination caused perhaps partly by the anti-arthritic drugs she had been taking. He said this was unlikely; however he prescribed a new drug, which he hoped would help her legs too. She must let him know how she got on with it. He said goodbye to her very pleasantly. And by the time she returned home again, having first taken the bus into the town to have the prescription made up by the chemist, she was almost wholly convinced that her nightmare had been of no, or very little, medical importance.

She didn't suspect there was any connection between it and her sudden ability, as she sat with Abigail on her lap the following evening, to begin to remember things about Maurice during the final year of the Great War. The first thing she clearly remembered was his being at home in the vicarage drawing-room wearing his army uniform. Their mother and father and several friends were there and so was Mavis Prosser, whom he'd become engaged to just before he was sent to France. Mavis was looking up at his face in an adoringly admiring way, which was perfectly genuine, and was asking him to tell them about some of the things he had done in battle. He flushed, and wouldn't say anything. The others probably thought this was due to modesty, but Esther could detect an extreme distaste in his look. After he was demobbed he broke off his engagement with Mavis. He never got married. It was as if the war had turned him against all the ways of the adult world. He even stopped going to church, in spite of the distress this gave their father and mother. He refused to take any job which would have put him in a position of authority over other people. He didn't become soured, or a rebel; he simply seemed to regard the adult world as a joke, a rather stupid joke. He once told her that the epitaph he would like to have inscribed on his tomb-stone was John Gay's: 'Life is a jest, and all things show it; I thought so once, but now I know it.' He never lost his liking for verse, nor his other boyhood interests. Nor his affection for her. Had some particular happening during the war been the cause of the lifelong change in him afterwards? Or would he have developed just as he did if there had been no war? She couldn't believe he would have. Perhaps the death of his friend Louis was the cause. As Esther said this in her thoughts she had a premonitory feeling that the nightmare pain she had experienced two evenings ago was about to come upon her again, though this time she was wide awake.

She quickly lifted Abigail down from her lap to safety on the floor, and at the moment she did so she understood that the pain which was threatening to return had been connected with Louis. But there was a difference now: she was aware of the connection, as she hadn't been two evenings ago, and a hope came to her that she might be able to use her awareness to fend off the pain, or at least to change it, to convert it from a physical pain which she could not deal with to one in the mind which she possibly could. She began to tell herself the story of Louis. He was Maurice's best friend at school, and Maurice had invited him to stay at the vicarage for a day or two during several of the school holidays. He was a musician, a very promising pianist. She was learning to play the piano then. She used to turn over the pages of the music for him as he played Mozart sonatas on her mother's baby-grand Blüthner in the drawing-room. The day he came to say goodbye to them before he was sent to France she was alone with him in the drawing-room for a minute or two. They were standing near the piano, facing each other. The words rose into her mind, 'You are in love with me, Louis.' She came very near to speaking them to him. She had no doubt they were true, and she knew she was in love with him. But he did not say anything either. He may have thought that at the age of fifteen and a half she was too young to become engaged to him, and that he would wait for another half year before asking her father's permission to marry her. He was killed four days after he was sent to the Front. She never in later years became engaged to anyone, although there were two men at different times who wanted to marry her. She could not be in love with either of them, and she was not the sort of woman who believes that almost any husband is better than none. But she had wanted to be married, and now she was old and getting older and more arthritic and Margery her friend was seldom able to come to see her, and the rector, Mr Liddicott, never did.

'That's quite enough of that,' she told herself, and immediately afterwards she realised she had said it aloud; so she stroked Abigail, who might have recognised reproof in the tone of it, and she added aloud, 'I was speaking to myself, not to you, Abigail dear.' Then she went on, not aloud, to tell herself she ought to be thankful that things weren't worse than they were with her, that she was still able to go to church, to do her own shopping, to visit Margery, to weed and to plant in the garden with her knee-pads on, that there was a boy from the hamlet who mowed the lawn for her, that even the adults in the hamlet had seemed friendlier to her since Maurice had died. And although she had never married she had been able for nearly twenty-five years of her life to do work which she loved as a teacher of young children at a preparatory school. Her father had expected her as an unmarried daughter to stay at home with her parents, but in fact it was their bachelor son Maurice who found an office job near enough to the vicarage for him to continue living with them, and when Mother had to leave the vicarage after Father died Maurice moved with her to another house in London not far from the office. Esther was very successful in her teaching of eight- and nine-year-old children, as everyone recognised, not least Commander Eversley, the chairman of the governing body which her headmaster, Mr Winford, had got together so that his school should acquire charitable status (and the tax advantages this brought with it). Nevertheless when Mother died and Maurice promptly gave up his job as an insurance broker's clerk and said he wanted to get out of London, Esther agreed to retire from teaching and to set up house with him in the country somewhere. Her last end-of-term at the school was a sad one, made sadder by Commander

Eversley's goodbye talk alone with her. 'You won't need a pension from the school, of course,' he said, after praising her work. No doubt he had been told by Mr Winford that her mother had left her enough to live on, but she knew that two of the men teachers who had retired since the governing body had come into existence, and neither of whom was without private means, were receiving small pensions from the school. She had burst into tears in front of the Commander, and she still – to this day, to this evening – felt ashamed of that. But she had felt no bitterness at the time about her treatment by the governors, and she must not let herself feel any now – nor about Mr Liddicott's failure to come and visit her at the station house, though she couldn't help comparing him unfavourably with her father, who would never have neglected one of his elderly and solitary parishioners in this way. She must count her blessings, and Abigail was not the least of these. She must put the remainder of her life to good use, try each day to do the things she knew she ought to do. And one of these things – as she had been increasingly aware recently – was to see her solicitor about certain changes that needed to be made in her will. After all, even if her nightmare pain had not been due to any fatal physical malady, she was not going to live for ever.

On a Friday morning – Friday being a usual shopping day for her – she visited the solicitor; and that evening with Abigail on her lap again she began to speak, at first only in her thoughts, about the two codicils she had asked the solicitor to add to her will. She would rather not have spoken about them at all; because one of them was painful for her to think of, but as it concerned Abigail who was lying warm on her lap she would have felt like a deceiver if she had kept it out of her talk now. She nevertheless delayingly spoke to begin with about the other codicil, which bequeathed most of her estate to the fund for repairing the seventeenth-century church that she loved and continued worshipping at each Sunday morning in spite of the rector's neglect of her. At last she said out loud, 'Abigail dear, oh Abigail, there is something I need to tell you though I know you are not able to understand me. If only you could understand, I could discuss it with you and get your agreement to what I have done. Or perhaps you would disagree. Then I would respect your disagreement, and I would make the solicitor cancel the codicil about you that I told him to add to my will when I saw him this morning. But as I have not become senile enough yet to think that you and I can really talk to each other, Abigail dear, I know I must rely on my own judgement, and it tells me that if I died tomorrow there would be no one to care for you and to feed you. I would have asked Margery, who gave you to me when you were a kitten, to take you back if I were to die before her, but I grieve to say that her arthritis is becoming so bad that soon she may no longer be able to care even for herself. So I felt I had no alternative to doing what I did this morning. Oh Abigail, I have added a request to my will that as soon as I am dead the vet should come here and put you to sleep. Oh Abigail, forgive me, forgive me, and believe that I have done what I'm sure will be best for you, though if you could understand what I'm saying you might tell me you would rather risk trying to survive without me.'

She stopped speaking aloud. She recognised that if she went on like this she might before long get herself into a state of believing that Abigail could after all understand everything she said. And it might be better for her to stop talking to Abigail even in her thoughts. It might be better if she stopped talking in her thoughts altogether and found an evening occupation more likely to do no harm to her health of mind. There had never been television in the house for her to watch, because Maurice wouldn't have been able to bear it, and the wireless which he could just tolerate made him restless and she used it so seldom that when it got out of order a year ago she hadn't bothered to have it repaired. They relied on *The Times* and the local paper for their news. She still took both of these, but she couldn't occupy whole evenings reading them. She decided she would have the wireless repaired. Also she would start reading her favourite author, Jane Austen, again.

Next morning, though it was a Saturday and the town would be crowded with shoppers, she took the bus and went to ask the man at the small electricity shop if he would collect and repair her wireless set, which she told him was an old one too heavy for her to carry. He said he would come on Monday. She went straight back to the bus stop, having no shopping to do as she had done it all on

Friday. When she got back to the hamlet she was a little disappointed not to find Abigail waiting for her at the gate of the station house garden. Abigail was nowhere in the garden and remained away from the house all day. Before dark Esther went to the back door just as Maurice used to do when the two cats were late in returning for their evening milk, and she called out the name of Abigail, her voice rising as his used to rise if the cats did not return quickly to his call, though her call was shriller than his; yet Abigail did not come. She was about to give up, when suddenly a cat peered in through the garden gate. Although she soon knew it wasn't Abigail it caused her to remain here and to continue calling for a while, but without effect. Abigail did not come back that night and Esther did not sleep.

She was up early in the morning, well before the milkman had begun his round. There was still no sign of Abigail. When the milkman came to the door she asked him if he had seen anything of her cat, which she described to him. He told her he would recognise Abigail anywhere. He was a kind-faced, youngish man with a dark beard and a high bald forehead. 'I'm afraid I've not seen her this morning,' he said. 'But I'll keep a good look-out in future.' After he had gone Esther wrote out in large letters on a piece of white card a notice headed with the word MISSING and mentioning Abigail's unusual markings and friendly nature. She wrapped the notice in a transparent plastic bag, as a protection against bad weather, and she pinned it with drawing pins to the outside of the garden gate where everyone walking by would see it. Several of the neighbours spoke to her about it during the next few days, though only to ask whether she had had any news yet of where Abigail might have got to. The days and the nights passed, and Abigail did not return.

One morning the moment came when she gave up hope of ever seeing Abigail again. She was at the back door, paying the milkman what she owed him for the week's milk. He told her that on his rounds he had asked at every house whether anyone had caught sight of her cat anywhere, and no one had. There was real sympathy in his voice. She had difficulty in holding back her tears. Her sadness was made worse by a sudden thought that Abigail while not understanding her words about the codicil in her will might somehow have sensed danger in them and might instinctively have chosen to 'go feral' rather than remain with her. Only by immediately reminding herself of another favourite saying of Maurice's, 'Few things are more frequent than coincidences', was she able to become sure that Abigail's disappearance had not been an instinctive act of self-preservation but a dreadful coincidence. Yet her sureness could not prevent her from having an intense brief feeling that there was nothing ahead for her now except ageing and aloneness and illness and death. The kind and helpful milkman, just before going off to his next customer, said to her, 'I won't give up keeping a look-out for Abigail.' Words came into her mind which she might almost have spoken to him if he had stayed a little longer at her door. As she carried into the kitchen the bottle of milk he had left for her she spoke them aloud to herself, 'If I didn't believe that my heavenly father is watching over me I don't know what I would do.'

An Unmentionable Man

The casualty was brought into the hospital some while after he was mugged. As a result of Government pressure on the local Health Authority to economise, the number of ambulances available had been drastically cut and there was a considerable delay before one of them arrived to pick the injured elderly man up from the pavement. The ambulance-men gave him what first aid they could, but when they delivered him to the hospital he was left without any treatment for nearly half an hour on a stretcher in the corridor where a junior nurse now and then took a look at him. Recently 'in the interests of efficiency' one of the wards had been closed down, so the overworked house surgeon, in order to free a bed for the present urgent case, had to select a patient to send home who was not too obviously unfit to go (and who if having to return within a day or two could be counted as a new admission, thereby helping the business-minded hospital manager to assert that the hospital could take in more patients at present than it had been able to before the closure of the uneconomical ward).

The only injuries the house surgeon found, after as careful an examination as he had time for, were an apparently superficial grazing of the skin down one side of the face of the mugged man and a swelling just above his temple on the other side. He was unconscious and restless, moving his arms and legs about, and at intervals he spoke three words, always the same three, enunciated very unclearly. The house surgeon thought they might be, 'Where am I?'; and it was true that this man – who now believed that he was standing on the white esplanade of a vividly sunlit lakeside town he had never visited before, and that he was gazing up at snow-topped mountains across the blue water of the lake – did wonder what country he had arrived in.

An Unmentionable Man

An expensive-looking white motor cruiser on the lake drew up alongside the esplanade near to where he stood, and a casually yet fashionably dressed group of men and women, chatting and laughing, emerged from it to walk over towards a large café where green tables were shaded beneath a boldly striped awning. He became conscious that he too wanted something to eat, but he would have to find a café less extravagant to eat in than this one would certainly be. He began to stroll away from it along the esplanade. He was soon among other strollers who, he noticed, were most of them talking in other languages than English. None of the cafés he could see as he moved on, walking a little more quickly, looked inexpensive. He would probably have to leave the esplanade and go a little way into the town before he could find a cheaper one. But would they accept English money there? Then a panicking doubt whether he had any money on him at all brought him to a sharp stop in his walk. However, after a frantic search twice over of each of the pockets of his jacket he could think of, he found in a suddenly remembered inner pocket his soft leather wallet with quite a number of English banknotes inside. He was still shaking with relief when he saw coming directly towards him from among the strollers a formerly close friend of his – Peter Knightley.

Peter, for more than a few seconds after being greeted by him, stared unrecognisingly and warily at him, almost as though suspecting him of being a drug or brothel tout. Slowly, a look of recognition came up over Peter's face; and, at last, 'Stephen Highwood,' he was able to say, with a friendly smile. 'What are you doing here?'

'That's what I'm wondering,' Stephen said.

Peter seemed on the point of asking Stephen to explain this peculiar answer, and then checked himself. The suspicion may have come to him that Stephen wasn't being jocular but was perhaps suffering from some kind of psychiatric disorder, which might reveal itself more definitely later on as they continued talking.

'What would you say to our having lunch together?' Peter proposed.

'A good idea.'

'There's an excellent place quite near here.'

A Renegade in Springtime

Peter led the way towards a café which Stephen soon recognised as the very one he had just avoided because of the likelihood of its being extravagantly expensive. But since there was no escape for him now he tried to quell his alarm by telling himself that he would almost certainly not have too little money in his wallet to pay his share of the bill.

He followed Peter into the awning-shaded outer part of the café where the green tables were. A waiter in a black tailed-suit with a bow tie came briskly towards them, bowed, showed them to one of the tables and drew back the chairs for them. Stephen felt helplessly trapped. The waiter momentarily disappeared, then reappeared holding two gilt-lettered menu cards, one of which he handed to Peter before handing the other to Stephen, who glanced through it quickly for the least extravagant items.

'Well, what would you fancy for a starter?', Peter asked, in an inviting way that made Stephen wonder whether Peter might intend to stand him a free lunch; but, to be on the safe side, he said he would have chilled tomato juice. Peter beckoned the waiter and ordered this for Stephen and an hors d'oeuvre for himself consisting of anchovies, olives and whatnot else, which when it was all brought to the table looked like a complete meal on its own. However, it did not prevent Peter from talking, nor did any of the subsequent courses he chose, all of them more substantial than those chosen by Stephen.

'So you're not sure why you're here?' Peter said with smiling curiosity.

Stephen had a quick inspiration: 'I suppose I'm here mainly because at my present age of eighty-nine I hadn't yet seen this place, and I felt that if I didn't see it now I might not ever. And the journey here by air is only a short one.'

Peter, after getting this explanation, no longer appeared to suspect that Stephen might be psychiatrically ill. With a change of tone he asked, 'Didn't you think of visiting first some of the interesting ancient towns of Eastern Europe that you haven't seen yet?'

There was a hint of amicable irony in Peter's voice which Stephen did not like. Peter was no doubt getting at him on the assumption that he had a better opinion of the post-war Eastern

Block regimes than of those in the Capitalist West. Stephen, instead of answering, said: 'And what are you doing here, Peter?'

'I'm having a holiday; and combining it with looking for material I can use in an article I've been commissioned to write.'

'Are you writing anything now besides your articles for the Press?' Stephen asked, trying not so amicably to get at Peter who had once written poetry but who in spite of persistent efforts had been unable to continue writing any. Peter, however, did not appear to be in the least discomfited by Stephen's question.

'I am working on a book about us all,' he said. A fondness came into his voice, and a look overspreading his face seemed to have something of the same warm and vulnerable ingenuousness it had at times had in the years when Stephen and he were regarded as being in the same group of young left-wing nineteen-thirties writers. Peter had been the youngest of them all.

'Will you be mentioning me in it?'

'Why, of course,' Peter said, seeming very surprised and even a little hurt by this question.

For a moment Stephen thought of leaving it at that and changing the subject. But a resentment which for many years he had refrained from revealing to Peter welled up irresistibly in him now, and he said, 'I may not have read every article you've written or television talk you've given about the 'thirties, but I have read and heard more than a few, and there wasn't one of them that didn't completely ignore me.'

Peter looked put out for a moment; then he retorted, 'If I didn't mention you, it can only have been because I was writing about happenings that you weren't directly involved in – such as the Spanish Civil War.'

Not going to Spain, though the Party which Stephen was a member of had not expected him to go, was something he had always felt guilty about, and Peter intuitively knew this. Stephen did his best not to let his face show that Peter had succeeded in wounding him at all. 'You have written articles and given radio and television interviews which had nothing to do with Spain,' he said, 'but were about various 'thirties writers – with the exception always of myself.'

'The reason I avoided saying anything about you was that I didn't want to be unfriendly.'

Stephen gave him an uncomprehending look, and Peter went on, 'I could have told my readers how much I admired your skill as a writer, but I should also have felt bound to tell them how much I dislike the naïve and now completely out-of-date left-wing views that have always been so evident in your writings.'

Stephen, to avoid getting into a futile argument in defence of his politics, asked, 'What about the conventional Capitalist views you have reverted to as you have grown older. Are you happy with them now?'

'No, not *happy*. But what else is there?'

'There is Marxism, which you have rejected in spite of the fact that present day Capitalism is in just the kind of crisis that Marx so well understood and explained.'

Peter said nothing. He gave the impression that he would be bored by any further discussion of this subject. Stephen tried to goad him by saying, 'I wonder if you have ever thought of religion as a solution to your problem?'

'Never!' Peter said. He grinned. Suddenly this copiously white-haired broad-shouldered ruddy-faced man, who was only six years less old than Stephen himself, appeared to Stephen as someone he must not die unfriendly with. And he said to Peter, 'Whatever our differences, I do feel that few things could be more sordid and unseemly than for old friends like ourselves to quarrel in old age.'

'I'm glad to hear you say that. I have never intended to quarrel with you, and I shall always think of you with affection.' After a brief silence between them, Peter called to the waiter to bring him the bill. 'I'm sorry to be so sudden,' he said to Stephen, 'but I've just realised that if I sit here any longer I shall be late for an interview I'm to have with Herr Postler, the Mayor of this town.'

He paid the bill, and stood up. Stephen stood up too, and as they walked out of the café Stephen said, 'I'd like to pay for my part of the meal.'

'Of course not. It's all on my expense account.'

'Oh well, thanks very much all the same.'

An Unmentionable Man

'I'm so glad we met today,' Peter said. 'Unfortunately I'm booked on a plane back to England later this afternoon, but certainly we must meet again before too long.'

'Yes we must,' Stephen said, feeling far from certain about it.

Smilingly Peter turned from him, and with a brief confident goodbye wave of the hand he walked briskly off along the esplanade.

Stephen standing still, undecided what to do next, became aware of a young man with long blond hair who had come up from behind him and who spoke to him by name: 'Mr Highwood, I hope you won't think me impertinent, but I was sitting at the table next to yours in the café – you may well not have noticed me – and I couldn't help overhearing the conversation between you and Mr Knightley. I found it extremely interesting.' Stephen looked at him with distrust, and asked, 'How do you know my name?'

'I deduced it from the conversation.'

Stephen didn't try to prevent his face from showing that this failed to make him any less distrustful, but the young man went on undeterred, 'I am a lecturer at a Yorkshire Polytechnic which has just become a University' – he smiled – 'and I am collecting material for a book I have been given the go-ahead to write, which is to be about the touristic, banking, religious, literary, artistic and scientific associations of this town.'

'That seems rather a tall order,' Stephen said, interrupting him.

The young man laughed. 'It is,' he agreed. 'And I would be most grateful if you could help me by sparing a little of your time to give me your impressions of the place.'

'I've only just arrived here this morning. My impressions would be useless to anyone intending to produce a serious scholarly work.'

The young man ignored the unpromising tone of this. He continued, 'I could act as your guide. I have been here long enough to explore a number of the back streets as well as taking a look into most of the sumptuous hotels and other buildings open to the public along the esplanade.'

'Are you some kind of high-class tout?'

The young man did not take offence. 'No,' he said. 'I am an admirer – and have been for a long time – of your writing. And I would greatly value even your first impressions.'

'Which books of mine have you read?' Stephen challengingly asked.

'Every one of them that I could get hold of.'

Stephen was painfully reminded that all his books were out of print, and nearly all of them unobtainable in the majority of public libraries, but he was convinced now that the young man's admiration was sincere, and he was grateful to him for it.

'I'm sorry to have been so suspicious,' Stephen said to him.

'It's very understandable that you were,' the young man excusingly said.

'What is your name, by the way?' Stephen asked.

'Paul Irlam. I'm afraid I was more than a bit impertinent when I, a complete stranger to you, introduced myself by saying I had found your conversation with Peter Knightley extremely interesting.'

'Never mind,' Stephen said with a smile. 'But I'm curious to know what there was in it to interest you so much.'

'Several things; especially the fact that neither of the two reasons Knightley gave you, when he was trying to justify his never having mentioned you in his occasional articles and television interviews about the 'thirties, was the true one – though just possibly he may not have been conscious of this.'

'Well, what do you think was the true reason?' Stephen asked.

'He wasn't willing to go against the dominant opinion in Establishment circles now that it simply "isn't done" to mention you at all,' Paul Irlam said. 'There was a time when it would have been quite in order to refer to your work dismissively or disapprovingly, but that time has passed. They've decided now that you are to be obliterated – permanently.'

'You may be right,' Stephen agreed.

'I'm not suggesting that guidelines about you and certain other politically undesirable writers are passed down to loyal subordinates by a few topmost people meeting in the Carlton Club,' Paul Irlam said, 'but somehow it becomes generally understood that such writers are as far as possible to become non-existent.'

'I don't doubt that the people who would like to obliterate me would like even more to obliterate the political ideas I have supported in my writings.'

An Unmentionable Man

'They won't succeed in that,' Paul said. 'And your work has other admirers besides myself who are just as determined as I am to ensure that it isn't forgotten.'

'I'm happy to hear that,' Stephen said, 'and I shall always be grateful to you all; but I know that you have the economic crisis against you, and there is the probability of a devastating war which you and I will rightly regard as immeasurably more important than any writings of mine.'

'That's not the sort of talk that should come from a Marxist,' Paul said reprovingly. 'We shall never win if we don't confidently expect we can. But you must be a little tired after your journey. Would you be willing to go with me now to the inexpensive hotel I've found for myself in a back street? I'm sure they'll have a room for you, and the hotel isn't a bordel.'

'Thanks, yes. I would be glad to rest for an hour or two.'

They started at once to walk to the hotel.

It was a small one in a narrow street not far from the traffic-infested surroundings of a railway terminus, and it was clean besides being cheap. Stephen's room there had a bed covered with a duvet which – though he'd never found duvets easy to sleep under – he was now soon able to doze comfortably on top of without undressing.

When Paul woke him by knocking on his door, and came into the room to ask whether he felt ready to go to a place where they could eat which was very different from the café they'd both been in that morning, Stephen said he felt thoroughly rested and would be glad to go.

'First we shall have to traverse the red light district,' Paul said as they came out of the hotel on to the street. 'You'd better firmly hold your hat on there or you'll risk having it snatched from your head.'

The upper windows of a number of the houses in the district were wide open displaying a well illuminated woman sitting inside, and the street doors too were open, but no pimp tried to snatch Stephen's hat and run upstairs with it.

'Have you ever in your long life been up to one of the women in a district like this?' Paul asked.

A Renegade in Springtime

'No.'

'Not even for the sake of an experience which could be useful to you as a writer?'

'No.'

'Why not?'

'Much too dangerous,' Stephen said.

They both laughed.

Quite soon Paul said, 'And here, just at the end of the street, is the restaurant we are going to eat in.'

'One thing I've been meaning to ask you,' Stephen said. 'Will they accept English bank notes?'

'You needn't worry,' Paul said. 'I'll be paying in the local currency for your share of the meal and you can recoup me in your money afterwards.'

'Thanks.'

'It's when we reach the places I'd like to take you to later this evening that you will need to worry about your money – and to keep a tight hold on it too.'

The restaurant was small and comfortable, and the waiter, who recognised Paul, was friendly. For their first course both Stephen and Paul chose artichokes of the thistle-like type with soft parts which are very edible when dipped in melted butter. The waiter, before going off to place their orders with the chef for the artichokes and the other courses they'd chosen, brought to their table a basket full of brioche rolls and a large carafe of red wine.

'This stuff seems remarkably strong,' Stephen commented after drinking less than a quarter of a glass.

'It is,' Paul said.

'And I should guess its quality is pretty good.'

'I'm sure it is,' Paul said. 'But don't let your liking for it be lessened by any fears that we're going to have a huge bill to pay. This restaurant is almost unbelievably modest in its charges.'

At the end of the meal the amount that Stephen and Paul had to pay was as modest as Paul had said it would be, considering the quantity as well as the quality of what he and Irlam had eaten and drunk. But after they went out from the restaurant into the open air Stephen felt very unsteady. As an old man he had become gradually less keen on alcoholic drinking, and when he did have a drink with friends it was never anything like as much as he'd had this evening. He decided to try not to let his inner unsteadiness become an outward staggering that Paul would notice; and in fact Paul did not seem to guess how Stephen felt.

'Now we'll visit the Arts Quarter,' he said.

'You told me earlier on that after our meal we would be going somewhere where I would need to keep a tight hold on my money,' Stephen said. 'Did you mean the Arts Quarter?'

'Yes, I did. But, apart from pickpockets and a few other more sinister characters including drug-peddlers, not everyone in the Quarter is simply out to fleece the tourists. I'll take you to two of the studios where we shall be able to look around and to talk to artists who won't press us to buy anything.'

'Do you think we shall see anything I might want to buy?'

'I doubt it,' Paul said. 'Certainly not from the first studio we're on our way to visit now; but I think I can promise you that you'll find it interesting.'

They didn't have to walk far. Paul came to a stop at one of the gaps in the railings that stretched along the front of a terrace of perhaps once fashionable though now decaying homes. 'The studio is down these steps here,' he told Stephen. 'Be very careful how you go. The street lamp above us is appallingly dim.'

They descended slowly to a rubbish-cluttered basement area which looked like the backside of a sleazy hotel. At the far end there was an open door from which light shone and a smell issued that was sweetly fragrant yet at the same time malodorous.

'Is this a studio?' Stephen asked.

Paul pointed to a cursively written brown inscription on white-painted plaster above the open doorway.

Stephen read the words, *THE EXCREMENTALISTS*.

'This is the "manufacturing" outer part of the studio,' Paul said quietly as they paused before going in through the doorway. 'The workers here call themselves "practical artists". The main part where the actual paintings are done is separated from this by double-doors. It can be reached also by steps going down to the next – and much less dirty – basement area farther along the street.

A Renegade in Springtime

That is the entrance used by nearly all the tourists who visit the studio. They are eager to see the famous/notorious painters at work in the main part of the studio; but few of them ask to see the "practical artists" at work in the outer part of it.'

'What exactly is manufactured here in the outer part?' Stephen asked.

'The peculiar material required by the "painter artists",' Paul answered. 'The "practical artists" create this from raw human excrement, some of which they themselves provide – though help from paid outside volunteers is needed to top it up. Of course it has to be deodorised and otherwise processed before it's fit to be conveyed through the double doors to the painters. But we'd better not hover here outside any longer, as one of the practicals might spot us and become suspicious. Or,' Paul quickly added, 'would you perhaps rather visit somewhere less disgusting?'

'Oh no,' Stephen said. 'What you've told me has made me extremely curious about these Excrementalists.'

He and Paul were noticed as soon as they entered the studio. A bulky youngish man in a dark brown overall came towards them, staring with undisguised suspicion at Stephen.

'He's all right, Crags,' Paul said, evidently on good enough terms with the man to call him without offence by what Stephen thought likely to be his nickname. 'My friend Mr Stephen Highwood isn't a police spy. He is a distinguished writer, and he's very keen to be shown over both parts of this unique studio.'

'How do,' Crags said, and Stephen was fastidiously relieved that he didn't offer to shake hands.

On the centre of the concrete floor in this 'practical' part of the studio were two large upright corrugated metal cylinders with a wooden bung near the bottom of each. A man who wore the same kind of brown overall as Crags did was standing beside one of the cylinders.

'Jock,' Crags called out to him, 'we've a visitor with Mr Irlam here wanting to see how the process works.'

Jock glanced only briefly at Stephen, nodded recognisingly to Paul, then bent down and released the bung from the cylinder. A slurry of excrement flowed thickly out into a capacious flat metal tray below it, and as it did so he turned on a brass tap which sprayed the flow with a scent so powerful that Stephen momentarily had difficulty in restraining himself from vomiting.

When the tray was filled almost to the brim Jock replaced the bung. Next he stepped back from the cylinder and went to pull a small lever among the dials of a black panel fixed against the wall. Crags, without needing to be asked by Stephen, readily explained this latest stage of the process. 'The lever controls the heating of the slurry,' he said. 'The liquidness has to be lessened, but the slurry must not be baked. It must be soft, and its softness has to be of a kind that will allow the painters to apply it to their canvases with a small trowel, or with a brush if they soften it further by adding oil to it. And it must be capable of retaining any colour they choose to give it.'

Stephen, thinking he detected a note of jealousy in the way that Crags spoke of the painters, dared to ask him, 'What is there for you in this work you are doing?'

Crags did not take offence. 'Well,' he said, 'I won't pretend that I'm not attracted by the pay I'm getting here, which is far better than I'd get for any equally mucky job elsewhere, and many "clean" white-collar office workers are paid far worse. Also, since my prospering employers in the painters' part of the studio know that I do my job here pretty efficiently, I can feel quite secure in it.'

At this point Jock abruptly showed that while regulating the heating of the slurry he had been listening to Stephen and Crags. 'There's much more for me in the work I do here than that,' he said. 'I have the same views about the world as the painters have who founded this studio, and I think of myself as a practical *artist* without whose basic help they would be unable to create paintings which embody these views.' He turned to Stephen, and he added, 'But you must talk with the painters themselves. They can explain these things to you from first hand experience.'

'Thank you very much,' Stephen said.

'He's a philosopher, our Jock is,' Crags jokily told Stephen, 'and he speaks like one.'

Paul said, 'Well, thank you both very much for telling us about your work, and now I think we should leave you to it and take a look at the inner part of the studio.'

He led Stephen to the double doors, and surprised him by saying, 'Go in ahead of me.' Stephen pushed open the first door, which was handleless and had a covering of red baize. He found himself in a space that would have been completely dark if some of the light from the outer studio hadn't followed him into it while Paul still held the door open behind him. Stephen tried to push open the second door but failed, even though he pushed hard. When Paul closed the first door and he and Stephen were in complete darkness, there was a startlingly loud whirring sound just above their heads.

'What's that?' Stephen asked.

'That's an electric extractor,' Paul said, 'which is automatically started up by the shutting of the first door and removes all the smells of the manufacturing studio from the air in here.'

After a minute or two the noise abruptly stopped. 'Now I shall push the second door and you'll see that it will open with ease,' he said. 'The doors are controlled by a clever device which ensures that they can never be open at the same time and that both remain shut for as long as the extractor is still switched on.'

He opened the second door, which appeared to be made of heavy oak, and it closed behind them automatically when they stepped out into the artists' studio. Stephen had an impression of many people moving about, some pausing to watch the artists painting at their easels, others gazing at the various framed canvases, large and small, hanging numerously on the studio walls. No one seemed to notice Paul and Stephen for a while, until suddenly a young woman detached herself from the crowd and came straight towards them. She welcomingly recognised Paul; but like Crags before her, though much less crudely, she showed an unmistakable suspiciousness of Stephen. Paul, however, was quickly able to dispel this when he introduced him to her.

'Kirsty,' he said to her, 'this is my friend Stephen Highwood, the distinguished writer. He is eager to see the work of the painters here.'

She was honest enough not to pretend she had heard of him before, but her smile told him she was glad that he wanted to see the paintings.

He became conscious that she had an extraordinarily beautiful face.

'We have to be very watchful,' she said, in an apologetic tone which confessed that she had been unjustly suspicious of him. 'We do get the occasional police officer in disguise who is reconnoitring in preparation for a raid by the vice squad. Several of our painters and even a visitor or two have been arrested before now and have been quite brutally interrogated in police cells, though all of them so far have been released without any charge being brought against them. The fact is that the authorities in this world-known town are very reluctant to risk putting visitors off by appearing to have intolerantly old-fashioned views about modern art. But let us go and see the canvases now on display so that you' – she spoke to Stephen, not Paul – 'can form your own opinion of them.' (Presumably she already knew Paul's opinion.) 'We won't interrupt the artists at their work, unless of course you want to buy one of their paintings.'

'Are you yourself a painter, by the way?' Stephen asked.

'No. My job is simply to look after the visitors and to answer their questions. But I am very much in sympathy with the outlook which led these artists to found this studio.'

'What sort of outlook is that?' Stephen asked.

'A loathing for the whole anti-human ideology of the murderous present-day powers who rule the world,' she said.

'You make me even more eager than I already was to see these paintings,' he said, genuinely and not just to please her – though he felt a growing desire to please her.

Paul, aware that Stephen was attracted by her, tactfully took no part in his further talk with her after she had guided them through the crowd of visitors towards one of the larger framed canvases hanging from the wall.

'This is by Bradnock,' she said. 'It is his own favourite, and he has priced it so highly that perhaps he doesn't really want to part with it. But I suspect that some millionaire is bound to turn up sooner or later who will not hesitate to pay almost any price Bradnock may ask for it. What do you think of it?'

Stephen's first impression was of a great variety of colours heavily applied to the canvas, perhaps with a small trowel such as Crags had mentioned, and only after a while did he realise that the painting was representational. It exhibited a pinkish-fleshed human female rump across which, and also across the widely parted white thighs below it, there were deeply red raised lines such as could have been caused by a whip.

'Well, how do you like this?' Kirsty asked.

'Is the painter some kind of pathological pervert?' Stephen asked, aware of using an old-fashioned word.

'Not at all,' she said. 'He's perfectly "normal", and quite sane.'

'Does that mean he's just a pornographer cynically out to make money?'

'Of course not,' she said a little sharply. 'I've told you before that what unites all the artists here is a loathing of the world's criminal rulers.'

'Yes,' he said, 'but I can't see how these artists can claim to be attacking our rulers by producing paintings like this one.'

'They regard themselves as "super-subversionists",' she said. 'They believe that the visual images they create with excremental paint can significantly contribute to the already far-gone corruption of the present social and economic system, and can help to accelerate its final self-destruction.'

'I wouldn't rely on corruption, however ingeniously it may be deepened by Excremental artists, to break the power of our rulers over us,' Stephen said. 'That power needs to be forcibly overthrown by the working class.'

'To my admittedly disillusioned mind this seems a somewhat outdated notion,' Kirsty said.

'I agree with Stephen,' Paul said.

'Well,' she said, 'I wonder how Stephen will like the paintings in the studio of The Resuscitationists, if that's where you're taking him next?'

'Yes, I am.'

'Please don't feel I'm not grateful for the time you've given to explaining so clearly what the Excrementalists are aiming at,' Stephen said anxiously.

Kirsty gave him a nice smile. Then he asked, 'Could you tell me what you think of these Resuscitationist artists? We unfortunately shan't have you as a guide when we get to their studio.'

'They aim to revive the idea that true Art is never *about* anything in the external world, and especially never about politics. They consider that the Excrementalists are politically motivated, and they despise them. They argue that Art is a world in its own right.'

Kirsty would have continued, but at this instant a squad of stout leather-belted black-uniformed policemen, with handgun holsters attached to their belts, abruptly invaded the studio. Arbitrarily it seemed, they seized hold of a number of the visitors, including, to Stephen's horror, his new friend Paul. But Paul though roughly handled was able, before the policeman who held him could clap a hand over his mouth, to shout to Stephen, 'Get away quick!' And Stephen did get away, running as quickly as at his age he could towards the same door by which the police had entered the studio (he knew it would have been futile for him to try to get through the double doors that led into the outer studio); and, strangely, a solitary policeman who had been left behind on guard at the entrance made no attempt to prevent him from escaping.

There was something strange also about the street he found himself in when he got outside. It was very narrow, quite unlike the street he had walked along to the Excrementalists' 'manufacturing' studio earlier in the evening with Paul. Stranger still was its name, Town Lane, which he suddenly saw on an oblong enamel plate attached to the windowless wall of a small house. A moment later he realised he was in deadly danger. Two young men wearing identical tee-shirts which had the word BRITISH inscribed in crimson lettering across them, and identical dark blue shorts with union jacks vividly printed on them, were advancing menacingly towards him, and he knew he could have no hope of escape from them.

* * *

The hospital had at last contacted his wife, and she was standing at his bedside with the house surgeon now. Stephen's eyes were both partly open, and she had the feeling that he recognised her. Also he was saying something, but it was incoherent and unintelligible to her.

'He has been like this ever since he was brought in here,' the house surgeon said.

'But I do feel that he recognises me,' she said.

The house surgeon, looking at her with a compassion which was genuine enough, said, 'He may well recognise you, though I am afraid we must face up to the possibility that he may never make a full recovery.' He had a momentary impulse to add, 'The kindest thing that could happen to your husband might be to die now.' However, his conscience warned him that such a suggestion, besides being cruel to her, would be tainted by an irritable regret that he would not be able to tell the hospital manager that the old man's bed would be free for the next patient; so he went on to say to her, 'But he looks strong for his age, and it is not at all impossible that he could almost fully recover. I shall do the very best I can for him.'

The house surgeon, as she said goodbye and told him she would be coming to the hospital again on the following day, noticed tears in her eyes. Yet he could not refrain from saying, 'I hope you will not mind my asking if you know what made your husband go out alone at this time of night in this town where so many muggings are taking place.'

'Yes, I do know,' she said. 'It must have been due to one of those attacks of fury that sometimes came over him about the way his writing was being ignored, and whenever they came he just had to go out and pace the streets.'

A Ship in the Sky

On the fourth day after the street mugging of the elderly writer, Stephen Highwood, the house surgeon at the hospital was able to tell his anxious wife that her husband had made a further improvement since she had seen him on the previous day. Besides being completely coherent still, he had been speaking far more and in much greater detail than ever before.

'And, by the way, he several times spoke a woman's name,' the house surgeon added, and immediately wished he'd not told her this. How could he have been so obtuse as not to realise that the name might be of a rival trying to lure her husband away from her?

'What was the name?' she asked.

He had a momentary temptation to answer, 'I'm ashamed to say I've forgotten', but feeling that this would be unconvincing he told her the truth.

'Rosa,' he said.

'That is my name,' she said, and she was no longer able to hold back her tears.

He considerately waited for a while before asking, 'Would you like me to tell you now some of the other things he said?'

'Yes, I would.'

'I'm sorry I can't remember all of them – there were so many – but one that made a special impression on me was, "I have been forty years a nanny with the same family, and at last I have managed to save enough money to go on this mystery tour of the world before I die."'

'He seems to have been quoting the words of someone's nanny, but I'm fairly sure that in all our married years together he never mentioned such a person to me,' Rosa said.

A Renegade in Springtime

'Another thing I remember your husband saying was, "What is it that's so scaring about the word 'Andromeda'? I think it must be the hollow sound of that syllable 'drom'."'

'This is just the kind of imaginative conceit Stephen might have come out with in the old days,' she said, 'though I don't think I ever actually heard him say it.'

The house surgeon continued for some time longer to tell her of things her husband had been saying as he lay in the hospital bed, but Rosa continued to be unable to find any clear connection between most of these and what she knew of his real life.

While she and the house surgeon talked at Stephen's bedside he himself was sure that he was walking downhill towards the sea, and that high above the roofs of the houses of a small town ahead of him he saw an exceptionally large ship just on the horizon-line between sea and sky. He was trailing behind him a heavy suitcase with wheels attached to two of its lower corners, and he hadn't yet totally overcome the misgivings he'd felt when receiving two mornings ago a letter congratulating him on having won a free ticket for a voyage round the world in a famous liner. This liner, the letter told him, had been extensively and expensively repaired and refitted, and was now renamed *Andromeda*. To celebrate the occasion of its first voyage as *Andromeda* a number of inhabitants of this seaside town had been randomly chosen to receive free tickets, and he was among the lucky ones. Stephen, who was all too accustomed to get letters through the post telling him he'd won large sums of money, had looked very carefully through the small print of the congratulatory letter to see where the catch was, but he could find none. And now that he was actually on his way towards the ship his remaining misgivings began to be superseded by a growing excitement at the prospect of a voyage which he was certain would provide him with entirely fresh material for his writing.

Soon, as he continued walking downhill, the horizon-line between sea and sky became hidden from him by the town's rising house-roofs. He made his way downward still along several streets

A Ship in the Sky

to reach the sea front, rightly assuming that a smaller boat would be conveying the voyagers out to *Andromeda* from there.

Moored against the landing-stage at a pier-head was a large motor launch already carrying a number of passengers. A sailor, after beckoning to him to step on board, took hold of his heavy suitcase but clumsily let it slip over the side of the launch into the water, where it instantly sank out of sight.

The sailor quite unapologetically said, 'Well, you didn't really need it.'

Stephen was extremely indignant. 'Of course I needed it,' he shouted; and in his rage he was about to claim that there were things in it which he absolutely couldn't do without on a long sea voyage – but he noticed that he seemed not to have the sympathy of any of the other passengers on the launch, who none of them had suitcases with them.

'Weren't you informed in the letter you were sent,' the sailor calmly asked, 'that everything you could need on the voyage would be provided for you?'

'I don't think I was,' Stephen lamely said.

'You were,' the sailor said, 'and it will be.'

Stephen didn't speak another word during the short time the launch took to reach the liner, from the side of which, quite low down, a gangway was pushed out by members of the crew and was securely roped to the launch by the sailor.

Stephen was the last of the passengers to walk up the gangway. He wanted to have a word with the man who was collecting tickets at the top of it. Fortunately Stephen had not forgotten to bring his own ticket. The collector listened very sympathetically to his complaint about the loss of his suitcase, but assured him it was quite true that everything he needed would be provided for him; then told him, 'Beth Davies will show you to your cabin.'

A white-uniformed pleasantly smiling young woman came forward and asked him to follow her. She led him along an electrically lit corridor till at last she stopped at a door which had the small brass numerals 49 screwed on to it. 'This is your cabin,' she said, as she unlocked the door. He followed her in. She handed him a key, saying, 'And this is your key to your cabin. Now I'll show you where to find everything else you'll need for the voyage.'

He was amazed by the size of the cabin. Besides several large wardrobes and a very comfortable-looking bed, it also contained a bathroom. She took him into it and pointed out close to the silvery-tapped bath an ample pink towel draped over a rail which she told him was heated. 'A fresh towel will be provided for you every day,' she added. Then she showed him, on a glass-topped table next to a silvery-tapped hand basin, an array of toilet requisites including cellophane-wrapped toothbrushes of several sizes, a loofah, a real sponge, four small flannels of differing colours, and three rolls of lavatory paper – she slid back a door in a corner of the bathroom and revealed a shower and a bidet and also a lavatory pan which had a polished wooden seat instead of the usual cheap and chilly plastic one.

'Now we will take a look at the wardrobes,' she said, and she led him out of the bathroom. He noticed on their way out a yellow towel-like bathgown hanging from a hook on the wall opposite the bath.

The first wardrobe she opened contained dinner-jackets and trousers of various sizes. 'It is thought probable that most of the men will choose to wear them for dinner in the State Room every evening, but of course no objection will be raised to eccentrics who choose not to. When dances are held in the Grand Ballroom the men in general are likely to wear tails and white ties. You can see that this wardrobe contains a selection of various sizes of these tail suits too.'

She moved on to open another wardrobe. 'Here is a selection of casual and formal daytime suits,' she said, 'and very smart and fashionable they are.'

The third wardrobe she showed him contained underwear, even including a dark blue bikini-like minimal cache-sexe that men could wear when bathing in the liner's swimming pool.

'Complete nakedness is absolutely forbidden,' she said. 'And now I must leave you; but if there's anything else you want to know, just ring Reception. As you see, there's a phone – and a phone book –

on the table here beside the door. You could also at any time ring anywhere in England you might wish to.'

Then smilingly she went out of the cabin and left him on his own.

He chose first of all to try whether the bed was as comfortable as it looked. He leant on it with both his hands and he decided that its mattress was probably a genuine latex one and that the bed itself was properly sprung, instead of being as springlessly hard as the only beds obtainable in most contemporary furniture shops were. To test it further he took off his shoes and lay down on it with the eiderdown underneath him.

He was wakened by a knocking at his door. It seemed to have been going on for some while. 'Come in,' he was at last able to force himself to say.

A young girl appeared, who could have been in her late teens. 'I am your chambermaid, sir,' she told him. 'Shall I get your bath ready for you, sir, or will you have a shower?'

'What time is it?' he asked her.

'Dinner will be served in about three quarters of an hour from now, sir.'

'Please stop calling me "sir". It makes me feel nervous.'

'I am sorry, sir – I mean I am sorry,' she said, momentarily flustered.

Stephen tactfully changed the subject by asking, 'Is the ship moving? I suppose it must be by now but how does it manage to move so very smoothly?'

'It is gyroscopically controlled,' she said, pronouncing with some uncertainty a word she had perhaps only recently been taught. 'But what about your bath, s–,' she checked herself just in time, 'shall I fill it now?'

'Yes please. Half fill it with hot water, and I'll add as much cold as is needed.'

She did what he asked and then hurried out of the cabin.

As he bathed himself he began to feel bad about the way he had treated her. In calling him 'sir' she was only doing what she had been instructed to do after accepting her present job which she'd assumed to be a reputable one. He had humiliated her by a request that amounted to asking her to be on more familiar terms with him. After all, there were and always had been nasty risks in a chambermaid's job. He remembered a cartoon by Rowlandson showing an ugly night-shirted middle-aged man leaping lecherously from his bed as a nice-looking young girl enters the bedroom. Stephen decided he must think out some way of making amends to his chambermaid.

Drying himself after his bath he wondered whether he might like to be one of those tolerated eccentrics Beth Davies had mentioned who chose not to wear a dinner-jacket for dinner in the State Room; however he realised that this would call attention to himself, which he did not wish to do, so he selected a dinner-jacket of the right size from the wardrobe. But he had difficulty in tying his black bow-tie – ready-tied ties were not provided, presumably because they were regarded as unfashionably vulgar – and he was rather late getting to the State Room.

A waiter approached him as soon as he entered it and led him to a seat beside an elderly woman at one of the tables. She seemed glad of his arrival – the man sitting on the other side of her was preoccupied with another and younger woman – and Stephen was very willing to let her get into conversation with him.

She told him she had been a nanny to the same family for many years and had at last saved up enough money to go on this mystery tour of the world. 'But I became ill,' she said, 'and the mother of the family I'd looked after until they grew up one by one and left home had to look after me. She was getting old herself, quite a bit older than I was, and she felt the burden of it all, but she wouldn't have dreamed of having me put into a home. And then a morning came when I felt suddenly a lot better, and I escaped. I got up early, and made myself some breakfast, and walked out of the house.'

'You didn't say goodbye to her?' he couldn't refrain from asking.

'I didn't' she admitted, 'but I did write to her after I had bought my ticket and other things I would need for this mystery voyage.' He noticed that she was wearing a fashionably low-cut evening dress and that her bosom was unwithered. 'Do you think it was wrong of me to leave her like that?'

'Oh no,' he said. 'It would have been painful for you to tell her to her face that you were leaving her, and to resist her if she had pleaded with you not to go.'

'I do hope that any grief she may feel now I've gone will be less than her relief at no longer having to look after me,' the ex-nanny said.

Stephen, aware that this talk with him was giving her pleasure, dared to ask, 'Did you ever want to marry and have children of your own?'

'I hadn't really begun to think about it while I was looking after her children, and when they grew up and I did begin it was too late.'

'In your place,' Stephen dared further to say, 'I think I should have felt I had sacrificed the best part of my life to a middle-class family who did not value me at my true worth.'

She startled him by saying, 'I shall not die thinking to myself that I have never lived. I know this voyage is going to be an experience for me more wonderful than any that any of them have ever had.'

A strange uneasiness rose in him as she said this. They both became silent, and he became conscious of having finished his meal without being able to remember at all certainly what he had eaten.

They stood up, and as they were leaving the State Room together he asked her whether she would like to go for an exploratory walk round the ship with him.

'I would like to,' she said, 'but I am afraid I would find it rather too tiring just now. I think I'll go to my cabin and get myself ready for bed.'

As they parted in the corridor he said, 'Good night, and I hope I'll meet you again tomorrow.'

'Yes, I hope you will,' she said.

Within minutes he had forgotten all about her. He had gone up several flights of stairs to reach the open deck of the ship, and he was leaning forward over the wooden rail along the side of it to gaze at the remarkably calm moonlit sea. After a while he was aware that a woman had come to lean on the rail quite near to him. She could be in her forties. Her red hair had probably been dyed, and she wore a heavily jewelled necklace in several strands which gave only a few glimpses of the flesh that her low-cut evening gown would otherwise have revealed. She was perfumed, expensively perhaps, but the perfume failed to disguise a rich smell of alcohol.

'What a romantic setting,' she suddenly said, referring he assumed to the moonlit sea.

He didn't like the implication he believed he detected in this, and he commented unromantically that he could not remember having seen the planets Jupiter and Venus together with the moon before now. He added, 'They are the brightest of all the planets. When only one of them is in the sky would you know how to tell whether it was Venus or not?'

'No,' she said.

'The way you could tell,' he said, 'is that if you had any doubt about it at all it wouldn't be Venus.'

'Is that so?' she said, without any pretence of interest.

Then she startled him by asking, 'What is the number of your cabin?'

'Why should you want to know?' he coldly said.

'Well, one reason is that I've been wondering whether some of us passengers have been given numbers corresponding to our ages, – which would be an awful bit of cheek on the part of the tour organisers, – or whether it's just a coincidence that my number is 39, which happens to be exactly my age. Would you object to telling me what your age is?'

'Not in the slightest,' he said, with an indifference that had a trace of contempt in it; 'I am eighty-nine.'

'I can't believe it,' she exclaimed with exaggerated amazement. 'You look at least twenty years younger. Is the number of your cabin 89, by any chance?'

'No it isn't.'

'But you are quite determined not to tell me what your actual number is?'

'Why should I when you refuse to explain why you want to know?' he said.

'I want to know because I want to avoid knocking on the wrong door,' she said. 'Wouldn't you like me to come along and give you a bath tonight?'

A Ship in the Sky

'No I would not, thank you very much,' he said; but she looked so deeply insulted that he added, 'Please realise that I'm not rejecting your offer because of any special objection to you personally. I would have refused anyone else who might have made me the offer.' (He hastily restrained a momentary fanciful impulse to add, 'including Venus herself.')

'Would you have refused if your wife had been here and had made the offer?' she asked, and a maliciousness in her tone suggested she was chancing a guess that he had a wife and that he'd come on this tour to escape from her.

Stephen turned his back on the woman and walked quickly away. As he went down the several flights of stairs to reach his cabin an agony of guilt and grief came upon him. Until this moment he had completely forgotten Rosa, the wife he had been living with for over half a century and loved more than anyone else in the world. Without a word to her he had abandoned her, his own Rosa who needed him as much as he needed her, and he had started on a tour which was to last at least a year. What would become of her during all that time? No, he could escape from this ship as soon as it reached the first port it was due to stop at, and he would take a plane back home. But though he didn't doubt that when he returned to her she would forgive him, no matter how difficult this might be for her, would things ever be the same between them again? Would she ever again feel able to trust him as wholly as before his present desertion of her?

When he entered his cabin he was attacked by a sudden fear of going mad during the days he would still have to remain confined to this ship until it reached the first port it was making for. He was a little relieved to discover, next to the cellophane-wrapped toothbrushes of several sizes and the array of other toilet requisites on the glass-topped table beside the hand basin, a brown glass bottle labelled SLEEPING TABLETS. Without difficulty he unscrewed the top of the bottle – everything on this ship was made easy, and the top was not of the usual safety type designed to deter children from poisoning themselves – then he recklessly swallowed three of the pills. Their effect was almost instantaneous. He managed to stagger far enough to reach his bed, and to collapse backwards on to it. He was soon lying supinely asleep with his dinner-jacket, trousers and shoes unremoved.

He continued lying there for a while when he woke in the morning. The idea came to him of a way of keeping sane during the remaining time before he could escape at the ship's first port of call. Till then he would make a point of trying to investigate everything that was happening on board here. The idea appealed to him sufficiently to make him almost eagerly get up and, after shaving and washing, dress himself in the smartly casual clothes he found inside one of the wardrobes. Then he left his cabin and went to have breakfast.

He was not surprised to find how late he was for it. Only three of the other voyagers, sitting separately from each other, were in the State Room when he arrived there. The same waiter who had served him on the previous evening came forward to guide him to the same seat he had occupied then. This was possibly where he was expected to sit for every meal during the rest of the voyage, he thought. The waiter handed him a menu that had an astonishing variety of items on it, including beef and pheasant. Stephen chose what he normally had at home – porridge, milk, wholemeal bread, butter, marmalade and very weak tea. When the waiter returned with all these, Stephen asked whether the lady who'd sat next to him at dinner had already been down for breakfast.

'No, sir. I'm sorry to say she has been taken ill,' the waiter told him. 'If you would like to know more I could direct you after your breakfast to the ship's doctor, Dr Hector Mackenzie.'

Stephen left uneaten on his plate part of the first and all of the second slice of wholemeal bread he had cut, buttered and marmaladed.

Dr Mackenzie, to whose clinic the waiter directed him, was a serious-looking pleasantly ruddy-faced young man, who said when Stephen asked him about the 'elderly lady', 'Are you a relative of hers?'

'No, she was a complete stranger to me before I sat next to her at dinner last night, but I was very interested by the story she told me of her life.'

'She died two hours ago. She ought never to have come on this tour. She was quite unfit for it.'

'I'm sorry,' Stephen genuinely said.

'The organisers of the tour won't be happy about having a death on their ship,' Dr Mackenzie told him, and something in his tone suggested a dislike of the organisers.

'Well, thanks,' Stephen finally and rather inappropriately said before he walked out of the clinic.

As he went back into his cabin to use the lavatory there, he became deeply depressed, and then a sudden terror arose in him again of becoming insane during the time he would still be confined to the ship before it touched port. However, his renewed terror began to subside from the moment when a young man came up to him along the corridor just as he was stepping out from his cabin and was about to walk he didn't know where.

'Mr Stephen Highwood?' the young man said.

'Yes, I am Stephen Highwood.'

'I never thought I would have the luck to meet you on this voyage,' the young man said.

'How did you know who I was?' Stephen asked.

'I've just read your name – and room number – in the list of passengers, and more than once I've seen your photograph in the left-wing press.'

'And why do you think you are lucky to meet me?'

'Because my closest friends and I have always admired you as one of the very few left-wing imaginative writers of literary ability who have not betrayed their principles.'

'I'm afraid your admiration has been misplaced,' Stephen said with shame. 'The truth is I was given a free ticket for this world tour and I was glad to accept it because I thought the voyage would be a long holiday for me which I could confidently expect to provide me with entirely fresh material for my writing.'

Then seeing the disappointment in the young man's face, he added, 'I've already realised how disgracefully thoughtless I was. I abandoned my wife without saying goodbye or telling her a word

A Renegade in Springtime

about where I was going. But I've made up my mind to escape from this ship as soon as it reaches the first port it's due to stop at, and I shall take a plane back home to her.'

'We know from her past letters to the press that she has never ceased to be a left-wing activist, and there is no reason why you yourself shouldn't become one again even before the ship reaches its first port.'

'How could that be possible?' Stephen asked a little sharply, noticing the authoritative tone in which this young man, who had previously expressed such respectful admiration for him, was now speaking to him.

'I wouldn't be wise to begin to give you an explanation while we're continuing to stand in a corridor where other people may pass along and overhear me,' the young man said. 'Could we go into your cabin?'

'Of course,' Stephen said, and showed him into the bedroom in which two armchairs had been provided by the ever thoughtful tour-organisers.

As soon as the young man had sat down he said, 'By the way, what an interesting coincidence it is that the room you've been given is numbered 49. Wasn't 1949 the year when you and your wife finally realised that the British Communist Party you'd so long been members of had ceased to be revolutionary, and you got out of it for good?'

'Yes, you are right. You seem to have a remarkably detailed knowledge of our political lives.'

'I hope this doesn't make you distrustful of me at all,' the young man said, detecting suspicion in Stephen's tone. 'The admiration I and my friends have had of the way you and your wife stuck to your revolutionary left-wing principles in your later years has been our sole reason for wanting to find out as much as we could about your lives.'

'I am grateful to you for your interest in us,' Stephen contritely said. 'Now tell me more about your friends.'

'That is just what I wanted to do. One of the first things I need to make quite clear is that we call ourselves a group, not a party.'

'What is the name of your group?' Stephen asked. 'And for that matter what is your own name?'

'We call ourselves simply The Group, and my name is Kevin Finnimore. There are not many of us in England yet, and we don't advertise ourselves when we take part in progressive anti-capitalist activities here, but our influence is not insignificant, and we have international contacts.'

'It sounds almost as though you are a sort of secret society,' Stephen commented.

'No,' Kevin said, 'we don't hide our name or our aims, but we want above all to be known by our "deeds" – that's to say by our active support for the working-class wherever it is resisting capitalist attack.'

Stephen felt a growing sympathy with Kevin and he was able to overcome a brief new suspicion that The Group might be just another ultra-leftist organisation, and he also overcame the remnants of his earlier feeling that Kevin's tone was too authoritative.

'You must be wondering why I'm on this ship,' Kevin went on.

'I know I ought to have been wondering, but I'm afraid I've been preoccupied with my own situation.'

'Well, I'll tell you. I have been entrusted by The Group in England with a mission to our South American friends who are doing all they can to help the present insurrection.'

'And how are you going to get to them on this ship?' Stephen asked.

'The first port it is due to stop at is within a few miles of the town which is the epicentre of the insurrection. My mission is to bring support to our friends mainly in the form of money we have collected in England and also with the promise that we shall do everything we can to rouse opinion in England against the murderously reactionary Government that the insurrectionary peasants aim to overthrow.'

'How can I give the support you said I could?' Stephen asked.

'By giving me permission to tell our friends that you, a distinguished veteran writer, are wholly on the side of the insurrection, and that they can use your name to gain support from the wavering intellectuals they are trying to win over to the same side.'

'I shall be glad to have my name used in any way that can help,' Stephen said.

'I'm happy about that, and so will The Group be,' Kevin said. 'And now I'd better visit the ship's gymnasium to get some strenuous exercise – hoping it will help to keep me fit for whatever our South American friends may want me to do. After the gym I shall relax in the ship's swimming pool. Would the pool appeal to you?'

'Not really,' Stephen said. 'What I would most like to do would be to see the ship's engine room. When I was a boy I had holidays with my family each summer on an island, which we were ferried to by paddle-steamer. I used to be able to go down and watch with fascination the movement of the two huge glistening steel pistons that drove the paddles. I was also fascinated to watch the engineer, who operated a large lever resembling the levers in railway signalmen's cabins. It could slow down or reverse or accelerate the pistons according to orders from the Captain's bridge conveyed to him on an engine room dial which rang like an exceptionally loud cash-register. The engine room of this super-ship will be very different, and I have to admit I am almost as keen to see it as if I were still a boy.'

'Well,' Kevin said, 'it seems we must go our separate ways, you to the engine room and myself to the gym.'

They came out of Stephen's cabin, and with smiles they parted.

As Stephen descended to the lowest part of the ship he couldn't help feeling a slight trepidation. This was intensified when a tall gaunt-looking man suddenly appeared and challengingly said, 'What can I do for you?'

'I hoped to be able to see the engine room,' Stephen said mildly.

'This is the one part of the ship where passengers are not allowed.'

'Oh, I'm so sorry,' Stephen said very apologetically.

The gaunt man seemed to relent. 'I can't let you see the engine room, but I can tell you something about it and about the ship in general.'

'That's very good of you,' Stephen said.

It was soon clear that this man had become willing to tell Stephen about the ship not so much because he wanted to be nice to

Stephen as because the telling enabled him to give vent to bitter feelings that had been accumulating in him about it.

'I am the Chief Engineer on this ship and I know that it should have been put through several more tests before the present tour started. I have serious doubts about the new type of welding that was used to replace the old riveting when the ship was being renovated and refitted. The steering mechanism too needs rigorous further testing, and I am far from confident about the new turbines. I warned the organisers of the tour about these things, but they ignored my advice. Their only concern was to get their widely advertised world tour started on time. They feared they could lose millions of pounds if it was delayed.'

He abruptly stopped. Then, looking almost menacingly at Stephen, he added, 'Don't repeat anything I've told you to any of the other passengers. It might create a panic. And perhaps a mistaken one. After all, the organisers may get away with the risks they are taking, and the tour could be completed without the slightest mishap.'

Stephen was silent.

'You must on no account repeat anything I've told you,' the Engineer insisted, speaking in an even more threatening tone than before.

'I shall think about it,' Stephen said with dignity.

He turned his back on his would-be intimidator, and walked away from him.

He decided to go to the swimming pool in the hope of finding Kevin there.

Kevin had finished his bathe and had dried and dressed himself by the time Stephen arrived. 'There's something serious I want to talk to you about,' Stephen said to him.

They went to Stephen's cabin and sat in the same armchairs as previously.

Stephen repeated to Kevin in detail what the Chief Engineer had told him, and then Kevin said, 'It seems to me that whether or not the ship survives the whole tour the probability of its failing to reach the first port we're making for is very slight. We must already be quite near there by now.'

Stephen found Kevin's reasoning convincing enough to help him overcome an uneasiness bordering on apprehension that he had been experiencing since his encounter with the Engineer.

'Well,' he said, 'I think I'll go and have lunch now. I feel extraordinarily hungry.'

'I don't,' Kevin said. 'I think I'll wait till a little later.'

With smiles again they parted outside the cabin, and Stephen went into the State Room for his lunch.

He sat in his usual seat, and while waiting for the menu to be brought to him he for the first time took note of the four favoured voyagers who sat at the Captain's table. Two of them were perhaps rich business men who had financed the renovating of this ship, and the other two could be the organisers of this world tour. Their faces were startlingly out-of-the-ordinary, and each face was strikingly different from any of the others. There was one man with an enormous head and tiny mouth and heavily drooping eyelids, another whose head looked as though it had been ironed flat on both sides, a third with a head which seemed almost globular and neckless, and a fourth with huge ears and bulging eyes and a deeply cleft protruding chin.

But Stephen was not able to meditate for long on these heads and faces. A sudden extremely loud ringing sound filled the air of the State Room, and the Captain – an inconspicuously ordinary-looking man – followed by his four table-sharers made their way out, trying unsuccessfully to disguise the need they felt to hurry. In no time almost all the rest of the voyagers left their lunch tables and crowded to get out too.

'Most of them haven't a chance. There aren't half enough lifeboats.'

The voice that bitterly said this close to Stephen's ear was the waiter's.

Soon there was a vast scraping sound as of sheets of iron being forced over one another. Stephen knew he hadn't the physical strength even to attempt to escape. The waiter had disappeared. Perhaps he was going to try to save himself by jumping into the sea with a life-belt on. Before very long Stephen noticed that water was visible all over the floor of the State Room. It was rising fast. In an agony of despair he called out, 'Rosa, Rosa.'

Stephen's wife was about to leave his bedside in the hospital on the day of her fourth visit to him there when he suddenly spoke her name. 'Rosa, Rosa,' he said very clearly and in a tone which seemed urgent.

The house surgeon standing at the other side of the bed nodded to her significantly as though to say, 'Didn't I tell you he had been speaking that name?'

Something made her want to test whether Stephen would show any signs of hearing her if she spoke to him. 'Yes darling,' she said, 'I am here.'

To her surprise and delight he answered, 'Oh Rosa, I am so glad.' But then he went on to say, 'Can you ever forgive me?'

'Darling, I have nothing to forgive you for.'

'Yes you have. I can never forgive myself, unless you can forgive me, for leaving you, my dear love, and going for a holiday tour on that ship without even saying goodbye.'

'What ship, darling?'

He did not answer and she could get no further response from him.

But her disappointment was lightened when the house surgeon said with conviction, 'Now we can feel sure that in good time your husband will fully recover and will be able to leave this hospital.'

Emily and Oswin

A 65-year-old well-to-do widow, Mrs Emily Harlowe, was glancing through her newspaper *The Daily Messenger* one morning when she came upon a brief paragraph stating that the poet Oswin Walden was now in a 'home' for old people. (Normally *The Daily Messenger* ignored Walden's existence – the editor and the notably rapacious proprietor of this 'quality' newspaper both detested him because of his politics – however his present misfortune was presumably not displeasing to them and the editor had considered it worthy of mention.) Emily liked poetry, and the few poems by him she had read in magazines and newspapers that published poetry had been more interesting to her than most of those they published by other poets. The paragraph about him in *The Daily Messenger* was strangely disturbing to her; and, as the days went by, a wish grew in her to do something to help him.

For quite a while now she had felt increasingly dissatisfied with the life she was living, in spite of the various pleasures it gave her – such as playing bridge several afternoons each week with local women friends, helping the amiable local vicar by doing flower arrangements (she could do these quite expertly) for special occasions at his church, and getting regular visits from her married daughters who lived in the north of England and brought with them their likeable children, her grandchildren. But she at last came to recognise with hardly any shame that what she needed above everything else was to have some excitement in her life before it was too late. She decided that she would try to rescue Oswin Walden from a 'home' which she didn't doubt he must abominate.

The paragraph in *The Daily Messenger* had been unhelpfully

imprecise as a guide to the whereabouts of the 'home', stating merely that it was in Sussex. She wrote to the editor saying she would be grateful if he could give her its address, and after a long delay his secretary answered that it was near Eastbourne and that it was called 'Sundown House'.

She told her friends she was going for a holiday in Sussex; and early one midweek morning, before the commuter traffic started from the London suburb where she and they lived, she packed her suitcase and set out in her expensive new Rover car to drive south via the Dartford crossing towards Eastbourne.

Sundown House was not too difficult for her to find. It was on a main road and its name was painted large over its front door. She parked her car in a side road and walked to the door and rang the bell. She had to wait what seemed more than a minute before the door was opened to her by a young woman dressed in clothes that made no pretence of resembling those of a trained nurse. When Emily asked to see Mr Oswin Walden, the young woman gave her a nervously doubtful look.' I'll ask Mr Imray,' she said.

Mr Imray, tall in a smart grey suit, came quickly down a curving flight of stairs towards Emily. He had evidently overheard from above what she'd said to the young woman.

With a look of undisguised suspicion he asked her, 'Are you an investigative journalist?'

'No', Emily said, surprised, and then becoming suspicious herself she said,'Why do you ask? Is there something here that you would rather not have investigated?'

'Of course there isn't,' he said, 'but all of us who run private residential homes mainly for the elderly are on the alert against freelance journalists intending to get sensational reports about us published in the tabloid press.'

'You can set your mind at rest as to my intentions,' she said. 'I am simply someone who admires Oswin Walden's poetry, and I would like to meet him and to see if I can do anything to help him.'

'Would you mind telling me your name?'

'Mrs Harlowe.'

'Very well,' Mr Imray said, 'I'll go and ask him.'

Imray was soon back again, saying, 'He's quite indifferent whether he sees you or not.'

'I would like to see him,' Emily said.

Imray led her along a passageway which had a number of similar-seeming doors on either side of it. He stopped at one of these and without knocking on it he showed her into a room where Oswin Walden was sitting in an armchair, wearing pyjamas and a dressing-gown and holding a closed notebook on his lap.

Imray went out of the room without completely shutting the door, and she was left alone with the poet.

'I hope you don't mind my intruding on you,' she said, 'but I am an admirer of your poetry, and when I read in *The Messenger* that you were in this home I felt I must come down here to see if I could be of any use to you.'

He said nothing.

There was a second armchair near his, and after some hesitation she sat down in it.

'I could get you out of here today at once if you wished.'

'I would have nowhere to go,' he said. 'They have sold my house.'

She gazed at him, and he gazed at her.

He found her attractive to look at, though he judged that she was probably in her middle sixties or older. She did not think him particularly good-looking, but she felt sure that he couldn't be less than thirty years younger than herself.

'Are you given enough to eat here?' she asked him.

'The food is uninteresting, to say the least, and is atrociously cooked, but we are not starved.'

'Wouldn't you like a holiday?'

'A holiday from my present state of mind – yes, I certainly would,' he said with a hint of irony.

'A change of place might help to change your state of mind,' she said.

'A change of place could even worsen my state of mind,' he said. 'I might feel wholly lost and disorientated.'

'I could take you to a place of your own choice which you've known well and liked in the past and where you would not feel disorientated at all,' she said.

'I can't think of any such place,' he said, 'though I might like Rouen. Before the War my elder brother stayed several months there, and he was enthusiastic about it.'

'All right, we will travel there tomorrow.'

Oswin looked at her with disbelief.

'Where are your outdoor clothes?' she asked.

'Imray keeps them locked away.'

'I'll get them from him.' She stood up and walked quickly out of the room.

Imray asked what right she thought she had to remove one of his residents from here. For all he knew she might be a member of one of those pseudo-religious cults that would submit him to a repulsive 'cure' which would convert his neurosis into real insanity. 'I may be exaggerating,' Imray said, 'but you can appreciate why I am not keen to let him be taken from Sundown House by someone I know nothing about.'

'I can appreciate that you are not keen to lose the money you are paid for keeping him here,' she said, 'but I have several influential friends, and I think that if I were to give them a not entirely unfavourable report on the running of Sundown House you might feel sufficiently compensated.'

Without a word he went from the room to fetch Oswin's outdoor clothes. He returned and handed them to her; and she handed them to Oswin, who seemed unwilling to put them on. Guessing that he did not want to change in her presence she left him alone with Imray.

After a considerable while he emerged fully dressed into the hall, carrying the suitcase that contained the rest of his belongings. Imray in silence ushered Emily and Oswin out of the front door, which he closed behind them.

She led him to her impressive-looking car in the side-street, and opening the large boot at the rear of it she told him to put his suitcase into this next to her own that was already there. Then she got him to sit down in the front seat beside her.

'Where are we going?' he asked as she drove out on to the main road.

'To Southampton,' she said.

During the journey to Southampton she asked him various questions about himself, which she found he was very ready to answer.

One of the first of these was, 'How did it happen that you were sent from your own house to Sundown House?'

Oswin, before answering this, mentioned that his 'house' was really only an ordinary rural cottage, not a house. Then he said, 'It happened when I got myself into such a neurotic state that a retired pharmacist, Mr Robinson, who lived in a nearby cottage and occasionally looked in on me for a brief neighbourly chat, went to see the local GP, Dr Parsons, about me. I willingly agreed to be visited by Dr Parsons, but after he'd asked me various questions he was uncertain what should be done with me. I didn't seem to be the sort of case he should send to a mental hospital, but on the other hand he felt I couldn't just be left where I was. Finally I accepted a suggestion of his that I should go into Sundown House at least temporarily. I didn't foresee that during the time I was there my cottage would be sold to help pay for my keep.'

'What made you get yourself into such a neurotic state?'

'I was trying every day and all day to write a better kind of poetry than I'd written before, and I wasn't succeeding. I drove myself harder and harder, and at last several nights came when I couldn't sleep at all. It was then that Robinson asked Parsons to come and visit me.'

'Were you able to sleep at Sundown House?'

'Oh yes; they gave me dope. I've still got quite a lot with me now. But I always managed to avoid taking any in the daytime, however bad I felt.'

'There was a closed notebook on your lap when I first saw you. Do you mind my asking whether you still hope to write a poem of the new kind you wanted to?'

'I think I do. But I haven't yet got any farther than occasionally discussing in my notebook what was wrong with my previous attempts.'

She asked him what he thought was wrong with his previous attempts.

He explained that they were still too explicitly political. What he aimed to do was to write poems which though they would most of them continue to be political would never be other than implicitly so.

'I suppose I've realised that the poems of yours I've read and admired were explicitly political, but this didn't bother me in the least,' she said. 'For me the impressive thing about them was how well they were written and how comprehensible they were.'

He noticed that all the while she was speaking she kept a careful eye on the road. She was a good driver, better than he had been when he had owned a car (an antiquated third-hand one).

She went on to ask him at what age he became a poet.

He found himself speaking freely to her about his boyhood and his social origins. He was born in 1924 in an Essex town within twelve miles of London. His father, he told her, was a railway signalman and his mother a teacher whose parents had been working-class. His elder brother, Henry, their only other child, was four years older than him. They went to the same elementary school, and both did well there, Henry going on to a good secondary school where he was quite happy, and Oswin to a posh grammar school where he was made to feel socially inferior, though he did well academically. While he was there he fell in love with a middle-class girl at a girls' high school in the same town, and the first poem he ever wrote was a love poem inspired by her, but he never dared to show it to her or to tell her he was in love with her. Henry was killed early on in the 1939 war. Oswin himself was called up in 1942 and joined the fire service. In 1945 after the war he was able to go to a redbrick university where he got a good degree in English. He left in 1948 at the age of 24 and he earned a bare living for some years as a journalist writing under an assumed name for a local newspaper whose proprietor could be described as a liberal Tory. He had two books of his poems published by a reputable publisher which were reviewed dismissively or hostilely in several 'quality' papers and magazines, but he got good reviews from two reviewers who thought him promising.

Abruptly he stopped talking, afraid that he might have been boring her and that she wasn't really listening. But she had been listening with sympathetic interest and she asked him to go on.

He told her that he had never got married, and why. He had had affairs with three women, but found he'd not enough in common with any of the three to want to settle down with her. Then he had fallen quite seriously in love with a fourth and would have liked to marry her, but he discovered he was sharing her with another man of his own age who had a better income than his and who did eventually marry her. It was soon after this that his mother died (his father had died a year earlier) and she left him a little money, which helped him to buy the quiet cottage in Sussex where he hoped to concentrate on solving his poetic problem.

All at once Oswin became conscious that he knew nothing about the life of the woman he had been speaking to so unreservedly about his own life, and who had chosen to drive him to Southampton in her car now.

He decided to ask her to tell him about herself.

She readily did. 'I am the widow of a workaholic,' she said. 'Don't misunderstand me. Charles was a good husband to me, as the saying goes, and I had two lovely children by him, but he was the chairman of an important company and more of his time and energy was given to his work than he was physically able to bear. One morning not more than an hour after he had said goodbye to me and left the house, his secretary rang up to tell me he had died suddenly of heart failure while at work.'

'How dreadfully upsetting for you,' Oswin said.

'Yes, the immediate shock was dreadful, but my daughters who by then had grown up and got married were very supportive – so were my friends – and I felt almost ashamed that I recovered from it as soon as I did.'

'Though after recovering from it you must have had a feeling of loss which you couldn't recover from so soon,' Oswin said, sympathetically.

'I have to admit that I didn't grieve as greatly for him as I expected to. I suppose the truth is I never deeply loved him,' she said. 'I thought just as my parents did that he would be a suitable husband for me because he was very well-off, and so were they. "Money marries money" was one of my father's favourite sayings. And I didn't find Charles actually unattractive. He was about the same age as I was, quite good-looking, and very considerate.'

Oswin was astonished at her having, casually almost, revealed all this about her married life to him. He would have liked to ask whether she had ever at any time fallen in love with anyone, but he dared not.

A silence, except for occasional remarks about the scenery or the behaviour of other motorists on the road, fell between them during the rest of their drive to Southampton.

Emily stopped her car in a parking-space that fronted an expensive-looking hotel. After getting out from her driving seat she opened the car door for him on his side of the car and then went to unlock the car boot where their suitcases were. She told him to follow her into the hotel, but Oswin, wishing to be helpful, lifted the two suitcases from the boot and was about to carry them into the hotel.

'No,' she said peremptorily. 'A servant from the hotel can do that.'

He put the cases down and followed her into the entrance hall of the hotel, where she approached a young woman who sat at a desk to which was affixed the word 'Reception', printed in gold on a wavy-edged piece of polished brown wood. Emily announced that she wanted two separate rooms. She wrote her name and address in the visitors' book, and Oswin wrote his name, but he hesitated a moment before deciding to give Sundown House as his address. Then, after the Receptionist had presented her with the key for room number 7, and Oswin with the key for number 8, Emily asked that the two suitcases which were standing close to the boot of her black Rover car in the forecourt should be brought into the hotel at once.

A uniformed young man carried the cases up a short flight of stairs, and deposited them in rooms 7 and 8, Emily and Oswin having unlocked the doors for him. Emily gave the man a tip, and this slightly embarrassed Oswin who couldn't help feeling that in paying for his stay at this hotel she would be giving him a kind of tip.

Emily went into her room and Oswin went into his, where quite soon, however, she joined him.

'Well, what do you think of it?' she asked.

Oswin didn't immediately know what to say he thought of it, but he was aware that it was an 'en suite' room and that beyond the rather broad chintzy single bed there was a smaller room containing a wash-basin, a shower, and a 'toilet'.

'I think I'll take advantage of the facilities here,' he said.

'That's a good idea,' she said. 'I'll return to my room and do likewise. Then we will go downstairs together to find out when dinner is served.'

They walked down the wide stairs side by side, she holding his arm and wearing an evening dress, low-cut and with what looked like a triple diamond necklace (presumably the diamonds weren't real) partially covering her neck; whereas he wore the everyday, far from smart or even very clean, clothes he had been wearing on the day he had been taken from his cottage to Sundown House.

Emily asked the Receptionist what time dinner would be served. 'Within twenty minutes,' the Receptionist said, 'and meanwhile perhaps you might like to go and sit in the lounge through the arch over there.' She pointed to the arch. Emily detected a hint of disrespect in the Receptionist's manner, but deciding to appear not to have noticed it she was soon leading Oswin through the arch into a lounge which was already quite crowded with guests of both sexes, who all of them seemed to Oswin to be as well-dressed for dinner as Emily was.

'I can't help feeling a bit out of place here in these clothes of mine,' he murmured to her only semi-humorously.

She turned on him with more than semi-serious scorn: 'So much for your explicit or implicit political principles,' she said. 'You ought not to care a damn about what these no doubt mostly Conservative types here may think of the way you are dressed.'

'You are right,' he said contritely.

'Very well,' she said, 'I'll let you do penance by buying the drinks for us both. I know you've got just about enough money of your own to buy them with. And if your conduct improves in future, I may even consider recouping you.'

'What will you have?' he asked her.

'A large gin-and-tonic,' she said.

He went to the bar and bought this for her and a schooner of dry sherry for himself. He felt better after drinking the sherry, and when she had finished her gin-and-tonic he wanted to go and buy a repeat for her and for himself, but she would not let him.

However, between them they drank a whole bottle of excellent Burgundy with their tolerably good dinner. At the end of it she said, 'I don't feel much like retiring to the lounge now, do you? I think bed might be best after our long drive today.'

'Yes, I agree it might be,' he said.

They went up the broad stairway together, ignoring the Receptionist who was still at her desk.

Outside their rooms they stopped and turned to face each other.

'Well, good-night, Oswin,' she said.

'Good-night,' he said.

She went into her room and he went into his.

He gave himself a shower; after which he put on his pyjamas and got into his chintzily coverleted hotel bed. It was comfortable, but he had no intention of trying to go to sleep in it. He waited for a time that he calculated would be long enough to allow Emily to finish her preparations and to get into the bed in her room. Then, with his dressing gown on over his pyjamas, he cautiously opened his door to make sure that none of the other guests was in the passageway. He saw no one. He hurried to her door, quickly and quietly opened it and was inside her room.

She was sitting up in her bed wearing a silk nightgown. She looked relieved and glad to see him.

'I hoped this would happen,' she said.

He took off his dressing gown, placed it on a bedside chair and got into bed with her. He had a strange feeling that now he would be able to avenge himself for some of the humiliations she had inflicted on him. He embraced her and she held him tight against her, almost as though to prevent him from making any further movement. As though she feared it. And she did suddenly fear being inadequate after her many years of sexless widowhood. But he was gentle with her, and her fears gave way to a prolonged intense delight such as she had never experienced with Charles. It was repeated several times that night, and she knew when they woke in the morning that she was helplessly in love with him.

She drove him in her car to an AA-approved garage where it could remain until they returned from Rouen. They then walked arm-in-arm together along the streets of Southampton, window-shopping and also visiting the ancient Guildhall and the Maritime Museum. They had lunch together in a famous pub, where she was unwise enough after drinking two glasses of red wine with her meal to make the would-be humorous remark that some of the other eaters present might refer to him among themselves as her 'toy-boy'.

He was angry with her, and said, 'Perhaps that's how you too think of me.'

'Oh no, Oswin,' she said, distressed. 'I love you.'

He said nothing. He felt embarrassed.

But they had got over the tiff between them by the time they came to the ticket office where she booked two first-class berths on the boat which was to take them on the six-hour night crossing from Southampton to Le Havre.

They arrived early in the morning and were drowsy during their comfortable train journey to Rouen.

'French trains were very different in my brother Henry's day,' Oswin told her. 'He used to say that when they were going at speed they rocked from side to side and he was terrified that they might come off the rails at any moment. But it seems that nowadays they are more comfortable and less alarming than the English trains are.'

'You could be right about that,' she said, 'though you're judging only by your experience of the one French train we are on at present.'

'I do think that English railways are less efficient than they were in my father's day,' he said, 'and I think that the Government's deliberate policy of favouring the roads at the expense of the railways is to blame for it.'

'If the English railways have become less efficient it's the fault of the people who manage them and not of the Government's pro-road policy,' she told him.

'There are times when I get the impression that you are politically a little bit reactionary,' he said mildly.

'No,' she said. 'I'm just an unpolitical person who likes owning and driving an up-to-date car.'

Emily and Oswin

They took a taxi from the station at Rouen to a large and newly-built hotel recommended by the proprietor of the garage in Southampton where Emily had left her car. (Oswin wondered whether the Hôtel de la Poste, which his brother Henry had spoken of as being favoured by English tourists, still existed.) A guide-book obtained by Emily at the new hotel told her and Oswin how severely the city had been damaged during the war, and proudly stressed the recent reconstruction of a number of its famous medieval buildings. Mostly these were what they spent their next few days in going to see. First its two cathedrals, the 14th-century Abbey Church of St-Ouen and the 13th to 16th-century gothic Notre-Dame with the high green metal spire inside which a winding stair rose towards the summit. From this stair Henry had released over the city a piece of lavatory paper inscribed with a blasphemous statement capable of getting him into serious trouble if it had floated down into hostile hands. (Henry ashamedly admitted to Oswin that he was then, like many another British contemporary of his, little more than an overgrown schoolboy compared with the adult-minded continental young men of approximately his own age he would soon meet.) Emily was keen also to see La Tour Jeanne d'Arc, the tower where Joan of Arc was, incorrectly perhaps, said to have been imprisoned for a while before being burnt at the stake; but what interested Oswin more than La Tour was Le Gros-Horloge – because this big ornate clock was above a narrow street in which there had been a restaurant where Henry had eaten artichokes that he claimed had poisoned him for three days. However, there was something Oswin was keener to see than anything else unmentioned in the guide-book – a 'pension' with the address 'Le Vert Logis, Impasse des Arquebusiers, Boulevard St-Hilaire'. Henry had once told Oswin that during his stay here he was happier than he had ever been before.

Yet Oswin shrank from telling Emily that he wanted to see it. He was afraid of the deep disappointment he would feel if he found that it was no longer there. The map in the guide-book clearly showed the Boulevard St-Hilaire, but not the Impasse des Arquebusiers.

He did not tell her and they did not try to find it. His mind however was dominated by thoughts and feelings about it wherever they went. She was well aware that he wasn't fully attentive to what they were actually seeing; but also she sensed an exaltation in him, and she forgave him. After all he was a poet, and he might at last be beginning to dream up a poem of the kind he had for so long been unsuccessfully trying to write.

The truth was that Oswin in his imagination, and with the aid of what his brother Henry had told him, had become his brother Henry.

On his first morning at the pension he was woken by a beautiful young girl saying in a gentle voice, 'Bonjour Monsieur', before drawing back his bedroom curtains. (He was soon to discover that she was a peasant girl and a slavey at the beck and call of an astonishing woman rarely seen above stairs who cooked the excellent meals which the girl brought to the pension table.) He seemed from the start to be on a new plane of existence, liberating and superior to almost anything he had ever experienced in England. Even the aroma arising from the bowl of French coffee served at petit déjeuner, and especially the taste of the coffee itself and of the croissant he ate with it, had this same liberating effect on him, so different were they from the cruder though appetising enough smell and flavour of a more substantial English breakfast.

Meeting the other guests at the pension – with the exception of the only Englishman (who was a typical 'public-school' product) – was also exciting to him. There were the three Scandinavians, a Norwegian young woman and two Swedish males, one of them a little older than the other, who played footsie-footsie with her under the table, and she couldn't refrain from grinning. There was a young Frenchman, André Poncet, very upright in his bearing, smartly dressed and precise in pronouncing the words he used, who mockingly took to calling Henry 'Monsieur le Philosophe'. But he was friendly too, admitting to Henry that the prospect of having to do two years' military training in the French army, as other young Frenchmen of his age also had to, did not please him. Then a young woman arrived from Finland, with fair hair and a pretty face, whose surname was Pletchnikov. (Henry never knew her first name.)

Poncet was soon quite often in her room, and the puritanical English ex-School Prefect, Paget, spied on them. Poncet one day discovering this was understandably furious.

Poncet worked in the town for a commercial firm, and occasionally he went home for a couple of days to stay with his parents. Whenever this happened Pletchnikov was unhappy. Henry wrote a mocking verse, which to his disgrace he showed to Paget:

> *Pletchnikov and Poncet*
> *Are flirting all the day*
> *And Pletchnikov is homesick*
> *When Poncet goes away.*

Undoubtedly Paget was envious, but Henry genuinely was not. What mattered to him more than anything else was his poetry, and he found that the Vert Logis with its many peculiarities was a poetically stimulating place to be staying in.

Why did it defy ordinary French grammar by placing the word 'Vert' before instead of after the word 'Logis'? Why, high up at right angles to the front of the building, was there a garden bright with shrubs in flower, and immediately below this two heavy wooden padlocked doors which concealed a cellar containing wine barrels? Every now and then a lorry with a not very large tank on it would arrive in the Impasse. The driver would get down from his driving-seat and, drawing out with one hand from the lorry a long rubber hose, he would unlock with a key in his other hand the big padlock that kept the doors of the cellar closed. Then he would enter the cellar and after unbunging one of the barrels he would suck at that end of the hose until a siphoning process had been established and he could spit out the small quantity of wine that remained in his mouth while he directed its full flow into the bung-hole of the barrel.

But Henry was not sure of having correctly understood what had been happening. Did another lorry perhaps come in the middle of the night to take the full barrels away and replace them with other empty ones? Or might he be even more wrong and might the wine be flowing from the barrels into the tanker?

A Renegade in Springtime

One of the things he could be certain about was that he was never given wine to drink at the pension. Nor water either, apart from the boiled water with which his morning coffee was presumably made. And at the main meal of the day the guests were always provided with a glass of pink syrupy liquid, likely to be grenadine diluted with cooled water that had been boiled. The proprietors of the pension, Monsieur and Madame Morel, seemed to be as distrustful of the quality of French water as the British then were. At any rate, none of their guests was known to have been afflicted with typhoid after returning home.

Henry, when describing such details to Oswin made clear that for himself they were not trivial. They all in their own way contributed to the special poetic appeal that Rouen had for him. This was true even of the *Vidange*, a lorry that used to be driven round to various houses in Rouen for the purpose of pumping out sewage from domestic cesspits through a long, capacious and flexible metal hose. The hose as it trailed its way out down the stairs of Le Vert Logis leaked slightly, Henry said.

Oswin commented that he couldn't easily understand how the *Vidange* could have much poetic appeal, but Henry answered that there had been comic scenes in some of the greatest of Marlowe's and Shakespeare's Tragedies.

* * *

Often Oswin had wondered what Henry's feelings had been in the months preceding the war that was to kill him.

The poetry he wrote at school, and continued to write almost until the actual outbreak of the war, was unpolitical and showed no sign of concern about the rise of Nazism in Europe.

* * *

Oswin's experience as a fire fighter during the war had strengthened his will to write poetry in support of the working-class he had been born into, but after the war he had failed to write the kind of poems he wanted to, and if it hadn't been for the help of a member of the upper-middle class he might have remained in Sundown House and have become slowly insane.

* * *

Now the time had arrived for him and Emily to return from Rouen to England. What were they going to do when they got there?

He had avoided asking her while they remained in France, but she herself raised the subject while they were on the boat back to Southampton.

She said that to begin with they could stay in the same Southampton hotel they had stayed in before crossing to France.

'And after that?' he asked.

'I shall find you a house.'

'What about your own house?'

'Quite impossible,' she said with alarm, 'The scandal it would cause in the village would make our lives there unbearable.'

'Yes, of course it would,' he agreed. 'I was only joking.'

'Where would you like to have a house?'

'Somewhere in or near the Essex town where I was born,' he said. 'But I wouldn't want it as a gift. I would want to pay you for it.'

'I could make you an interest-free loan which you could pay off gradually as soon as you could afford to.'

'That is very generous of you,' he said.

* * *

Soon after their return to England they motored to Oswin's home town. They stayed in a local hotel – at Emily's expense – while visiting various Estate Agents and being taken to look at, and into, various houses that were up for sale. The small house once owned by Oswin's signalman father in which Oswin had been born had now been demolished, but quite near the site of it there was a not-too-large house that Oswin thought suitable. It was the end house of a terrace which was 'on the wrong side of the tracks' (an American phrase meaning 'situated in the lower-class part of the

A Renegade in Springtime

town on the wrong side of the railway'), and he particularly liked to use the phrase because of its conciseness.

* * *

Much of the furniture necessary to him – bed, a table, a few chairs – was sold with the house, as were a fridge and various facilities for cooking. Other requirements, including discarded (though by no means too worn) bedclothes and curtains were supplied by Emily, who also gave him a typewriter in good condition that had belonged to her husband.

By means of some private tutoring of teenagers working for exams, and some journalism for the editor of the local newspaper, he was able to keep up his payments to Emily, and she quite often came to see him.

Then he got to know a small group of people whose political views were similar to his own.

Being with them enabled him at last to begin writing the kind of poetry he had for so many months been unsuccessfully trying to write. And after a while he and a young woman in the group, who was younger than himself, fell for each other.

He let Emily know about this, and she wished him well. She even came to meet them both. But she was broken-hearted, and before long she decided to move from her village and to go and end her days in an extremely expensive 'home'.

She found that it had wonderfully spacious grounds and a marvellous view of trees beyond which swans could be seen swimming on a blue sky-reflecting lake. She wrote to describe all this to him, and to tell him that he need no longer continue to pay off the money she had lent him.

* * *

What she was never to tell him was that at this 'home' she met a beautiful man, a little older than herself, and that they became platonic lovers.

Imaginative Men & Women

Early one fine autumnal Saturday afternoon, during the Second World War, Dr Andrew Elford was waiting for the ferryboat which would take him across from the south to the north side of the estuary. Almost always, whatever the time of year might be, the south side was very windy, and today he was looking forward both to meeting old friends living on the north side and to escaping into the remarkably milder climate that prevailed there. Quite possibly the northern weather now might still be warm enough for them and him to sit and talk and eat together out-of-doors.

* * *

Andrew's wait for the ferry-boat was much longer than he had expected. He had arrived too soon at the small pier on the south side, probably because of an over-eagerness to reach what he hoped to be the calmer north. He was deterred from feeling irritably restive, however, by remembering that the force of the wind which was buffeting him here on the pier was as nothing compared with its violence when he had to bicycle against it in a rain-proof suit to visit his patients.

* * *

At last a swirling column of thick black smoke mounting into the clean blustery air told him that the high-funnelled antiquated ferryboat was making its way back from the far side towards him as he stood waiting.

* * *

On its deck during its return to the northern pier he was hardly conscious at all of the wind which was blowing more strongly than ever. Then, after he had landed, and had left the pier behind him, the word 'paradise' rose into his mind at his first glimpse – beyond trees that had several Cedars of Lebanon among them – of the house his friends Sid and Gladys Palmer lived in.

He found them digging in their garden. They didn't believe in possessing a telephone, so he had not been able to let them know in advance of his decision to visit them today. They were surprised to see him, but there could be no doubt about the complete genuineness of their delight that he had come.

'But why hasn't Mary come with you?' Gladys asked.

'Mary would very much have liked to come,' Andrew said, 'but all three of the children have got colds and one of us parents had to stay with them. Mary insisted that I had been working too hard during the week and it would do no harm if I were to ask Dr Ragnell, my senior partner in our practice, to take over from me this weekend for a change. So here I am on my own.' Then he added with a grin, 'And, anyway, looking after the children is her official war work: if it weren't for them she would have been conscripted into the army.'

'But what about yourself?' Gladys asked him with concern. 'Mightn't you still get conscripted?'

'Well, it could happen,' Andrew admitted. 'I have been thinking of myself as being a little too old to be called up now, just as I was a little too young to be called up in the First War. But if there were heavy losses among younger doctors who have been conscripted I think I would be quite likely to be taken – and I would go willingly enough because I believe that the Nazis are a far deadlier menace to the human race than the Kaiser's Germany ever was. This present war is very different from the First.'

Andrew, luckily, realised almost instantly that his remark about the difference between the two wars might get him into the kind of fruitlessly obstinate argument with Sid that he especially wanted to avoid. He quickly said to Sid, 'But I think I remember your telling me that in the First War no one seemed to regard you as too old to enlist, though you must have been at least as old then as I am now.'

'How right you are,' Sid said. 'I was employed as an assistant gardener by an Anglican Rector who came of a very aristocratic family, and he was proud to see me go. I fancy he would have been even prouder if I'd been killed and he'd been able to put up a bronze plaque in his church to my memory.' Sid laughed, and added, 'But things didn't work out like that at all. I was captured by the enemy only a day or two after we reached the front.'

'You sound as though you weren't too sorry about it?'

'I wasn't. I let them know I'd been a gardener in civil life, and they allowed me to do a little work for a German farmer some way behind their lines, under military guard of course.'

Grinning, Andrew quoted,

> *and one, to use the word of 'ypocrites*
> *'ad the misfortoon to be took by Fritz.*

'I like that,' Sid said.

'It comes from a poem written by our best war poet.'

But Sid showed no sign of caring who wrote the poem. There was something important to him that he wanted to let Andrew know. 'It is a strange thing,' he said, 'that when I was a prisoner of war on a German farm I first became keen on agriculture.'

'Would you have liked to stay on after the war and become a farmer in Germany?'

'Good Lord, no.' Sid laughed loudly.

'That could be taken to mean you don't like Germans.'

'I liked them – those I got to know – very much,' Sid said forcefully. 'Including my military guard. But this home here is where I want to live. With Gladys of course. And to dig our garden.'

She gave Andrew an interested look; and the thought came to him, as it had never done before, that she might agree with those early socialists who believed in 'free love'.

He quickly got back to the subject of nationalities by saying, 'I knew a man who had been a German prisoner of war in this country and who chose to stay on here. One summer Mary and I were having a fortnight's holiday together in the south of England. We'd found a very pleasant house which had only one disadvantage:

A Renegade in Springtime

the owner who rented it to us, and was himself going away for a holiday, kept chickens in a wire enclosure at the end of his garden, and he asked us to do something for them, give them water or grain – I can't remember exactly what.'

Sid commented with affable sarcasm, 'You must have enjoyed that.'

'The owner assured us we could get help from his neighbour, the German prisoner who had stayed on, if we had any trouble with the chickens.'

'And I suppose you did,' Gladys guessed from Andrew's tone of voice.

'Yes,' he said. 'We were horrified to see that one of the chickens was being mercilessly attacked by the others who were viciously pecking its neck. "They'll kill it," Mary said.'

'The German ex-prisoner, a very friendly man, came along and lifted up the attacked chicken in his arms and took it away with him. Two or three days later he brought it back and dropped it in among the others, who accepted it without the least hostility. He explained that it had been suffering from something like what might be called a cold in the nose, and that he'd been able to cure this.'

* * *

'And what moral do you expect us to draw from your holiday story?' a man's voice suddenly and a little truculently asked. He was Clem Marsden, a friend of the Palmers, living with his wife Alice in a small nearby cottage. Andrew, who had met him once before, said amicably, 'I don't know of any moral I would draw from it, though perhaps it does suggest to me that if I had the time to spare I might like to take up the study of the behaviour of birds in general.'

'You could *make* the time, if you wanted to,' Marsden said almost severely.

Gladys changed the subject for them by saying, 'I think it might be a good idea for all of us now to have tea.'

Andrew had learnt from his middle-class (but politically very left-wing) wife Mary that for the middle class 'to have tea' meant having, between four and half-past in the afternoon a cup of tea, and a slice of cake, or even cucumber sandwiches, whereas for the great majority of the British population it was the main meal of the day, and was usually eaten between six and half-past.

Didn't this mean, Andrew half-humorously asked himself, that Sid and Gladys whose origins were certainly working-class had become bourgeoisified? And that he had become so too, his parents having been petty-bourgeois shopkeepers whose tea was at six thirty? Yes, but at least in their politics both he and Sid, and Gladys and bourgeois-born Mary, were wholeheartedly on the side of the exploited working class. However, what did or could they do politically now?

'I've brought some cherry cake,' Andrew said, intending not to tell them till after they'd eaten it that the cherries were really bits of beetroot.

'That's very sweet of you,' Gladys told him, 'or perhaps I should say it's very sweet of Mary who I daresay was the one who actually made the cake.'

'Yes, she did,' Andrew admitted.

'Clem and Alice are also kindly contributing,' Gladys went on, 'and now I think the time has come for us to fetch out the garden chairs and table from the garden shed; though when I say us I really mean all you, not including me, because I shall be bringing out from the house the actual tea – that's to say the hot liquid in a teapot – together with the milk.'

Soon after they had begun their tea-meal, Clem suddenly said, 'It is almost difficult to believe we are in the middle of a deadly war.'

'It may not go on for very much longer,' Sid said.

'More likely it will never stop,' Clem said, 'or not until most of the human race have succeeded in exterminating themselves.'

'Why is he so bitterly pessimistic?' Gladys asked his wife Alice.

'I may get into trouble with him for telling you what I think might partly account for it.' She turned to her husband and said, 'You have several times described to me how on one occasion you saw men blown to "bits of meat" by an exploding shell. I think the incident preyed on your mind.'

'Whose minds wouldn't it have preyed on, except those of – to quote the poet I'm told is Andrew's favourite war poet – "dullards whom no cannon stuns."'

Neither Andrew nor Sid nor Gladys asked Alice or Clem why this one horrible incident that preyed on his mind had convinced him that the present war would go on till most of the human race were exterminated by it.

* * *

Dr Andrew had an alarmed suspicion that Clem might be on the verge of a serious mental breakdown.

Ironically, Andrew did not remember that the war poet greatly admired by him and perfectly sane, Wilfred Owen, seemed in a poem entitled 'The End' to take an even more pessimistic view than Clem did.

But the old-time socialist Sid argued, as the meal went on, that in the not too distant future most of the human race would have learnt at last that wars were of no benefit to them, and there would then be no more wars.

Andrew, however, said, 'Although I agree with you that wars will ultimately be abolished I am convinced there will have to be a long and bitter struggle before this.'

* * *

He became aware, as they all sat comfortably enough around the garden table, that though the air remained warm it was growing darker. He would soon have to leave if he was to be in time to catch the last ferry to the south. Suddenly they all heard the throbbing drone of aircraft flying in formation high overhead, and then far to the north soon afterwards there were loud bright explosions while criss-crossing searchlights scissored the sky.

'They are bombing the shipyards,' Sid said. 'They are not interested in small fry like us living here.'

'We've sometimes heard those explosions and seen those searchlights from where we live,' Andrew said. 'They seemed very distant.

We ourselves are within three miles of a large chemical factory which in spite of its conspicuously high chimneys appears to be immune from attack. There are rumours that a similar factory in Germany is owned by the same powerful company and is equally immune.'

'Did you create the rumours, by any chance?' Clem bluntly asked.

'Well, perhaps I did contribute to them,' Andrew frankly said.

'Quite rightly,' Sid said vigorously. 'They are obviously true.'

When Andrew arrived home that evening he gave Mary an account of the talk at the tea party, and she was particularly interested to hear of Sid's vigorous assertion of belief in the 'rumour' that explained why the chemical factory remained unbombed.

But also she wondered whether its being a *chemical* factory was particularly repulsive to him.

She was wrong about this.

* * *

Sid had no objection to chemicals so long as they benefited agriculture without harming either the farm-workers who had to use them or the surrounding country and the people who lived there – 'the environment', as it was officially called, to Sid's distaste.

Sid thought often about workers on the land. He thought, as he dug in his garden, about those working in other countries besides Britain, women as well as men. His mind pictured women in the flooded paddy fields stooping to implant the rice-plants beneath the shallow water which covered their bare feet, and he knew that this bareness could cause disease, and he thought of the poverty which prevented the women from providing themselves with protective high boots. He thought of Africa and of farmers there who were forced to abandon their farming by wars that the rivalry of outside Powers had caused, and he thought of the starving African children with swollen bellies.

* * *

He thought too of England in the past, and he felt an affinity with Gerrard Winstanley, 'the Digger', who during the period of the

A Renegade in Springtime

Commonwealth had insisted that all the land belonged to the whole people of England. Sid imagined Winstanley's setting out one Sunday morning with a few followers to dig the waste land on St George's Hill in Surrey and to begin the establishment of a community there, and he vividly saw their brutal ejection a fortnight later by Cromwell's soldiers.

* * *

But of land-workers in twentieth-century countries he thought mostly about those rebelling in South America. His mind saw the death-squads in action and horrifically murdered bodies flung into roadside ditches. Then his mind foresaw at last a decisive battle won in a South American country by rebel peasants who thereafter ceased to be peasants and became free. And Sid dreamed as he dug in his garden that the same thing, perhaps all the sooner because of their example, would happen in every country where there were peasants still, and that the transition would be less murderous when land-owners understood how profitably they could exploit 'free' waged labourers.

* * *

Sid dreamed further of laws that would curb and finally put an end to such exploitation and would bring about the common ownership of all the land by all the people. He dreamed of richly green fields and of preserved hedges and of cared-for woodlands. He dreamed of new agricultural machines which without polluting the air or the soil would make work far easier for the farm workers who operated them. He never doubted, and Gladys agreed with him, that wars would come and wars would go, but the cultivation of the earth would continue and would save the human race from self-extinction.

* * *

Mary often daydreamed of a future in which all discrimination against women was brought to an end. When her three children were grown up and had left home she felt she had the time and the duty to do something to help the cause of women's 'liberation'. She found several local women who were willing to co-operate with her in arranging public meetings. Their heroine was Mary Wollstonecraft, who wrote *A Vindication of the Rights of Woman*.

Andrew was entirely in favour of Mary's work, but he thought he'd better not show this, because some patients if he did might suspect him of caring a bit less for them than for politics.

* * *

And what about Clem Marsden? Did he still say wars would go on till most humans were extinct? Yes, but his wife found out he was daydreaming of being in a space vehicle travelling far faster than light and arriving outside the supposedly finite 'universe' at a place where life existed in a physical form much less disadvantaged than the human body, and where he would be happier than he could ever have been on the earth.

The Scenic Railway

The early afternoon was warmly bright, the grey-white autumnal clematis was profuse on the roadside hedges, the views of sea and country became more extensive as the car went up the hill, and the tones of the voices of the five disabled passengers who were being driven by Leslie Brellis to the Happiland Amusement Park were cheerfully expectant; but Leslie began to suspect he might not have fully recovered yet from the attack of giddiness he'd had soon after getting out of bed this morning. When the trees of the Park, with the red-and-white-striped dome of the Pleasure Palace conspicuous among them, came into sight not far ahead in a valley descending steeply to the coastline below the hill, he noticed that the dome appeared to sway slightly as if shaken by a minor earth tremor, though the high cedars around it were quite unmoved. The appearance might be due to a trick of the afternoon sunlight on the spirally twisted stripes of the dome. But if the swaying he seemed to see had no objective reality at all, not even the reality of an externally caused deceptive appearance, and was due solely to the distortion of his seeing by a dizzy shakiness in himself, he ought not to be driving these disabled people in this car. Perhaps he ought to stop at once.

He thought of asking Willie Tyler, who sat beside him staring raptly ahead through the windscreen of the car, some not too particularised question which would lead Willie to reveal whether he too had noticed an apparent swaying of the dome. But Willie was an inveterate romancer and quite capable, if he guessed what Leslie was trying to find out, of saying he was sure the dome was moving up and down as well as from side to side. Also an answer of any kind from Willie would take time to get, because he had a speech defect, a stammer which every now and then when he seemed to be speaking almost easily would bring him to a dead stop, with his mouth open, agonisingly trying to utter a next word and absolutely unable to say anything more until someone else spoke the word for him and he was gratefully able to go on again. And Leslie in any case did not really need to ask Willie about the dome. He was becoming all too certain that its swaying was an illusion produced by his own physical state. But he knew that if he stopped his large estate car anywhere here on this narrow curving road along the hillside it would be a hazard to other traffic.

He drove on, much more slowly than before. He realised how right his wife Lana had been at breakfast to warn him that his vertigo this morning, like his similar attack last month, was mainly caused by his putting extra pressure on himself recently and that he must give up this weekly driving he had volunteered to do for a local 'caring' organisation, or else he would become incapable of going on any longer with the political activities which had mattered more than anything else to him and to her ever since their retirement to the South Coast fifteen years before. But by the end of breakfast, though he had promised her he would not drive for the organisation again after today, he had told her he mustn't fail to transport his disabled group this afternoon, because their outing to the Happiland Park was the one they looked forward to above every other in the year. And now on this narrow road along the hillside he might at any moment, owing to an optical misjudgement, steer the car over the edge of the road and plunge it with himself and his group inside it to the bottom of the hill. However, the road in front of him did not appear to sway, nor did he feel at all dizzy. He decided to drive carefully on for as long as he felt no worse.

The Park was quite near at last. He was seeing it from above, looking down even on the high dome of the Pleasure Palace. The spirally twisted red-and-white stripes were reassuringly steady, and so was the minaret-like top of a helter-skelter tower just beyond the Palace, and so were the hugely elongated grey neck and disproportionately small head of a perhaps life-size model of a dinosaur whose body was hidden behind low trees beyond the helter-skelter. He began to feel safer, almost as if he had already brought the car to within a few hundred yards of the turnstiles at the Park entrance. But he remembered that in the road ahead there was a steep double zigzag he would have to steer the car down before it would be on the same level as the entrance. Surprisingly soon the road began to dip and in a moment the car was on the zigzag and more surprisingly still he had so little doubt of his ability to steer successfully that he even accelerated slightly when rounding the zigzag's final bend.

He brought the car safely to a stop in one of the few remaining empty spaces at the far end of the large asphalt-surfaced car-park opposite the turnstiles. He quickly opened the door beside his driving seat with the intention of going round immediately to open the other three doors for his disabled passengers. At the instant when he stood fully upright after leaving his seat he felt the same kind of preliminary giddiness that had come upon him this morning just before he had fallen strengthlessly backwards flat on to the carpeted bedroom floor; but now a panic fear of hitting the back of his head on the hard ground surged up in him and gave him the strength to remain standing. He managed to walk round the bonnet of the car with hardly any unsteadiness, though he felt an extreme acceleration in the beating of his heart. Fortunately only one of his passengers needed to be helped to get out of the car, Miss Bilston, whose legs were abnormally short, and he found he could lift her without difficulty gently down from the front seat. The others – Miss Dover, who had a heart condition, Mr Unwin, a sufferer from Parkinson's disease, Mrs Unwin with rheumatoid arthritis – though they were slow in getting out (Mrs Unwin slid out backwards) – did not expect or want a steadying hand from Leslie; and Willie Tyler, giving no outward sign of disability at all, was almost running as he came round the car from the driver's door, which he could reach because the front seat was a long undivided one made for three people including the driver. Soon they were all walking at the pace of the slowest, Miss Bilston, towards the turnstiles across the asphalt, and Leslie succeeded in willing himself to begin talking with simulated enthusiasm about the Scenic Railway they would be going on this afternoon. He told them he was greatly looking forward to it, as he knew it had been wonderfully changed

The Scenic Railway

since he had last been on it ten years before and it was now said to be the most remarkable of its kind anywhere in the world. Wanting to make amends to them for his long silence during the drive he persevered in forcing himself to be cheerfully talkative until, with a little relief, he was aware of having arrived within a few yards of the entrance of the Happiland Park, inside which he would before long be meeting other drivers for the organisation who would already have got there with their groups, and his responsibility for his own group would be shared, or if necessary the main organiser, Nigel Crowbridge, could take over from him altogether.

Under the barkless and highly varnished criss-crossing tree branches of the big rustic entrance arch Crowbridge was standing near the thatch-roofed hut from which the turnstiles were controlled. At the sight of him, unshakily upright in spite of being in his middle eighties, Leslie knew it would not be easy to complain to him of feeling shaky himself, and it would be even less easy to suggest to him that some of the other drivers should be asked to make room in their cars for Mr and Mrs Unwin and Miss Dover and Miss Bilston and Willie when the time came to take all the disabled people home again. But though Leslie did not feel unsteady on his feet now, this might be only because fear of falling was still keeping him tensely upright; and for how much longer would his fear, even if it were to rise to the level of panic again, have power to suppress the extreme vertigo that might be lurking in him? He might be more seriously unwell than he had yet suspected. He would be guilty of criminal irresponsibility if, out of shame at the thought of having to reveal his weakness to Crowbridge, he failed to tell him anything about it and took the risk of driving his own group back to their homes. Undoubtedly the revelation would come as a shock to Crowbridge, who looked all too pleased to see Leslie's group approaching (perhaps they were late and he'd been wondering whether Leslie's car had broken down). 'The Scenic Train is waiting for you in the station', he told them as he welcomingly waved them on through the turnstile nearest to the hut – he must have arranged beforehand that they, and Leslie, should go through without having to buy entrance tickets – and while Crowbridge stayed behind at the hut to pay the ticket man there

Leslie's group began to move off on their own, Mrs Unwin holding Miss Bilston's hand, towards the glass-roofed and glass-walled station less than a hundred yards away across a gravelled open space. Leslie lingered until Crowbridge joined him, but before he could bring himself to say anything about his giddiness Crowbridge said,

'A ride on the Scenic Railway is the ideal amusement for them here – quite exciting without being at all bumpy or alarming.'

He spoke in the confidential tone of one public school man talking to another about people he did not regard as their social equals. For a moment this antagonised Leslie so acutely that it could have spurred him to say immediately that he wouldn't be driving his disabled group back home today, but he noticed that Willie Tyler had lagged behind the others and was still within earshot. He did not want Willie to hear something which could spoil his enjoyment of the Happiland Park from the start.

The reason for Willie's lagging behind was most probably that he was keen to continue being near Leslie, who unlike any of the other drivers for the organisation, including Crowbridge, did not treat him as a compulsive fibber to be tolerantly humoured but accepted his exaggerations and inventions with something of the kind of interest and willing suspension of disbelief required by serious works of fiction. Leslie decided, as he and Crowbridge caught up with Willie on their way to the Scenic Train, that he would not tell Crowbridge about his giddiness till after the whole party of the disabled people and their drivers had finished the 'high tea' Crowbridge had ordered for them at the terminus restaurant, and that he would make the telling easier by offering to pay for a taxi to take his own group back to their homes. But even before he and Crowbridge and Willie caught up with the rest of his group the slight feeling of relief his decision gave him was followed by a sudden new premonitory dizziness which in turn, almost instantly, was countered by a powerful renewal of fear in him. He wasn't diverted at all from this fear when he saw, just outside the station and jutting up from the steep valley beyond, the head and shoulders of a gigantic glossily coloured plastic effigy of a famous film-cartoon character, a sailorman whose name Leslie could not at once remember, with puckered-up cheeks indicating a hidden clenching of toothless gums and with a short-stemmed clay pipe stuffed so far into his pursed-up mouth that the clay bowl almost touched his bulbous nose – an effigy which helped to intensify Leslie's fear because in its hugeness it was strange enough to have been an hallucination produced by a dizzy derangement of his eyesight, though he was as sure as he could be that it was objectively real. And when he came with Crowbridge and Willie and the rest of his group into the station, the green-tailed and vermilion-mouthed dragon train waiting at the platform seemed similarly sinister.

The small roofless darkly shiny carriages, linked closely together like green-painted vertebrae of a monstrous snake, were mostly occupied already by other disabled groups in the organisation, and while Crowbridge went forward to speak to and sit beside one of the other drivers – Colonel Disley – Leslie's group got into the last carriage in the train. When Leslie carefully lifted Miss Bilston on to a seat beside Mrs Unwin he was again conscious of the violent beating of his heart, and this did not at once become any less violent after he had quickly sat down next to Willie who had chosen to sit with an empty seat beside him no doubt in the hope that Leslie would take it.

Their seats were the rearmost ones in the train. The tail of the dragon, with what appeared to be a large metal arrowhead at the tip of it, curved up over their heads from behind them. Willie was pointing up at this and trying to say something, but he was unable to enunciate a single word. He got no help from Leslie who, soon after sitting down securely on this seat that had a high outer side designed presumably to hinder anyone from falling out of the carriage accidentally, felt a new dread which for a while distracted his attention from everything other than itself. It supplanted his fear of falling and it had misery in it combined with a different fear. It was a dread that he might not succeed in avoiding attacks of vertigo after today merely by giving up his work for the organisation, and that the extra pressure he had been putting on himself for two months now might already have done him an injury severe and lasting enough to force him to give up his political activities too. At a time when the anti-capitalist cause, which for so many years had been more important to him and Lana than anything else in their lives,

A Renegade in Springtime

was at its lowest ebb yet in the advanced capitalist countries of the world and needed the utmost help its supporters could give it, he had in all probability made himself permanently useless to it. He was so deeply depressed by this thought that he lost all awareness of Willie sitting beside him, and he hardly noticed the train starting to move and the scenery coming into view just outside the station.

Or was it the scenery, not the train, that was moving? Certainly he felt a vibration which could have been transmitted to his uncushioned wooden seat from wheels turning on rails beneath the carriage. But the high grass alongside the track was passing at a speed impossible for the train itself to have achieved so soon, except at a rate of acceleration that would have brought excessive discomfort to its passengers. Yes, relatively to the track, the scenery was moving – and so was the train, but much more slowly – and the grass beside the track was moving faster than the more distant scenery, though this too seemed to move less slowly backwards than the train moved forwards. The difference in speed between the passing of the trackside grass and of the blueish romantic-looking hills in the background must have been intended by the designer of the railway to create an illusion that the hills were at a distance of many miles from the train, whereas actually they were unlikely to be as much as twenty yards away and had possibly been painted on the canvas of a long high horizontal backdrop which was kept moving by vertical rollers revolving behind it. How ridiculous the blueish hills seemed, and how inferior to the reality they were hiding – the real tree'd valley descending steeply to the sea. For a while he stared at the backward moving artificial scenery – though without clearly focusing it, because now almost everything in his immediate surroundings was becoming excluded from his consciousness again, this time by a misery which was less about the unlikelihood of his being able to continue his political activities than about the present state of the cause whose triumph he and Lana had once so confidently hoped would extend all over the world before they died. Yet, as he half-unseeingly stared, an imaginary scene based partly on the actual artificial one though much more alerting and substantial-seeming became visible in his mind.

The blueish hills were replaced by a wide mud-coloured treeless

The Scenic Railway

and grassless landscape that was sloping downwards from the foreground on the right and rising again to a horizon not less than a mile away in the background on the left, and two parallel military trenches that had been dug a hundred yards or so apart went down the slope and then up to and over the horizon. He remained well aware that none of this was in actuality being shown by the moving backdrop he stared towards, but the imagined scene was incomparably more vivid and significant than the actual external one which was still visible to him, though faintly, beneath it. From along the whole viewable length of the trenches unarmed soldiers began to emerge, only a few at first but soon many, who met in the no-man's-land between the trenches. He was seeing the beginning of the fraternisation of British and German troops on the first Christmas Day of the First World War, and he was seeing it because it had always been for him and Lana one of the guarantees history had given that the ordinary people of all nations would eventually join together against the rulers in whose interests they had been tricked into killing one another. He watched the British and German soldiers exchange helmets, show family photographs to each other, visit each other's trenches, start playing a game of football in no-man's-land. But a feeling which might have become elation was quickly aborted in him by his foreknowledge, as he watched these men, that the generals on both sides would soon regain control of them and mutual slaughter would be resumed and would be continued through three more Christmases without any further fraternising breaks and that he would live on into and through a Second World War brought about like the First by imperialistic capitalism, which would survive it to prepare for a Third.

However, the misery reviving in him now was checked by his awareness of a change that was coming over the imagined scene. He was still looking at a wide treeless, houseless and hedgeless stretch of land, but here the ground was dark to the point of being black, and instead of trenches there were innumerable parallel plough-furrows in it which reached from the railway uninterruptedly up to the horizon. It was apparently boundless in all directions like the sea, or like a landscape in another world. It was a Ukrainian field he had seen from a train when he had been on a visit to the Soviet

A Renegade in Springtime

Union during the spring of 1932, in ignorance of the famine that had followed the peasants' resistance to Stalin's forced collectivisation policy and before the assassination of Kirov and the beginning of Stalin's pre-Second World War political purges. It had been all the more impressive and exhilarating because he had seen it as a field in a vast country where for the first time anywhere the domination of the capitalist class had been broken and power had been taken over by a government which had proclaimed solidarity with the workers everywhere in the world. But he was seeing it now as a field in a country where great-nation patriotism had for too long been more evident than Leninist internationalism. The thought of this, and of the decline of international working-class support for the Soviet Union that the retreat from Leninism there had both caused and been prolonged by, renewed the misery Leslie had been feeling just before the Christmas Day trenches began to change to the furrows of the ploughed field. That imagined field was fading now, making him aware again of the actual dragon train he seemed to have been travelling in for quite a long while already with Willie beside him, and of the continuously moving artificial scenery showing at present an assemblage of holiday motorcoaches parked under palm trees on a Mediterranean-like seafront, though before long his imagination was once again transforming the scenery.

He was looking at an expanse of rough countryside with low hills gorse-covered except where the slopes had been cleared to make way for vineyards and for groves of olive trees. A motorcoach which came up along a valley road stopped in the foreground. As its passengers got out of it almost the only thing to distinguish them immediately from an ordinary random group of mainly elderly late-summer-holiday tourists was that there were more men among them than women, but he knew that he was seeing in his imagination a party of British veterans of the International Brigade who with a few of their relatives were able at last, after the death of the Spanish fascist dictator Franco, to revisit the Jarama valley where forty years earlier the British battalion had taken part in halting the fascist offensive against the vital road linking Valencia with Madrid, and on the first day of going into action had lost three hundred men out of six hundred. He saw they were singing now as they and the few women with them walked up the valley away from the motor-coach, and in his mind he heard the tune and the words of their song, the words of the original version of the famous Jarama song they had first sung during the three months they had been ordered to stay on in the valley after the fascist offensive had been checked – 'For 'tis here that we wasted our manhood / And most of our old age as well.' They came to a stop in front of a single tree on an open space of higher ground, and standing in a semicircle they sang a verse of the Internationale. One of the men stepped forward towards the tree, then turned to face the rest of the group. He was holding with both his hands a small oblong packet which was tightly sheathed in a covering of thick plastic. He had difficulty in opening the packet but he persisted without awkwardness and drew out a small wooden casket and scattered the ashes it contained. Leslie knew that these were the ashes of a veteran who had wanted to join the others here but had died in England only a few days before their coach tour had begun. The feelings of the veterans watching the scattering of the ashes did not plainly show in their faces – until suddenly a tall man standing at the far side of the semi-circle bowed his head and bitterly wept. He was grieving, Leslie knew, not only for the comrade they were commemorating here, nor only for the many comrades who had been killed during the war against fascism in Spain, but also for the cause of working-class internationalism that had suffered a defeat then from which, after more than forty years, it had not yet recovered.

Leslie realised that he too was weeping, and at the same time he was aware that the dragon train in which he was riding was drawing into the terminus station of the Scenic Railway. He was sure that Willie must have seen him weeping, but he hoped that the other four members of his group occupying the seats immediately in front of him had not seen. With difficulty he pretended to be about to sneeze, and bringing out a handkerchief from his pocket as if to blow his nose he wiped his eyes and his cheeks. By the time the train came to a stop at the terminus platform his eyes and cheeks were dry, and he was able to assume a look which he hoped was at least unmiserable if not actually cheerful as he helped Miss Bilston down from her seat in the train. He got the impression that neither

A Renegade in Springtime

she nor Miss Dover nor the Unwins had seen his tears; possibly their attention had been hypnotically held by the artificial scenery they had been staring at. Walking with them along the platform he was surprised to find himself free both from any premonition of vertigo and from the intense fear of falling that had kept him upright on his way to the train. And now he saw something that inexplicably freed him also from the grief he had been feeling in the train.

It was a tree. Not one depicted on the artificial scenery nor one created by his imagination but a real tree rooted in the steep slope of the real valley and visible through the high glass side-wall of the station. He saw it only for a moment as he followed his own group and the other disabled groups out of the station on their way to the Aviary, famous especially for its birds of prey, which was to be the first of several other exciting though not too alarming or physically risky amusements they were to be treated to before they had their 'high tea' at the terminus restaurant. He could not understand why the tree had affected him in the way it had, and a need to understand this grew strong in him before he reached the entrance to the Aviary, where Colonel Disley stood waiting for him. Broadly short, hatless, large-spectacled and with a face like Rudyard Kipling's though there was nothing else literary about him (Leslie had discovered that he had never heard of D. H. Lawrence), Disley was about to say something to Leslie, who however got in first with, 'Do you mind keeping an eye on my group for a short while? I want to go and pay a visit back at the station.' Leslie hadn't noticed whether or not there was a Gents at the station but if there wasn't Disley luckily didn't seem to know there wasn't. 'See you later,' he said, 'and perhaps you'll drop in at my house for a drink when this jaunt's over.' Leslie, putting on a look of urgency which he hoped would be taken as a convincing excuse for his not answering this invitation, hurried away from Disley in the direction of the station.

The tree was a sycamore, autumnal, with the wings of its seeds showing clearly among its not yet fallen leaves, a very tall tree rising from a projecting grassy ledge many feet below in the steeply sloping side of the valley and reaching up as high as the top of the glass roof of the glass-walled terminus. It reminded him of a tree that had been outside the railway station of his home town, the town where he had been born, though the tree there had not been a sycamore but an ash and had grown out of the side of the high embankment on which the station had been built. At the bottom of the embankment a road had led to a taxi-cab rank, whereas at the bottom of the valley here and almost directly below the sycamore was a pond, a surprisingly large one with reeds growing round it and with birds – could they be ducks? – swimming on it. Its water was too high above sea-level to be sea water and must have accumulated gradually in an impermeable hollow created by a landslide some while ago. He remembered the reedy pond in the public park of his home town. He noticed quite near the terminus entrance a narrow path leading down along the side of the valley to the foot of the sycamore and then curving on down to the pond. He decided to go a little way along this path to get a better view of the pond. He felt sure that neither Disley nor Crowbridge would take it amiss if he left his group in their charge rather longer than he had given Disley to expect.

Disley, who was greatly interested in birds of prey, did not notice that Leslie at least ten minutes after leaving him to 'pay a visit' at the station had not yet returned; but Willie did notice, and his curiosity about what Leslie might be doing overcame the keen interest he too had in condors and vultures and eagles. He was able to walk out of the Aviary without being immediately missed by Disley or Crowbridge or by any of his disabled friends – somewhat like a little boy who gets lost in a zoo when the attention of his parents and his siblings is monopolised for a moment too long by the antics of one of the animals – though Willie was away for so short a time that only the sight of him running as fast as he was capable of when he came in again through the Aviary entrance made Disley aware that he had been away at all.

He was desperately trying to say something, and totally failing. Disley, who prided himself on his skill in helping Willie to talk, experimentally suggested various words to him to get him started, such as 'money', 'pocket', 'train', but Willie shook his head each time until Disley said 'Mr Brellis', and then he vigorously nodded. Eventually Disley got out of him that Mr Brellis was paddling, not in the sea but in a pond with ducks on it, and that the pond was half-way down the side of the valley. Disley repeated this story, with an ill-disguised wink, to Crowbridge who had come up to him to propose that they should take the party on to see the Smugglers' Cave and also the Aquarium before taking them to the restaurant. Then Disley said to Willie, 'Mr Brellis would have had to look pretty slippy to get down there in the short time since he was with us here.' 'He did slip,' Willie said, enunciating the words very clearly. Disley and Crowbridge exchanged inconspicuous smiles. But they didn't feel inclined to go on humouring Willie, who was unsuccessfully and agonisingly trying to add something to his story.

Leslie knew that he did slip, at the top of the path leading downwards to the foot of the sycamore. With astonishing velocity he sat down on a hard surface somewhere below the path, jarring his spine. His legs dangled into a softness as of high grass. He was surprised to feel no pain, and the ease with which he was able after a minute or two to stand up again seemed to prove that he had not injured himself at all. On the contrary he felt strangely invigorated, and not only physically. His imagination became even more strongly alive than when he had watched the artificial scenery from the dragon train, and the scene he began to imagine now was so vivid that it completely replaced in his consciousness the real sycamore and the real valley.

* * *

He was standing at the top of a long covered footway that sloped down from the station platform-exit towards the side road leading leftward to the taxi-cab rank and rightward to the main street of his home town. The unwalled gaps between the iron pillars that upheld the curved roof over the footway gave a high clear view of the brewery tower and the church spire and even of the short bridge under which flowed (though he couldn't yet see it) the small river whose course through the town, whether briefly in the open or more often concealed in culverts, he remembered so well that he could almost have sketched a rapid map of it in his notebook as he stood here now. But sketching anything at all would have been made impossible for him by his emotion at the sight of his home town.

The Scenic Railway

He felt gladness, and he felt sorrow, and above all he felt love – not only his own love for this town he had been too long away from but its love (which seemed to emanate from everything he saw now) for him. Yet when he walked down the footway and came out on to the side road, the love he felt began to have anxiety in it. He was afraid that during all the years since he had last been here the town might have changed too much for him to find his way back to those places he most of all needed to revisit.

For a while nothing appeared unfamiliar to him. He crossed the main street near where it went beneath the brown brick railway bridge, and after turning away from the bridge to walk along the pavement towards the town centre he soon reached Southern Road, which ran parallel to the railway and looked entirely unchanged, with the trees all along both sides of it and even up to the far end of it easily recognisable as London planes by the light-coloured patches where the bark had flaked off from their trunks. The plane trees helped to assure him, as he crossed the entrance to Southern Road and walked on along the main street, that he was taking the right route to find what he first of all wanted to find, and the assurance they gave him was strengthened as he passed the house of Dr Woodcote and the old Corn Exchange building, which were exactly where they used to be. For a moment he was alarmed when, staring ahead along the main street towards the town centre, he discovered that the market-place which should have been just beyond the crossroads had disappeared and that the whole scene had become unrecognisable. But in the next moment he found he had reached the entrance to the road he had not allowed himself till now to be fully conscious of yearning to reach: Northern Road – and looking along this he could see on one side the wicket gate, as he had privately and romantically named it in his boyhood, which led into a market garden by the back way, and on the opposite side the small convent school which even some Anglican parents (middle-class ones for whom the lower class local Church of England elementary school would have been unthinkable as an alternative) sent their girl children to until they were old enough for the high school – but he could not yet see the house he longed to see.

The street lamps came on soon after he had started walking up Northern Road. He had not realised how late the afternoon had become. There was still no sign of darkness in the air when he passed the convent and reached the first of a group of identical-looking houses, one of which used to be named Braemar. He walked more and more slowly, unable to remember where it had been positioned among the other houses and increasingly apprehensive that he would not be able to recognise it if its name had been changed. But its name had not been changed, was inscribed just as formerly in gilded cursive lettering on the glass above its front door. He dared to stop soon after having very slowly passed the house, and then he turned back and stopped again, this time within a few paces of the gate which he would have to open if he were to decide to walk up the short tiled path to the door.

He stood looking towards the bay window of the front sitting-room. The curtains had not yet been drawn across nor had the light been switched on inside. In his boyhood more than fifty years before he would never have had the courage even to linger for a moment or two here, far less to stand staring as he was now. At most he would have walked or more probably bicycled slowly past the house – but not so slowly that his slowness would have been obvious – hoping that he might get at least a glimpse of Isabelle, or even that she might see him passing, though he was afraid this could make her think worse rather than better of him if he appeared to her to be merely on his way along Northern Road to somewhere else. He was never able to overcome the awed timidity that was caused by the very intensity of his love for her and led him at last to write her the letter which put an end for ever to his hope of being loved by her in return. Standing here near the gate outside her house this evening half a century afterwards he could not forget the final shameful fortnight that had begun when he had dared to post to her, anonymously, a book of poems by Rupert Brooke, bound in brown suede leather. Within a few days this had brought him a brief letter from her saying, sarcastically as it seemed to him, that someone had sent her a beautiful book but unfortunately had 'omitted to enclose their name'. He had written her a panicking answer improbably explaining that he had sent her the book because he had thought she had sent him one but he had realised later that the book he had received must have come from Mr Hobson, an old friend of his family. He never saw or heard from her again. Yet now as he continued staring at the window the memory of this unhappy ending became incomparably less important to him than the scene his imagination soon took him to see inside the room: Isabelle smiling with the lit candles of the Christmas tree behind her when he had arrived for the party where he had met her again for the first time since their childhood at kindergarten together ten years earlier, and before the evening of dancing had been over he had known he was utterly in love with her. How insignificant his miserable timidity was made to seem now by that remembered happiness.

He took a step towards the front gate. He hadn't the least expectation that Isabelle would still be living in this house. Yet if he were to open the gate and go up the path and ring the front door bell, someone who knew something about her might come to the door. He did not open the gate. He remembered that her house had not been the ultimate destination he had aimed to reach when he had set out from the station into the town. He must move on. He could come back here later, perhaps tomorrow. The evening was getting darker, and though he was confident as he began walking again that he was taking the right route, he wanted to see clearly any changes that might have been made to the houses that had once been familiar to him along it. He came to the end of Northern Road and saw on the far side of the T-junction there a large square-shaped yellow-brick house recognisable to him immediately as the one where Mr Hobson had lived. He walked towards it across a road which meant more to him than any other in this town – Junction Road, at the end of which his own home had been. In the lower rooms of Mr Hobson's house the lights were on. It might not be impossible, he thought, that in these times when more people than formerly reached a very advanced age Mr Hobson was still alive. Leslie did not stop to stare at the windows here but walking on he remembered Mr Hobson's offer to him long ago of a job which could have led eventually to a partnership in Mr Hobson's prosperous and by bourgeois standards reputable firm. If he had accepted that offer he might have become a success, highly respected in the town, though even supposing the prospect of that success might have persuaded Isabelle to forgive him and to marry him he was as certain still as he had been then that he would have found such a job unbearable. And Isabelle could never have been what Lana had been to him. But as he continued walking he thought with gratitude and warmth of Mr Hobson who, childless, had at one time seemed to regard him almost as a son and had genuinely wanted to help him.

* * *

From the moment when he got a first glimpse of his own home ahead at the corner of Junction Road he could no longer think of Mr Hobson or even of Isabelle. Nor could he think about his home: he could only feel, and his feeling was of fear as well as of yearning. He was not, or would not let himself be, fully aware of what he was afraid of. The exterior of the house, so far as he could see by the light of nearby street lamps when he reached the corner of the road, had suffered no hideous change since he had last seen it. The virginia creeper at its red autumnal best now was still thick on the house walls, and where the wide gravel path leading from the double front gate to the front door narrowed as it went on beyond the bow-window of the drawing-room he saw that the two privet hedges were still densely there hiding the sunken garden which the path zig-zaggingly reached through the gap between their overlapping ends. How often in his childhood he had trickily steered his pedal motorcar at speed down that zigzag and how often the chain had slipped off the cogs as he had struggled to pedal it up again. The remembrance helped him temporarily to forget his fear as he opened the customarily used right-hand half of the double gate – (had the other half ever been used?) – and went along the very short gravel 'drive' to the front door. But when he stood in the porch and was facing the door his fear returned.

The light visible through the thick wavy semi-transparent glass panels of the door was as dim almost as it had been during blackout hours in the Second World War (though it had never been really bright even when he had lived here before the war). Like a stranger now he had to press the bell-push beside the door instead of being able to let himself into the house with his latch key. He did not hear the bell ring and no one came to the door. He found just above the door-handle the familiar unpolished bronze knocker, shaped like the head of an Egyptian pharaoh, blacker than ever, and he knocked twice with this, not too loudly. Soon he saw someone moving slowly in the hall who loomed up towards the glass panels and at last reached the door. He did not instantly recognise his mother when she opened the door, because he had hardly had the remotest hope that she would still be here, but she knew him at once. 'Oh Leslie,' she said, and she put her arms round his shoulders and kissed him. 'I'm so glad.'

'I wish I could have let you know beforehand that I would be coming,' he said.

She seemed not to hear this. 'I'm so glad,' she said again, and then she called out into the hall, 'Arthur, it's Leslie.'

His father came out from the morning-room at the back of the hall. He shook hands with Leslie. Long ago Leslie had felt hurt that after he had reached the age of thirteen his father when welcoming him home from boarding-school or saying goodbye at the end of the holidays had taken to shaking hands with him instead of kissing him, but the warmth of his father's handshake now did away finally with Leslie's fear. His parents were both of them not only still alive but looked not so very much older than when he had last seen them.

'You are just in time for tea,' his mother said, leading the way into the large room which she had long ago named the south room. The light here was a little less dim than in the hall. There was a teapot covered with a knitted woollen cosy on the antique small round table in the middle of the room. His mother went to the dark oak corner cupboard at the end of the room to fetch an extra teacup and saucer and a plate. He sat down in the brown leather armchair he so well remembered. His father sat down opposite him in an almost identical chair, though with an inflated rubber ring for a cushion just as formerly. Leslie had a feeling of safety such as he believed would not have been possible for him anywhere else than here.

A Renegade in Springtime

The things he had especially wanted to tell his parents began to seem less urgent as he rested so comfortably in this chair. He must not let himself forget what these things were, however. He wanted to say how sorry he was that because of the work he had been doing he had not been able to come home before today. He wanted to say how sorry he was that he had disappointed them long ago by not taking the job Mr Hobson had offered him, and to explain that he could not have endured it and that the life he had chosen had been the only tolerable one for him. He wanted to admit that this work he had given his best energies to had not been a success, nor had the cause he had worked for, though also he would tell them he had never doubted – and was more convinced than ever – that it would triumph in the end. But why should he risk upsetting his parents by saying any of these things? Their happiness at having him here with them again was so evident. And why should he risk disturbing his own happy drowsiness which was increasing in him every moment as he sat here? 'Home is a place where I am well thought of,' he said to himself as he sank into the comfort of his armchair, as he slid more deeply, more and more deeply, downwards into its safety.

Appendix 1

Publication Details
The publication details for the twelve stories in this volume are given below. Further information may be found in *Edward Upward: A Bibliography 1920-2000* by Alan Walker (Enitharmon Press, 2000).

The Railway Accident was written in 1928 at Lockerbie, Scotland, where Upward was employed as a tutor (Upward's experience in this job would later provide the setting for *Journey to the Border*). It was the last and longest of the Mortmere stories, and circulated among Upward's friends in manuscript form during the 1930s. The story was not published until 1949, when it appeared in the United States in *New Directions in Prose and Poetry: Number Eleven* under the pseudonym of Allen Chalmers, with a foreword by Christopher Isherwood. It first appeared under Upward's own name in *The Railway Accident and Other Stories* (Heinemann, 1969), and was reprinted in the paperback volume by Penguin Modern Classics in 1972 and 1988. Finally the story was anthologised in *The Mortmere Stories* (with Christopher Isherwood; Enitharmon Press, 1994).

The original manuscript of the story featured sexually explicit and violent details which were expurgated for its first publication in 1949. This manuscript was later destroyed by Edward Upward, along with those of other Mortmere stories. Some indication of the deleted content is given by Upward in his memoir *Christopher Isherwood: Notes in Remembrance of a Friendship* (Enitharmon Press, 1996). The interested reader should also consult Christopher Isherwood's *Lions and Shadows* and his introduction to Mortmere contained in *The Railway Accident and Other Stories*; Katherine Bucknell's introduction to *The Mortmere Stories*; *Remembering Mortmere* by Edward Upward (*London Magazine* Vol 27 No 11, February 1988); and *Laily, Mortmere and All That* by Brian Finney (*Twentieth Century Literature*, Vol 22 No 3, October 1976).

Sunday was written in 1931 and first published in *New Country: Prose and Poetry by the Authors of "New Signatures"* (The Hogarth Press, 1933). It was included in *The Railway Accident and Other Stories* (Heinemann, 1969), which was reprinted in the Penguin Modern Classics series in 1972 and 1988.

The Island was written in 1934 and first published in *Left Review* Vol 1 No 4, January 1935. It was reprinted as a contribution to the left-wing anthology *In Letters of Red*, published by Michael Joseph in 1938. It was later included in *The Railway Accident and Other Stories* (Heinemann, 1969), which was reprinted in the Penguin Modern Classics series in 1972 and 1988.

The Procession first appeared in *The Guardian* on 3 May 1980, with an illustration by John Holder. It was later collected in *The Night Walk and Other Stories* (Heinemann, 1987).

An Old-Established School first appeared in *The London Magazine* Vol 21 Nos 1 & 2, April-May 1981. It was later published in *The Night Walk and Other Stories* (Heinemann, 1987).

The White-Pinafored Black Cat was published for the first time in *The Night Walk and Other Stories* (Heinemann, 1987). It had previously been adapted and abridged under the title *The Sister Who Survived* and broadcast on BBC Radio 3 on 5 August 1985. The story was read by Mary Wimbush and the programme produced by Maurice Leitch.

At the Ferry Inn first appeared in *The London Magazine* Vol 25 No 4, July 1985. It was later published in *The Night Walk and Other Stories* (Heinemann, 1987).

Appendix 1

An Unmentionable Man was published for the first time in its namesake volume of short stories (Enitharmon Press, 1994).

A Ship in the Sky was published for the first time in *An Unmentionable Man* (Enitharmon Press, 1994).

Emily and Oswin was completed in October 1996 and published for the first time in *The Scenic Railway* (Enitharmon Press, 1997).

Imaginative Men & Women was published for the first time in *The Coming Day and Other Stories* (Enitharmon Press, 2000).

The Scenic Railway was completed in June 1987 and first appeared in *The London Magazine* Vol 28 No 3, June 1988. It was reprinted in *Best Short Stories 1989* (Heinemann, 1989), edited by Giles Gordon and David Hughes, and as *Paesaggi di cartapesta*, translated by Roberta Scarabelli and introduced by Francesco Binni, in *Linea d'Ombra* No 73, July-August 1992. It was later published as the title story of *The Scenic Railway* (Enitharmon Press, 1997).

Appendix 2

Short Story Collections by Edward Upward

The five published collections of short stories by Edward Upward are listed below.

The Railway Accident and Other Stories (introduced by W. H. Sellers; Heinemann, 1969; reprinted in Penguin Modern Classics, 1972 and 1988)

The Railway Accident
The Colleagues
Sunday
Journey to the Border
The Island
New Order

The Night Walk and Other Stories (Heinemann, 1987)

Her Day
The Procession
An Old-Established School
From a Seaside Notebook (Nine Political Prose Pieces: 1976-1979)
   The Juror
   An Intruder at Night
   The Poet Who Died
   I Dreamt of a Valley
   Love Is Nice
   We Call Them Grockles
   The Spectacle

Appendix 2

The Last Good Thing That a Bad Reporter Should Heed
Do Others
Over the Cliff
The Interview
The White-Pinafored Black Cat
At the Ferry Inn
The Night Walk

An Unmentionable Man (introduced by Frank Kermode; Enitharmon Press, 1994)

An Unmentionable Man
The Unmentionable Thing
Into the Dark
A Ship in the Sky
Fred and Lil
With Alan to the Fair

The Scenic Railway (Enitharmon Press, 1997)

The Scenic Railway
Investigation after Midnight
People Hate Me
The World Revolution
Emily and Oswin

The Coming Day and Other Stories (Enitharmon Press, 2000)

The Coming Day
The War Widow
Imaginative Men & Women
The Serial Dreamer
The Intangible Man
A Better Job
The Suspect